Praise for Charlotte Lamb

'A potent mixture of murder, mystery and intrigue . . .
you simply won't be able to put the book down'
Woman's Realm

'Interesting characters and a satisfyingly structured
story, as polished as ever'   *Bolton Evening News*

'Her novels are rip-roaringly, mind-bogglingly . . .
heart-poundingly successful'   *Radio Times*

'One of the secrets of [her] phenomenal success is
her magnificent moody heroes'   *News of the World*

Angel of
Death

Charlotte Lamb

coronet

CORONET BOOKS
Hodder & Stoughton

First published in 2000 by Hodder & Stoughton
A division of Hodder Headline
First published in paperback in 2001 by Hodder & Stoughton
A Coronet paperback

10 9 8 7 6 5 4

A CIP catalogue record for this title is available
from the British Library

ISBN 0 340 76731 6

Typeset by Palimpsest Book Production Limited,
Polmont, Stirlingshire
Printed and bound in Great Britain by
Mackays of Chatham plc, Chatham, Kent

Hodder & Stoughton Ltd
A division of Hodder Headline
338 Euston Road
London NW1 3BH

Prologue

Miranda knew she was dreaming, at one level of her mind, and tried to wake up, but was held too deeply by the dream. Her body was heavy, as if she were paralysed.

A tumult of dark green, marbled, foam-flecked water carried her along, turning her this way and that, upside down, then right side up, weightless, flotsam crashing helplessly along. The sea, she thought, smelling salt. She was in the sea.

She could hear someone else, nearby, gasping, choking.

He called out to her. 'Miranda! Where are you? Miranda! Help me!'

He had never been a strong swimmer, whereas it had always been her favourite sport.

Her heart leapt in dread and anguish.

'Tom, I'm coming, hang on!' Fear for him made her fight harder. She struggled against the waves but she couldn't see him.

'Tom, where are you?' she screamed, and with a final effort surfaced.

But not in the sea. Awake now, she realised she was in bed, in a strange room – a narrow, boxlike little room. Her body was damp with sweat. The sheets stuck to her. Blankly, she stared around. Where on earth was she?

There was very little furniture; just the bed she lay in, a low cupboard next to it, on which stood a jug of water and a glass, and against the wall a wooden chair. The walls were white. Beige blinds covered the small window. There was a lamp on a table by the door, casting a veiled light, and somewhere she heard muffled footsteps. Her nose wrinkled – there was that familiar institutional scent of wax polish she remembered from school, from public libraries, but mingled with a pungent, antiseptic smell. Disinfectant? Was she in a hospital?

What was she doing here? How had she got here?

Panic rose up inside her. The sea. She remembered the dream, or had it just been a dream? She had been in the sea. How long ago? Tom. Where was Tom?

She had fought to reach him, then someone else

had appeared, had grabbed her by the shoulders to turn her over on to her back.

'Leave me alone,' she had yelled, trying to break free of him. 'I'll be OK. My husband. Save Tom. He's in trouble. He isn't a good swimmer, he needs help.'

He didn't answer, and she couldn't hear Tom any more. Fear made her desperate, but the powerful hands wouldn't release her. He began towing her through the water. When she screamed at him water sloshed into her mouth, half-choking her.

He seemed tireless, breasting the waves while he dragged her behind him, up on to a beach. At last he let go of her and she lay, face down, salt water spewing out of her, hurting her throat, her body shuddering and heaving. Rough sand had grazed her frozen skin, she saw blood smears on her legs.

The man who had saved her knelt, massaging her back and shoulders with firm fingers. He raised her and put his arms round her to keep her warm against his body. She tried to push him away, but he would not let go. She was too tired to fight. She sat rigid in the circle of his grasp, hearing his body, his breathing, his heartbeat.

She hated him. He was alive. Tom was dead.

She turned her head to look down the beach at the dark, devouring sea. There was no sign of the yacht. It must have gone to the bottom.

Her eyes closed to shut out the sight. Images of Tom's blond hair filled her head. It was so alive; it moved constantly, curling strands spread out in the water, floating away from the face with its closed, blind eyes, and she saw little blue and silver fish darting in and out of the curls.

Shuddering, she refused to think any more about that and drifted away like Tom on a remorseless tide.

How long had it been before rescue arrived? By the time it did, she must have been unconscious. She could remember nothing of what happened next.

All she knew was that she was here, in this silent little room. Alive and alone. Tears filled her eyes. Oh, Tom, Tom – how could she go on living, without him?

A sob broke out of her. She wished she were dead, too. She should have drowned out there, with him. She would have done if that man had not dragged her away.

In the corner of the room something moved. Her heart seemed to stop. Her head swung in shock.

'Who's there?' she whispered.

He got up from a chair and came towards her. She recognised him at once. All in black, as usual – tieless shirt, trousers, jacket. His hair almost the same colour, springing back from a widow's peak, short at the side, the back curling into his nape.

He stood beside the bed and she looked up with dread into his pale, cold face. His eyes were the colour of a grey winter's day.

'I was afraid of you the minute I first saw you,' she said. 'Now I know why. You're the angel of death, aren't you? You took Tom. Have you come for me now?'

He put a hand out towards her, long, tapering fingers curling to take her and she shrank away.

'Don't touch me! I couldn't bear it if you touched me!' she screamed.

Outside in a corridor footsteps quickened into a run. The door was flung open. Lights blazed in the room.

A nurse hurried over to her.

'What's wrong? Are you in pain, Mrs Grey?'

'Get him away from me!'

'Who?' The nurse looked round the room.

It was empty. There was nobody there. Miranda lay down again, trembling violently. Had she still been dreaming, after all?

The nurse gave her an injection. Miranda went back into her dream; into the cold, green sea. The angel of death was waiting for her there. That night and for many nights afterwards.

But she never saw him again when she was awake.

Chapter One

Until three years later.

Miranda drove down to Sussex one bright May morning feeling better than she had for a very long time. It was a lovely day and she was pleased with the way she looked in her new pale mauve suit. She had given herself a little more height by buying high-heeled white sandals. It would be a mistake to try to walk far in them. She knew she was a little unsteady on them but their delicacy and style made her feel really elegant, and what she needed was a boost to her self-confidence, which had been at an all-time low for a long time.

It had surprised her to be invited to the engagement party of her boss's son. She barely knew Sean, who was eight years younger than her; a good-looking, very sophisticated twenty-one-year-old who already knew it all, judging by his manner and the condescending way he spoke to her, as if she was a halfwit, or an old granny.

She had a sneaking feeling Sean did not even know she was on the invitation list. Her boss had sent out the invitations – to personal friends of his own, or Sean's buddies, or friends of the new fiancée, and, of course, to relatives from either side. There was a lot of excitement in the firm about who would be invited and who would not, but Miranda had not expected to be on the list.

She had accepted, of course – how could she refuse? Only later did it dawn on her that she had nothing to wear except clothes she had already worn to work and it would never do to wear any of them.

It was years since she had taken any interest in how she looked, but for a party like that she had to have something really good. People might notice. Her boss certainly would. He noticed everything; sharp as a tack, as her mother would say. So, last week she had taken a long lunch hour and gone to Oxford Street. After wandering from shop to shop, walking for half an hour, she had finally seen this suit. The soft colour suited her own pigmentation. She was no beauty, but she knew she had fresh, clear skin, a loose brunette swirl of shoulder-length hair and light hazel eyes. She had not inherited her mother's stunning looks. As a girl, she had kept hoping her hair would turn that shiny golden blonde colour, that her eyes would go grass green, that she would somehow acquire the ability to make men's heads turn, but she had her father's colouring and features, and the magic transformation had never happened. Life was full of disappointments.

In one of those odd coincidences she had spotted the shoes in a shop right next door and known at once that they would be the perfect match. She had been back at her office more or less on time, after all, and had eaten a yoghurt and a pear at her desk before starting work.

She had got a job with the firm six months after Tom's death. She suspected — no, she was certain — Terry had offered it to her out of a sense of guilt. Tom had worked for Terry's firm. They had been on the yacht at Terry's invitation — he had chartered it as a floating conference centre and brought on board a dozen of his top executives, with their wives and girlfriends, as well as some of his best customers. The others had all been saved when the yacht broke up on rocks. Only Tom had drowned.

She had been ill for months afterwards. When she was sent home she found she had lost her post with a large public relations firm. They were apologetic, but explained that they had not been able to keep her job open for ever, especially as they had no idea how long she would be kept in hospital.

The uneasy expression on their faces had told her they thought she was going to make trouble. That she was possibly a bit nuts. And maybe she had been, at first.

But she was back to normal when she left hospital and, after she had spent a fortnight convalescing with her mother down in Dorset, she was calm and rational. She saw there was no point in arguing or protesting. Her firm did not want her back.

She started applying for jobs at once, without much success at first, until, a few days later, Terry had visited her, heard about her predicament, and asked her to take on his firm's public relations.

'We haven't had a PR department, before, but we're growing, fast, and I think we probably need one now, to handle advertising and dealings with the media.'

Neither of them mentioned Tom's death. She had looked into Terry's warm, brown eyes and decided she liked him. They had first met on the yacht and she barely knew him, but she sensed he was a good man.

Big, muscled, with a pleasantly ugly face which was angular, bony and confident, he had a strength and cheerfulness which was instantly likeable. His very short, brown hair curled all over his head in little curls like the horns of a small goat. His grins and barks of laughter aroused answering smiles from most people he met.

He wore casual, light suits, in shades of blue or cream, with coloured shirts, pink or turquoise, and expensive silk ties. Conventional businessmen in striped grey city suits found his outfits worrying. Could he be serious when he dressed like that?

The success of his company was sufficient answer. Terry Finnigan was an electronic genius and understood both what he sold and how to make money selling it. He had founded his company ten years ago with a small legacy from the sale of his dead father's house.

Miranda wasn't sure how he had made a living before that. She had the idea that he hadn't been well off. Everything in his house was new, oddly impersonal in spite of being bright, modern, and very expensive.

Today, the company was worth millions, and Terry owned a majority of the shares. He also owned a large country house, a number of very expensive cars, and leased an office complex in which he had a flat that he and his son used when they were in London. Divorced, Terry dated quite often, but did not seem interested in marrying again, although he liked women.

His preference seemed to be for tall, curvy, show-biz girls, curiously similar in type to his first wife, Sandra, a nightclub singer. Maybe men always picked the same sort of women?

Sandra was now living in Spain with her second partner, to whom she was not married.

'A crook,' Terry always said of Jack Lee. 'And a cheap crook at that. You could buy him outright for a packet of crisps and a glass of beer. What does she see in him?'

Miranda never attempted to reply, she knew he was talking rhetorically, but she imagined Sandra liked Jack's party-going attitude to life. He joked, laughed, took nothing seriously, and he had a rough sort of sexuality, an instinctive body language with women.

He was, Miranda had decided long ago, very like Terry except that he didn't have Terry's brains or aptitude for business. So perhaps women also chose the same type, too? It wouldn't be surprising – it was all based on character, wasn't it? Everyone saw through their own eyes, and chose a partner accordingly.

Jack had money, and spent it with a free hand – but it was never clear how he made it. Maybe Terry was right. Jack might well be a crook. Was that why he lived in a villa somewhere in Spain? Miranda had heard the stories about British criminals migrating to Spain to spend their loot outside the reach of the British police.

She had only met Jack and Sandra a couple of times. They were both deeply tanned, wore a lot of gold, bracelets on wrists, necklaces around throats, rings on fingers. They glittered when they moved, and they hated the cooler temperatures of southern England.

'They can't wait to get back to Spain,' Terry commented, last time they were in London and called at the firm. 'Thank God. The less I see of them the better. If she wasn't Sean's mother I'd never let her through the door.'

Sean, though, seemed very fond of his mother. His taste in girls reflected this – he clearly liked the showy blondes his father did. Yet the girl he planned to marry was very different.

Nicola was nineteen, tiny, fragile, sweet; with sleek black hair which framed a heart-shaped face dominated by big, wide, innocent, blue eyes. She was the only child of a wealthy merchant banker, Francis Belcannon, whose bank had been very involved with Terry's company from the beginning.

Wearing an elegant blue and white organza out-fit which made her look like a Barbie doll, she met Miranda at the front door of Terry's country house, Blue Gables. Behind her the rooms swirled with people in beautiful clothes, talking, laughing, drinking champagne.

'Thank you so much for coming,' Nicola said with such warmth that Miranda almost believed she meant it, except that they had only met a handful of times and Nicola probably hadn't even known she was invited.

She handed over the silver-wrapped box of wine glasses she had bought and Nicola eagerly unwrapped it, held one of the glasses up to the light to watch it sparkle.

'Oh, they're gorgeous, so classy – thank you so much, I love them. Sean will adore them too.'

She looked round and waved a hand at one of Sean's friends, a great hulk of a boy with cropped gingery fair hair and features set in concrete.

'Georgie, will you get Miranda a drink and take care of her for me?'

'Sure,' George Stow growled. He might look like a stone wall but Miranda saw from his glance at Nicola that he worshipped the girl. She was so very much his opposite – tiny, where he was huge, gentle where he was tough, articulate where George was barely able to utter a word.

Miranda hoped Sean loved the girl that way, but

she wouldn't bet on it. She had a sinking feeling that Terry had put the idea of marrying Nicola into his son's head because it would be so very convenient for the business. Nicola was going to inherit a great deal of money one day, and meanwhile her father was vital to the firm's finances. Medieval as it might be, the idea of the marriage made a lot of sense – but would Sean make Nicola a good husband?

George steered her through the throng, produced a glass of champagne for her and hovered.

'You work for Terry, don't you? Are you his secretary?'

'No, I run the PR department. Nicola looks happy, doesn't she?'

George shot her a glower. 'Sean had better make her happy or I'll smash his face in.'

Startled but liking his honesty, Miranda smiled at him. 'I know what you mean. Hurting her would be like running over a kitten, wouldn't it?'

George made a growling noise in his throat. 'She's too good for Sean, that's for sure.' He was clearly besotted by the girl and very jealous of Sean – did Sean realise it?

A moment later, Miranda saw the angel of death on the other side of the room and stopped in her tracks, taking a sharp, indrawn, painful breath.

It couldn't be! She closed her eyes, took another deep breath, and opened them again.

She wasn't imagining it. It was him. He was wearing black again, but with a difference. Today he was wearing an immaculate black jersey wool suit, with a crisp white shirt, a dark blue silk tie. She saw other women in the room watching him with eager, covetous eyes. Couldn't they see that brooding air of threat about him?

'Something wrong?' George asked.

She swallowed, managed to wave a hand. 'Who is that? The guy talking to the woman in a pink hat.'

George looked, frowned. 'Never seen him before in my life. He must be a friend of Terry Finnigan or maybe Nicola's father. Or do you think he's a gatecrasher? Shall I go and ask to see his invitation?'

'No, leave it. I think he's probably a friend of Terry's.' He had been on the yacht after all – and Terry must have invited him. She knew he was not one of the company executives, she hadn't seen him at work, either before or since the yacht foundered.

She had been introduced to him briefly, during the cruise, but couldn't remember his name. That was weird, wasn't it? He had haunted her dreams ever since, yet she didn't even know his name.

Terry pushed his way through the crowds of guests, bringing another glass of champagne for her.

He was wearing a rainbow: sunshine yellow shirt, blue jacket, hot pink and green tie, blue trousers.

Huskily, tearing her gaze away from the angel of death, she managed to smile. 'You look ... dazzling!'

He grinned. 'You mean I have vulgar tastes in clothes! I know. But I love bright colours, they cheer me up when I'm feeling down.'

He threw a glance over her. 'You don't look bad yourself. A bit subdued, all that mauve and white, but it suits you. My old Gran used to wear mauve all the time – it was what widows wore fifty years ago. Black at first, then mauve after six months.'

Their eyes met and he groaned.

'Hush my mouth! Sorry, Miranda. I spoke without thinking. I'd forgotten Tom.'

'That's OK,' she managed to get out, thinking, how could he forget Tom? But three years is a long time and people do forget. She wished she could, but Tom still showed up in her dreams, especially when she was very tired or under a strain.

'You look lovely,' Terry said in a sweetly obvious attempt to change the subject and cheer her up. 'What are you doing this Sunday?'

'Nothing much.' Was he going to ask her out? Now and then she picked up the impression that Terry fancied her and might be going to ask her for a date, but so far it hadn't happened, and she was not certain whether or not she would welcome his approach if it came.

She liked Terry, but she did not want to get involved with anyone. She was sure she would know if she were ready for a new relationship. So far she wasn't.

He gave her a coaxing smile. 'I'd like you to work on projected publicity for the new printer. I don't want anyone to have an idea what we're doing, yet, which means you can't do this during the week with people walking in and out of the office all day. Could you do it on Sunday afternoon?'

'OK,' she said, laughing at herself silently. So much for her daydreaming. It had been work on Terry's mind, after all, not romance. She should have known it would be. Terry was a workaholic.

The day to day workload for her job was not exactly heavy. She had to arrange advertising and publicity, of course, but Terry kept a very small budget for either of those. Advertising was largely in trade magazines, and bought in blocks for so many weeks or months, and publicity came up only from time to time, usually when they introduced a new product.

She had to have a certain technical literacy in order to work out copy for advertising, although

Terry usually gave her a sketch of what he wanted her to write, puffing new features of a machine. She would have to know all about the new printer when she dealt with the marketing campaign later that year, so it made sense for her to familiarise herself with the details now.

Somebody loomed up beside them and her nerves leapt.

'Hello, Terry.'

'Alex! Great to see you, thanks for coming.' Terry beamed from ear to ear. He either liked this man a lot or the man was rich and important. Or both.

Seeing the other man staring at her, Terry introduced them. 'Alex, this is the head of our Public Relations department, Miranda Grey. Miranda, this is Alex.'

'Alexandros Manoussi,' the other man expanded, proffering his hand. 'But we've met before, haven't we?'

So that was his name. It sounded like the hiss of a snake. Sibilant, yet frighteningly sexy. She was sure she had never heard it before. She hesitated to take his hand, to touch him; long enough for Terry to notice.

'Alex is one of our best customers,' he told her pointedly, frowning. 'We make all the navigational computers Alex puts into his yachts.'

'Of course,' she said, realising she had dealt with

queries about such instruments, which were being put into boats in countries other than Greece, including Britain.

She had no choice; she had to put out her hand, let it be taken into the cool, supple fingers. A shiver went down her spine at the touch of his skin.

'I'm a boatbuilder,' he explained and the sound of his voice was bitterly familiar. She had never forgotten it; had heard it in her dreams for years.

'Alex makes his boats over in Greece, at Piraeus,' Terry told her. 'I've been there to see how he works, and discuss with his designers what they need the computers to do for them.'

She was looking into Alex Manoussi's dark eyes. 'You built the yacht?' Had he built the yacht they had been sailing on when it was wrecked and Tom drowned. There had been an inquest some months later but she had not been present, she had been too ill.

Only afterwards did she hear that the firm from whom Terry had chartered the yacht had been accused of negligence. That must have been Alex Manoussi's firm.

What had happened after the inquest? She had never been told. This man must be rich and powerful. Had he had to face consequences? Or had his employees been blamed?

Over the years since, she had never wanted to discuss it, with Terry, or anyone else. When she came out of hospital she had only wanted to forget. The doctors had told her to put the past behind, try to forget, and she had not wanted to think too much about what happened after the wreck, although sometimes she was not sure the medical advice had been sensible. Perhaps refusing to think about something so traumatic allowed it to fester in the mind?

Terry interrupted before the Greek could answer her. 'Have you seen Sean, Miranda? He should be taking care of Nicola. Why is she alone, over by the front door? Find him and tell him to stick beside his fiancée for the rest of the party, would you? We don't want her getting upset at being neglected, do we? Her father would be furious.'

Miranda nodded. 'Of course.' She half-glanced at Alex Manoussi with a polite pretence of regret. 'Would you excuse me?'

Did he guess how relieved she was to escape? There was a spark of cynicism in those eyes of his. Or was he simply noticing the way Terry coolly despatched her, like a servant, to do his bidding? Sometimes she resented Terry's habit of treating her that way, but since her illness she never had the energy to protest or argue.

It didn't take her long to find Sean in the Victorian-style conservatory at the back of the house, joking and drinking with his friends.

She whispered her message and he groaned. 'OK, OK, I'll go and find her. Why doesn't my father get off my case?'

She frowned disapproval at him. 'She's so sweet, Sean; be nice to her.' It didn't sound as if Sean cared much about Nicola and Miranda found that sad. The girl deserved better than a reluctant, indifferent fiancé.

'Don't you start! Dad's bad enough.' Sean glowered, his lower lip petulant. He hated being criticised.

He had his mother's colouring – blond hair, rough and curly, bright, selfish, vain blue eyes, and a fresh complexion. If he didn't stop drinking he would run to fat, his face would turn blotchy, those good looks of his would be destroyed and his liver would start giving him problems.

It was not her problem, though. She was paid to keep the firm in the public eye and make sure it had a good reputation. She was not paid to keep an eye on her boss's son.

Shrugging, she rejoined the party, keeping well away from Terry and the Greek man, who were still talking on the other side of the room.

Miranda circulated, picking up discarded glasses and taking them out to the kitchen to be loaded into the dishwasher by one of the catering team in charge of the party.

The buffet was served half an hour later. She got herself a plate of food and retreated into a corner with it.

Prawns and curls of white turbot crusted with red peppercorns; strips of chicken in a creamy lemon sauce, a few spoonfuls of warm rice mixed with peas and ham and chopped tomato – and a lot of salad. A perfect summer buffet.

While she ate she watched the other guests. The Greek was talking to Sean now, standing beside Nicola who looked faintly nervous of him. Her long eyelashes flickered up and down, her mouth was a little open, as if she had trouble breathing but she kept a polite smile on her mouth, which Miranda found touching.

She really was far too young to cope with Sean, who might not be much older than her but was much tougher. He stood there, one hand in the pocket of his white jacket, while he held a glass in the other, apparently listening to the Greek but all the time looking around the room with those bold, over-bright blue eyes at any attractive woman in view. Miranda felt anxious for Nicola. Someone like her should be cherished and protected, probably had been all her life. Sean would do neither. He would hurt her and make her miserable.

What was the girl's father doing, allowing this match? Couldn't he see what sort of man Sean was turning into?

Come to that, why didn't Terry see the way his son was shaping? Terry wasn't a fool, surely he must realise the danger of allowing Sean to run wild this way?

But it wasn't her business, she just worked for the company. Miranda decided to leave. She had run out of things to say to people she barely knew and she wanted to get home.

She saw Sean walk away, towards the hall, and went out to tell him she must be on her way but just before she reached him she heard the shrill peep-peep of a mobile in his pocket. He got it out, flipped it open.

'Hi. Of course it's me.' He frowned. 'I can't. No, I can't.'

Miranda waited, unsure what to do. Sean saw her hovering and gave her a nod.

'Hang on,' he said into his mobile, then looked at Miranda. 'Yeah? What now? Not another summons from my dad?'

'No, I just wanted to say I have to be going, I

have to drive back to London early. Will you give my apologies to Nicola?'

He cut her short. 'Sure, fine. Thanks for coming. I'll tell Nicola goodbye for you.'

She smiled politely and walked out of the house, hearing Sean talking into his mobile again.

'Look, I told you, I can't see you this weekend, OK? You know what's happening – I can't just walk out on my own party.'

He sounded even drunker now. Well, at least he did not need to drive anywhere. No doubt his father would help him up to bed before he fell over.

Miranda had been careful not to drink too much of the champagne so freely on offer and had just swallowed a mug of strong black coffee. Not that she ever did drink more than a glass or two of wine. But tonight it would have been irritating to have to get a taxi to the station and take the train back to town. It would leave her with the problem of picking up her car some other time.

Sean, however, was not in the habit of thinking about consequences. All his life his father had made his life easy. Miranda did not have parents to do that favour for her. Her father had vanished when she was ten, her mother had not been the sort of parent who believes in mollycoddling offspring. Miranda had left home at eighteen to get a job in London, and had only had herself to rely on for years. It would do Sean good to have to do his own thinking for once.

As she drove away, she caught a glimpse in her wing mirror of Alex Manoussi coming out of the house. From the way he stared after her car she guessed he had followed her, was looking for her, and shivered. Thank God she had escaped before he caught up with her.

He still had the same effect on her as he had had, even before the yacht foundered. Always in black, his face set in strong, hard lines, his manner cold, he was not a man anyone would take to on sight.

When he walked up to her and asked her to dance one evening, on the yacht, she had found being in his arms a disturbing experience and afterwards had avoided him whenever they were in the same room. He had not spoken to her during the dance; she had learnt nothing about him and been left curious.

'Who is he?' she had asked Tom.

'No idea. Obviously the boss knows him. Not exactly the life and soul of the party, is he?'

'He looks like the angel of death.'

Tom had laughed. 'You do say the oddest things, darling. What do you mean, the angel of death?'

'I saw a picture once, when I was about eight. My grandfather had it hanging on his wall. There was a little girl, lying on a bed, and beside the bed a man all in black.'

'An undertaker? A clergyman?'

'No, a man like that one there – with a face like stone, wearing some sort of armour. And he had big, black wings. Grandad said he was the angel of death, who had come for the child. It was really spooky. I hated it. And that guy looks just like the angel. All he needs is black wings.'

He had come for Tom, the very next night. Had he come for her today? Why had he suddenly reappeared, after three years?

A shiver ran down her back. Was she going to die?

Oh, don't be so ridiculous, she told herself. This is rank superstition. Grow up, why don't you?

That night, she dreamt the old nightmare and woke up with the sound of Tom drowning going on and on inside her head and tears running down her face.

She was glad to get up, take a shower, wash the memories out of her head.

It was hot and sunny that Sunday; a little humid. Miranda would not normally wear shorts and a t-shirt to work, but nobody else was around in the office to see her. The porter downstairs at reception, was reading the sports section of a Sunday newspaper with his feet up on the edge of the desk he sat behind. He looked up as she buzzed at the plate glass doors, recognised her and grinned before zapping the door open.

'Working on a Sunday? Hope you're on double time!'

'I hope so, too.' She walked towards the lift while he watched, enjoying his view of her neat behind in brief red cotton shorts which revealed most of her long, slender legs.

'You shouldn't let him take advantage of you!' he called, thinking that he would love to take advantage of her, himself. She had a curvy, sexy little bottom and he loved those legs.

She pressed the lift button, lifting the hair from her perspiring nape with her other hand, groaning. 'It's already really hot out there. We're going to have a scorcher.'

'Afraid the air-conditioning is switched off,' the porter apologised. 'I'm not allowed to have it on at weekends.'

'I'll keep the window open while I'm working.' She vanished into the lift, waving to him and he sighed, settling down to more long hours of tedium, a gold-fish in a glass bowl beyond which life swam freely.

The first thing Miranda did in her office was to open the window but lower the wide-banded linen blinds to keep the room cool and shady. The window looked out into a courtyard full of shrubs and flowers, lined with wooden benches where staff often ate sandwiches in warm weather. The scent of roses drifted up to her nostrils, a dizzying aroma.

She made some strong black coffee, then began keying documents into her word processor, scanning the drawings which went with them and putting them into the computer's memory too, printing them out afterwards, along with other pages of figures already in the machine's memory. Terry had also left her a sheet pointing out where the printer differed from their previous one.

She began to sketch out ideas for the campaign, but kept yawning. On the other side of the courtyard lay the family's apartment which was mostly used by Terry himself. Little golden specks of dust danced in the sunlight as Miranda sat at her desk.

Voices suddenly made her jump. Was that somebody in the courtyard? Nobody should be out there on a Sunday.

Then she realised that the voices came from the other side of the complex — from the family apartment. A window must be open.

'Get your clothes off or do you want me to do it for you?'

Miranda's eyes widened and her mouth opened in amazement. What on earth was going on over there? Had Terry brought a woman here?

No, that certainly was not Terry's voice. Surely it wasn't Sean? But who was with him? It couldn't be Nicola. Even Sean wouldn't talk to her that way. Or would he?

A girl's voice answered. 'Give us a kiss first!'

Miranda did not recognise this voice, but she was sure it did not belong to Sean's fiancée.

Nicola was not long out of one of the best girls' schools in England; shy, very unsure of herself despite her family's wealth. She had a faint lisp and stammered when she was nervous, but she had a typical, middle-class accent.

The voice Miranda had just heard was very confident, not to say oversure of itself, and it had a London accent, brash, pushy, huskily sensual. Of a very different class to Nicola.

Who had Sean got over there? His father would be furious if he found out his son was taking strange girls into the apartment.

'I'll give you something,' Sean said roughly and the girl began to giggle.

'You already have!'

Then came the unmistakable sound of a kiss. Miranda tried to concentrate on her work. She wished they would move away, go into another room. What were they doing in the bathroom?

The sound of running water came next. Oh, my God, were they planning to have a bath? Was that why Sean had told the girl to take her clothes off?

This was becoming very embarrassing. Miranda got up and went over to the window, to close it. As she lifted the blind to take hold of the window catch she saw Sean framed in the window opposite.

He was totally naked, his shoulders wide and powerful, his skin smooth, hairless. She could only see to his waist, but he had a strong, slim, very male body, with good muscle development in the arms and chest.

Behind him steam swirled and billowed. There was a sound of splashing.

'Come on, darling, get in with me!' the girl called.

Sean turned away, giving no sign of having noticed Miranda at the window opposite.

She almost closed the window but left it open enough to let some air circulate. It was too hot to have it shut.

She went back to her desk. Muffled now, the voices continued across the courtyard, laughter mingling with splashes.

Until Sean said sharply, 'What did you say?'

'I'm up the spout,' the girl told him defiantly. 'And it's your baby. You're going to have to marry me, Sean.'

There was a silence, then he snarled, 'You must be joking! Marry you? Even if I could, I wouldn't marry a greedy little tart like you.'

The girl's voice roughened, too. 'You bastard! I'm good enough for a fuck, but not good enough to marry, is that it?'

'You're damned right that's it! How do I even know it's my baby? You weren't a virgin when I met you, were you? You've spread it around since you were fourteen. I know all about you. How many men have you slept with this month? God knows who the father is.'

She sneered. 'These days it's easy to prove. You've heard of DNA, haven't you, Sean?'

'Yeah, but, even if it is my kid, I'm not marrying you. I'm marrying Nicola. At least I can be pretty sure she's a virgin.'

'Bloody hypocrite!'

'Look, I never promised you marriage, and I knew you'd been with half my mates. We were just having a bit of fun.'

'That was before I got pregnant. That changes everything.'

'The hell it does. I'll give you the money to get

rid of it, that's my best offer, so I'd take it, if I was you!'

'Oh, no! I'm not getting rid of my baby.'

'Suit yourself.'

'And you're not getting rid of me, Sean. You're going to have to break off your engagement and marry me. Or I'll talk to the press. I don't think your fiancée's father will be very happy to hear about your little bastard, do you? Your engagement isn't going to last long, once he hears about me and the baby.'

Miranda hated the ugly sound of their screaming at each other. She got up and ran to the window, then froze in shock.

The girl was still screaming, but now her voice was muffled. There were other, uglier noises now – flailing arms beating the water, a rhythmic banging as if hands were beating on the side of the bath.

She knew those gulping, choking sounds. Somebody was drowning.

The nightmare played again in her head. Those familiar, terrifying noises going on and on.

She was dragged backwards in time.

Tom was drowning. Tom was dying. She could not see him, could not reach him, but she heard him and felt sick and faint.

When everything was still again, when silence fell,

Miranda didn't move. Couldn't move. Just stood there, trembling, white as snow, icy cold.

Had she imagined what she just heard? Had it really happened? There had been so many nights when she had dreamt those sounds, woken to hear them in her room, only to be forced to admit she had imagined it.

She stood listening, waiting, staring at the bathroom opposite.

Sean reappeared at the open window. He was tying the belt of a black towelling robe as he reached forward to close the window. Behind him the steam had cleared, the room was horribly quiet.

This time he looked across and saw Miranda.

They stared at each other. His face filled with visible shock. He turned ashen.

Miranda's mind clouded. She had not imagined it. Someone had just drowned. A girl had died in that bathroom.

From the minute she saw that man at the party yesterday she had known a death would follow.

She slowly slipped to the floor in a dead faint.

Chapter Two

Miranda opened her eyes and stared up blankly at the plain white office ceiling. For a few seconds she could not understand where she was, or why she was lying on the floor. It was like a strange dream, except that she knew she was awake and wasn't in her flat.

She began to scramble to her feet unsteadily but as she stood up memory returned and she staggered, clutching at the desk.

Oh, God. Oh, God. Someone had drowned. Over there, across the courtyard, in the bathroom of Terry's flat, someone had drowned.

She lurched forward, pulled up the blinds. The window of the bathroom was closed and she could see nothing through the bubbled glass, not even the shadow of anyone in the room beyond. There wasn't a sound. The summer afternoon was languid and still.

In the distance she heard the drone of London traffic, like bees fumbling among flowers.

Had it really happened? It was dreamlike. Had she heard someone drowning? Or had she imagined it?

Confused, she stared across the courtyard. Suddenly out of the fog of memory and doubt she had a clear vision of Sean's face staring at her through that window, just before she fainted, and she knew she had not imagined anything. It had really happened.

First, she had heard them shouting at each other, and she winced at the memory of what they had said, then those awful, terrifyingly familiar noises had begun.

Panic welled up inside her. What was going on over there now? Was Sean still there, or had he left? What if he was coming round here, to confront her?

Her hands shook with nerves at the idea of seeing him after what she had overheard. What could she say? What would he do?

She wanted to run, but wouldn't give in to it. She had to do everything she always did before leaving the office. Ever since the shipwreck, she found life safer if she stuck to a careful routine. Habit was the hedge that kept out chaos. Leave out something you usually did and the boundaries burst and a deluge rushed in on you. That was what she had learnt in hospital. Get up at the same time, go to bed at the same time, eat at the same times, every day. Safety was a small oasis in the middle of a jungle. You had to stay inside those parameters or you would be lost.

So she lowered the blinds again, picked up the work she had been doing, put it into the safe, locked it, shut down her computer and locked the drawers of her desk. Only then did she pick up her handbag and leave.

As soon as she was out of the office, though, her iron control broke and she began to hurry, to run, her breath coming quickly. Must get away before Sean arrived, she thought. Must get away.

The porter was in his little cubbyhole making a pot of tea; she heard the kettle whistling, heard him rinsing a cup, clattering a spoon into a saucer.

He stuck his head round the door. 'Finished? Hang on, I'll let you out.'

She waited in a fury of impatience, watching the street which was almost empty except for the odd car driving past. Sean would have to come that way, but she couldn't see him yet. He would either have to go down to the car park or walk across the courtyard — there was no direct way through to the office complex from the private apartment. Terry had often complained about it, said how much time he lost having to go the roundabout route. One day soon he meant to get the builders in to make it easier, to put a door in each building so that it would be easier to walk out of the back of one into the back of the other. But it would cost a good deal, and cause a big upheaval, so he kept putting it off.

'There you go!' the porter said and the glass door clicked open.

'Thanks,' she called and hurried out, hearing the door shut behind her and lock.

Now she was out in the open, and vulnerable. She felt hunted. Her eyes flicked round the street but there were few people in view; she could see nobody looking back at her.

Her car was in the underground car park. She hesitated to enter the shadowy underpass, looking for movement, for a darker shadow down there, ears alert for the sound of footfalls, but nobody moved, there was no sound.

So she ran down the slope into the dimly lit interior. She couldn't see anyone and there were no other cars parked there, although on a weekday it would have been full.

Sean must have come by car, but he had no doubt parked on the far side of the complex.

Her car was parked close to the exit. It only took her a minute to reach it, press her automatic key ring to open the doors, and dive inside. She locked it again at once, started her engine and drove out, sick with relief at having escaped.

Sunlight dazzled her eyes. She fished in her glove compartment for dark glasses and put them on as she drove northwards. Inside her head the noises went on and on – if only she could turn them off, like a radio. She had often thought that, after Tom drowned; now she could not recall how long it had been before she slept a whole night without the dream, or spent a whole day without constantly thinking of her dead husband.

She didn't see the traffic she was driving through, or even hear it. Tom called her. She couldn't get to him, only hear the choking, gasping cries. Love and guilt overwhelmed her. If only she had been able to reach him, support him, Tom might never have died.

Tears filled her eyes until she couldn't drive any more, blinded and sobbing. She knew it was stupid and dangerous. She would have an accident if she went on driving in this state.

She pulled off the road and parked in the next layby. The traffic following her thundered on. She sat, trembling, rubbing her wet eyes.

Trying to ignore the other vehicles passing, she leaned her head back and stared fixedly at a sycamore which bent overhead, the lobed leaves shimmering in sunlight, five-pointed, dark green, veined, like hands reaching down to her.

If only she could stop shaking. Sweat poured down her back. Her shirt clung to her.

She had begun to think she was really better, that the nightmare was over, or at least, locked away for good, but here it was again.

Except that this time she had been awake. This time was different in other ways, too. She was not emotionally involved; she had not even known that girl.

She found a packet of paper hankies in her handbag and blew her nose, wiped her eyes, dried the perspiration from her forehead and face. After combing her hair she felt almost normal.

Staring at her face in the little mirror of her powder compact she couldn't believe how ordinary she looked when her mind was in such chaos. Who would guess what was going on inside her at this moment? Even her breathing had calmed down and she could think clearly again.

She should not have fled like that. She should have stayed in the office, rung the police, got help. That was what she should have done, not run away.

She would have to go back, call the police, tell them what she had heard and seen.

Should she first ring Terry and warn him? He

wouldn't be very happy if she called in the police without telling him. Sean was his son, his only child, and Terry thought the world of him.

He was such a good man. She enjoyed working for him; he was an excellent boss. Over the last couple of years he had been very kind to her. He didn't deserve this.

At that moment, Terry was enjoying a long, fluted glass of champagne, lying back in a lounger, on the lawn behind his large, glossy country home, which was being extensively cleaned after the party yesterday. He had come out into the garden to escape the drone of vacuum cleaners, the bang of doors, the hum of the dishwasher.

The bottle of champagne was thrust deep down into a bucket of ice standing on the grass beside him under his wide, dark green cotton umbrella. He could hear the cubes of silvery ice cracking, hear water dripping down into the bottom of the bucket. He loved the sound.

It was a hot afternoon. In spite of the shade in which he lay, dressed in a sleeveless t-shirt and brief shorts, perspiration pearled his skin and he decided he would take a swim in a minute. The doors of the swimming pool stood open, he could just catch the inviting blue gleam of the water within.

It was moments like this that he cherished. Here he was, drinking champagne, lying in the sun, about to go for a swim in his own pool – it was wonderful. A dream come true, most people would say, and they would be right.

This was the life he had always wanted for himself, had daydreamed about, ever since he could remember.

He had been born in a tiny, two-up, two-down, workman's cottage in a narrow, red-brick terrace in the back streets of Victorian Manchester. His father was a big, broad, clumsy man with a face the same dark red as their house, and eyes that were either dull and lethargic, or hot with temper.

Joe Finnigan wasn't a drunk, but he drank heavily, especially if he were out of work. He took bad luck personally, flew into rages, lashed out at anyone near enough to reach, used his fists on his wife and children in any of his moods of resentment and self-pity. Terry learnt at an early age to keep out of his father's way, especially if Dad had been in the pub.

He rarely had a job yet sometimes he had money, other times he had nothing. By the time Terry was five he had realised, partly through his own sharp wits and partly from accusations other boys threw at him, how his father got money.

'Your dad's a crook, Terry Finnigan.'

'Is not!'

'Is. Me dad says.'

'Your dad's a liar, and barmy into the bargain.'

'Is not.'

'Is.'

Sometimes the police came to the house. Terry and Jim were usually in bed by then, but would creep out on to the landing to peer down through the banisters. They got to know the policemen by face, even by name. They filled the tiny house as they shouldered in through the front door.

Terry could remember how his dad had sweated, seeing their hard, flinty faces and those tight, threatening smiles.

'Have you been out tonight, Joe?'

'No, I've been here all evening – haven't I, Nancy?'

'That's right,' Mum would agree. 'Been here all evening.'

She always backed him up in a confrontation of that kind, whatever she might say to him when they were alone.

'Somebody burgled the chemist's shop, Joe. You got any drugs in the house? Mind if we have a look?'

'Yeah, I do mind. Told you. Haven't been nowhere. You get a search warrant if you want to poke around my home.'

'Why would you mind us looking if there's nothing for us to find?'

'Would you like strangers coming into your house, going through your things?'

'I don't burgle other people's houses.'

'Neither do I, then. You can't prove I did.'

'Some day we will, Joe, don't worry.'

He was never caught, but Terry realised how uneasy life was for his parents, especially his mother, who lived in a state of worry and always had a frown of apprehension on her face, especially if someone knocked on the front door.

Terry and Jim would lie in bed, upstairs, listening, tense, anxious. They both loved their mother and were afraid of their father. Their childhood had been tough, they never had enough to eat and wore the cheapest clothes, but they could have borne that, if they had not lived in permanent fear.

When they were in their teens, Jim told him one Friday night, 'I'm off. I can't stand it any more. He's not knocking me about again. Next time I'll hit him back, I know I will. I nearly did, tonight. I wanted to kill him.'

Terry had been shocked. 'Where you going, then, our kid?'

'Getting a job down south.'

'Take me with you. Don't leave me here alone,' Terry had pleaded.

'You're not old enough,' Jim shrugged, then, seeing his white face, placated him. 'I'll come back for you when you're sixteen.'

He had not come. They never heard a word from him. His father threatened to skin him alive if he did come back. His mother was pale and silent. She wept when she thought nobody was in the house. Terry had heard her once or twice. Jim had always been her favourite, her first-born son.

Terry sighed. Was his brother still alive? He had sometimes thought of trying to find him, but it was all so long ago. A lifetime. His parents were both dead, years ago. That old world had gone. He and Jim would have nothing in common, except their shared childhood. What had Jim been doing all this time?

Terry's life was too good, too unbelievable, for him to risk adding an unpredictable element which might ruin everything. His father had become a crook – maybe Jim had, too? You could never tell with heredity.

Behind him he heard a door open and close, then footsteps on the patio.

He looked over his shoulder and relaxed, smiling in satisfaction at the boy coming towards him. That smooth, fresh, young skin, that slim, active body, the expensive grey suit, the gold cufflinks, polished shoes, dark red tie – he was such a good-looking kid. The way he walked, held his head, told you he had cool self-confidence.

A man could be proud of a son like Sean. Terry would have moved mountains for him. In a way, he had, over the past ten years. He had built the business up so that his boy should have a golden future. He had never laid a finger on him, either, from the day of his birth. He did not want his son scared of him, the way Terry had feared his own father. He wanted Sean to be his buddy, to like him, enjoy being with him.

'Hi, Sean – come and have a glass of champagne.'

There was no time to think about it. Miranda knew she had to go back. The road was empty. She drove out of the layby, turning the way she had come.

'Back again? Forgot something?' the porter said in surprise, letting her in again.

She managed a smile and hurried across the foyer to the lift. Up in the office again she glanced at the window. There wasn't a sound over in the flat now. Sean must have gone.

She picked up the phone and dialled the emergency number.

'Police, please,' she told the operator.

Almost at once a calm, measured voice said, 'Police emergency service — what is your phone number, please?'

She plunged straight into what she had to tell them. 'I overheard a fight in a room opposite. I think a girl is dead.'

'First, can I have your phone number, please?'

'What?'

She blanked on it — what was the number for the whole building? She could only think of her office extension. 'I . . . it . . .' she stammered. What on earth was the firm's main number? She knew it, of course she did. Why couldn't she remember it now?

The operator did not seem surprised by her dithering. 'Try to stay calm. Let's start with your name — what's that?'

'Miranda,' she said, relieved to have an easy answer to give. 'You see, I was working, doing overtime, just me — I was alone in the office, and then they arrived, I heard it all . . .'

'Sorry to interrupt, but I must know your surname, Miranda.'

'Oh, yes, sorry — Grey.' She spelt it and as she did so her eye was caught by the printed heading on the office writing paper, giving the address, telephone, fax and e-mail numbers.

Eagerly, she gave the phone number to the policeman at the other end of the line, then began again on her story. He seemed to take forever to take all the details, but eventually she was told to wait where she was, they would be there soon.

They arrived a quarter of an hour later. A CID sergeant, in his forties, grizzled, burly, and a young woman police constable with sculptured features and short, dark, straight hair, came to her office. Others went straight to Terry's flat. She saw them open the bathroom window and look across.

'Is that the window?' the sergeant asked her and she nodded, shivering.

'Yes. Yes, that's it.'

The sergeant opened her window and called across to one of his colleagues. 'OK, that's the room.'

They did not answer, but their expressions were odd and they immediately looked away. Miranda shivered. They seemed to be staring at something – the bath? What did someone look like when they had drowned?

She hadn't seen Tom afterwards, she had been too ill, but she had often thought . . . wondered . . . what he had looked like, how the sea had dealt with him.

That was the stuff of nightmares, the thought of

what the sea had done to Tom. It had kept her awake, night after night, torn between wishing she had seen him so that this everlasting question could be answered, so that it would stop beating in her head – and being glad she had not seen him dead, disfigured, terrible, as he must have been.

One of the men in the bathroom reappeared at the window, tapped, waved, beckoning in a peremptory way.

'They want us over there,' the sergeant said unnecessarily. 'Do you mind coming along, Miss?'

She grew agitated, her skin icy. 'Oh, no. No, I don't want to see her.' See a girl not much younger than herself, drowned, dead. Her stomach clenched in sickness. 'Can't I wait here?'

'I'm sorry, Miss, I'm afraid they would want you to be there, in person, whether or not you agree to identify someone.'

Her legs were wobbly, she could scarcely walk, and the sergeant suddenly put a protective, supportive arm around her.

'You'll be all right, Miss. You don't have to do anything you don't want to.'

Out of the corner of her eye she caught the sideways glance of the policewoman, a cool, strangely cynical look which bothered her, because what did it mean? Did the other woman think she was play-acting to get this male sympathy? Or did she think the sergeant was enjoying himself in this traditional, this age-old way, a man comforting a woman by holding her, talking softly to her.

The passages of the building flickered by in a strangely surreal way. She had rarely visited the private flat, the way to it from the office was circuitous and bewildering. It seemed to take ages to get there.

'Wait here, Miss,' the sergeant said at the flat's front door. 'Collins will stay with you.'

The policewoman gave her a polite smile, yet Miranda got the impression she was under observation, that WPC Collins was there to stop her bolting. Maybe she was imagining it, yet she distinctly felt as if they suspected her of something.

Did they think she was lying? But what about? Surely they didn't suspect she, herself, had drowned the girl? The idea gave her a jolt; she felt nervous, as if she were actually guilty of something.

The sergeant reappeared and now his face was very different. He looked at her in a worrying way, and Miranda felt panic beating in her throat. Why was he looking at her like that?

'Come in now, please, Miss,' he said with the same outward courtesy, yet with frost on every syllable.

She was too disturbed to argue. She went into

the flat and found herself facing another handful of policemen who all watched her, narrow-eyed and with distinct hostility.

One of them said curtly, 'Inspector Baines, Miss Grey. You reported a death, a possible murder. You claimed you had heard someone being drowned in the bathroom of this flat.'

She nodded, swallowing convulsively.

He waved a hand towards the bathroom door. 'Please look for yourself, Miss.'

Something was wrong. But what could it be? For a second she hesitated, still nervous, yet knew she was going to have to obey him. His face was too unyielding. She walked slowly forward and stood in the doorway, her eyes moving at once to the bath.

It was empty.

The smooth cream-coloured bath was spotless, as dry as a bone, gave no sign of having been used recently. There were no splash marks on the walls or on the carpet. The towels on the heated rail were clean, pristine, untouched. The bathroom was immaculate, as clean as a whistle.

She looked at the inspector. 'I don't understand. I tell you, I heard them in here, heard splashing, flailing about. I wasn't imagining it. He drowned the girl in this bath.'

'Then where is the body?' Inspector Baines curtly

asked, and she had no answer, simply stared blankly at him.

They took her back to the police station where she was interviewed for hours by a thin detective in a dark blue suit. When he switched on the tape machine he said into it, in a calm, quiet voice, 'Present, Sergeant Neil Maddrell,' and she noted his name, liking the tone he used.

He was perfectly pleasant, but the way he watched her, spoke to her, told her that he suspected her to be crazy or malicious, or both.

Her statement was typed; after reading it she signed it, and then she had to sit in a waiting room for another couple of hours. At last she had another interview with Sergeant Neil Maddrell.

His voice was gentler, almost soothing. 'Your husband, Mrs Grey, drowned three years ago — that is correct, isn't it?'

She nodded.

'And following on that, you spent some months in hospital, in a psychiatric department. During that time you had frequent hallucinations about people drowning.'

She saw immediately what he was suggesting. 'Yes, but I was ill then. I'm OK now. I've been better for years. What are you trying to imply? That I imagined what happened today? That I made it all up?'

'Did you?'

'No! It happened. I tell you, I heard the girl drowning!' Her voice rose, out of control, shaky. She swallowed, hating the sound of herself, got up, blundering against the table, barking her shins. 'I want to go home!'

'Very well, Mrs Grey, but we would like you to come back here tomorrow. We may need to interview you again.'

They sent her home in a police car. She had left her car at the office. The young policeman driving the car did not speak to her. She sat in the back seat, staring out of the window at passing shops, trying to make sense of everything that had happened.

How had they found out about Tom's death and her months in the hospital? They must have talked to Sean, and Terry, who would have told them her history.

She had accused his son of murder. He was going to be very angry. She couldn't blame him. He would fire her, of course — he would have to, she could see that. Not to fire her would be to appear to believe her.

She was so tired by the time she got home that she had a shower, put on a short cotton nightshirt, made herself some toast and peanut butter, and a mug of hot chocolate, her favourite comfort supper and went to bed. Chocolate was sensuous and soothing. She began to use the survival techniques she had learnt in hospital. To switch off your head. Stop thinking. Shut out worry, fear. Just do little tasks quietly, without thinking about them.

She sat up against banked pillows. The phone began ringing, kept on and on, but she had switched it on to the automatic answering system, so she could ignore it. She would hear the messages tomorrow. By then she might feel stronger.

But she could not shut off her head. Her mind kept ringing up questions, doubts, uncertainties. What had really happened in that bathroom? If the girl had drowned, where was her body?

She nibbled toast and sipped the warm, sweet milky drink, feeling the warmth of the bed seeping into her cold flesh.

She hadn't imagined what she saw and heard. Or had she? From the moment at the engagement party when she saw that man across the room she had been expecting a death, hadn't she? When death has come so close it is hard to believe you have shaken it off completely. You keep expecting it.

When she heard the screams, the splashes, in the bathroom across the courtyard, hadn't it all seemed inevitable, unrolling like a film she had seen before, knowing exactly what was going to happen? The echoes of past experience always made it easier to believe something was happening again, especially if you have been expecting it. The mind loves patterns, echoes, finding again what it has found before.

So, had she imagined everything that happened? For a second she doubted her sanity, then she angrily shook her head. No, no, she hadn't imagined any of it. That girl had drowned. But where was the body?

It made her head hurt to try to think; she kept going round and round in circles, reaching no real conclusion.

Opening a drawer in her bedside table she hunted for a bottle of sleeping pills that she had not needed to take for over a year and had hoped she would never need to take again. There were only a few. She shook two out into her palm, swallowed them with some water, and lay down in the shadowy room, her eyes wide open, the pupils dark with images she desperately wanted to forget, her head aching.

Had somebody drowned in that bathroom or had she dreamt the whole thing? If it had happened, where was the body? Or was she going mad again?

Next day she was up early to go to work. She put on muted grey; a trouser suit with a white shirt and flat, sensible shoes. The outfit made her feel responsible and sensible, but it would not make any difference, she knew that. Terry would terminate her contract. It was bound to happen.

Filled with dread, she left her apartment building and stopped in her tracks, recognising the dark red Jaguar parked outside.

Terry's usual smiling cheerfulness was absent. His features were drawn and grim. Her nerves jumped as he lowered his window and stared at her like an enemy.

'Get in, Miranda.'

She shivered, slowly walked round his car and got into the passenger seat. Terry started the engine again and drove off at speed, his tyres spinning on loose gravel in the road. He didn't speak until he had turned into a quiet road beside a small local park. Pulling up beside railings through which she could see well-mown grass, trees, spreading sycamores under which children were running, laughing, All so familiar and summery.

He turned to face her, his stare level and remote as if he didn't know her and did not like what he saw.

'You realise you'll have to leave the firm? I couldn't keep you on after this.'

She lowered her head and stared at her hands, biting her lip. What was there to say? She had been expecting this ever since she really started to think last night in bed, working out the reactions that were bound to follow her accusation against Sean.

After a pause Terry burst out, 'Haven't you got anything to say? My God, you've accused my son of murder. Murder! Why? Why did you do it? Are you off your rocker again? When I offered you a job people said I must be mad, said I was taking a terrible risk, employing someone who wasn't all there. But I thought you were over all that. I thought you were cured. But you weren't, were you? And now you've done this to my son, a mere boy, only twenty-one, his life just beginning, and you've accused him ...' He broke off, breathing roughly. 'Well, you'll have to go. I don't want you around me from now on. There's no room in my firm for crazy people. Do you understand?'

She sighed, nodded. Yes, she understood. She didn't blame him. Everyone knew how much Terry loved his son. Sean was the apple of his eye and he had great hopes for him. She had always admired Terry's love for his only child and had understood how he felt. Terry had built up a successful company by a lot of hard work, he was proud of what he had achieved, with good reason, and he wanted to leave it to his son, to give Sean all the things Terry, himself, had not had when he was growing up.

'I'm sorry, Terry – really. I thought about ringing you before I talked to the police, but I was in a terrible state. I had to make up my mind quickly and ... well, I couldn't just ignore it, could I? I had to do something fast. If you had heard her drowning ... it was horrible, Terry ...'

He burst out angrily. 'It never happened, you crazy bitch! You imagined the whole thing! And not for the first time, either. I told the police all about you. It's not the first time you've claimed to hear people drowning, is it? That's why they put you away.'

She flinched. 'I was ill, then, I'm not ill, now, Terry. I'm quite clear about what I heard and saw.'

'Sean was with me, at home,' he told her furiously. 'He wasn't in London at all. You know, I was sorry for you, after your husband's death, that's why I gave you the job, but now you're trying to destroy my son. Why are you doing it?'

She groaned. 'I don't want to harm Sean, I've always liked him, but I saw what I saw and I heard what I heard, it was not my imagination, it really happened.'

'You lying bitch! My boy wouldn't harm a fly, let alone drown a girl!' Terry put his flushed, strained face right next to hers, his eyes stared into hers, she could see the little yellow rays around his dark pupil, the deepset laughter lines cutting into his upper cheekbones. Terry was always laughing, smiling; that cheerfulness had carved out his flesh, made his features what they were. She had always liked his face, but suddenly she had a sickening feeling that his face was only some sort of mask, that if you peeled off the smile, the warm curves of cheek, nose, mouth, what you would have left would be something terrifying, The bony, rigid glare of an animal, primitive, predatory, with teeth that bit into you, jaws that could chew you up.

Fear seeped into Miranda. She tried to move away but Terry held on to her shoulders and shook her violently until her head wagged back and forth on her neck so that she began to be afraid it would fall off altogether.

His teeth clenched, he grated, 'Now, listen to me, and listen hard. I want you to vanish, go away, stay away – from the firm, from me and from my son, and especially from the police! And when I say I want you to do this, I'm warning you that if you don't, you'll regret it. Do you understand?'

He shook her again and Miranda cried out at the pain of his grip. His long, brown fingers dug into her and hurt.

'Do you understand?'

She nodded. Through the iron railings of the park she saw sunlight and flowers and laughing children, but here in this car there was a brooding, threatening darkness. Terry's physical bulk loomed over her. She was scared.

'I understand. Please, let go of me, Terry!'

He released her and straightened in his seat, started the engine. As he began to drive on, he said flatly, 'Get a job somewhere a long way off. I'll give you a good reference. And to help you with expenses, you can have three months salary on top of whatever you're entitled to. Just so long as you drop all this nonsense about Sean.'

'The police said they would want to see me again today.'

'Well, tell them you realise now that you imagined it all. You had a flashback. One of your crazy dreams. You know that now and you're sorry you gave them so much trouble.'

He stopped the car outside her flat. 'Don't come anywhere near the office again. If you've left any-thing personal, I'll have it packed up and brought here today.'

She got out of the car, closing the door behind her. His engine flared again; she stood watching him streak off into the oncoming traffic.

As stiffly as a wooden doll, she turned to go back into the building, then stopped as she saw someone standing on the other side of the road.

She wasn't even surprised to see him there. He was still haunting her. The angel of death.

Chapter Three

For a second she stood there, staring. He was still in black, but today his dress was casual – jeans, a t-shirt, a leather jacket. His head towered above those of people swirling around him. Whenever she saw him she was struck by his physical presence; his height, his good looks, the piercing dark eyes.

He took a step forward, as if to cross the road to meet her, and she panicked. Twice now she had seen him and death had followed.

Her eyes clouded with unshed tears of fear and misery, remembering the sounds in the bathroom, the way Terry had spoken to her, her lost job, her anxiety for the future. The tears made her almost blind, seeing through crystal, as she had seen shadows through the window of that bathroom when she was listening to the muffled groans of the dying girl.

She forgot she had been about to go into her apartment block. Without thinking where she was going, what she meant to do, she turned and ran towards the corner of the street. She had to get away from him before something happened.

Tearing round the corner she headed across the street towards a small alley which cut through to another road where there was a shopping centre she often visited. In there, she could hide, keep out of sight, sit at a café and observe who went past.

She ran flat out, breathing heavily, forgetting to make sure no car was coming. She was so absorbed that she didn't hear a car turn the corner, drive up behind her, until too late.

Only when a horn blared did she look over her shoulder. A black car, a foreign make, she thought, was very close; only a few feet away, coming fast. She lunged forward, sideways to the left, to get out of its path, but at the same instant, the car swung left, too, as if the driver was, in turn, trying to avoid her.

The car's bonnet hit her in her right side. Miranda wasn't even conscious of the impact. Fear and pain oddly muted her sensations. She did not know that she flew up into the air, arms flung wide, legs limp, body twisting in flight.

She did not know that she landed against the metal wing and was thrown off again instantly, fell on to the tarmac of the road and just lay there, arms and legs sprawled.

She had already lost consciousness.

She came back to awareness to see a ring of faces staring down at her. Miranda focused on the cold, remote, dark eyes, not surprised to see him there.

'Am I dead, or dying?' she asked him, and heard the others in the crowd take a sharp, indrawn breath of shock.

He didn't reply, just stared down at her. Pain beat through her, she found it hard to concentrate through the agony.

She couldn't be dead, or she wouldn't be in such pain, surely? Did dying hurt?

'Hello there,' a bald man in a green paramedic uniform said, smiling down as he knelt on the road, very close to her. 'I'm Derek. What's your name?'

Her lips fumbled sound which didn't really emerge. She was too tired to struggle to speak; the words she tried to say bubbled silently on her lips.

Living took too much energy – was it even worth it? Had she been happy for an instant since Tom died? She had tried to get over his death, but a day had not passed without her missing him, grieving for him. Maybe she had been meant to die with him? Was that why the angel of death kept haunting her?

'Haunting me, night and day,' she thought aloud.

'What's that, darling?' the paramedic asked, bending closer. 'Can you tell me your name? Then we can let your family know what's happened to you.'

She opened her mouth to speak but pain held her; she made a groaning sound instead. It hurts, it hurts, she tried to say, staring fixedly at the man's face. He had a big nose, rough skin like lemon peel, kind eyes. She felt him willing her to speak again and she wanted to, but she couldn't; she gave up and sank back instead into the well of pain.

The news of her accident reached Sergeant Neil Maddrell the following morning. It was handed to him by his inspector, a comfortably padded woman with startling ginger eyebrows. Neil read the faxed report several times, frowning.

'What do you think? Is it coincidence? Or what?' Inspector Burbage asked him in her deep, gravelly voice.

'Or what, I'd say,' Neil shrugged. 'I don't believe in coincidences this big. But I'd better interview the traffic guy who got there first, then I'll talk to the witnesses he took evidence from. At least one of them seems to suspect the hit and run was deliberate.'

'Depends whether the guy is paranoid, some people always suspect accidents are part of a plot. Anyway, there's something else you ought to see.' Inspector Burbage handed him another fax, a missing person report from an East End police station.

Neil half rose as he read, his face suddenly excited. 'I must talk to this girl at once. If she's the girl from the Finnigan case it changes everything.'

He began tidying up his desk, locking papers away in a top drawer.

'Let me know how you get on, don't forget the paperwork,' the inspector said, waddling away like a ginger duck.

Neil took some time to get through the clotted traffic on the main road through the East End, the Mile End road, but eventually turned into a narrow lane running down to the river and the long-abandoned dockland warehouses. He parked and went up in a graffiti-scribbled lift to the fourth floor.

A small girl with a face like a petulant kitten opened the front door of a flat on the corner looking over the river and the grey expanse of buildings on the south bank.

'Mmm?' she mewed at him, dyed blonde hair cascading down one side of her shoulders.

'Miss Liddie? Miss Delphine Liddie?' Was Delphine really her name? Or had she invented it to give herself a more interesting persona?

'Mmm,' she admitted warily. 'Who're you?'

He pulled out his warrant card and showed it to her. 'Sergeant Neil Maddrell.'

He saw her withdrawal, sensed she was thinking of slamming the door shut in his face, and added quickly, 'About your missing flatmate – has she shown up again yet?'

'Nah.'

A couple of women with shopping bags came past, staring.

'Nosy cows,' the blonde girl muttered. 'You'd better come in.'

The flat was so grotesquely untidy that for a moment he thought it had been burgled; litter on the floor, the furniture, cans of coke standing on radiators, full ashtrays on tables, magazines and CDs lying on the carpet.

Delphine Liddie swept stuff off an armchair to join the other rubbish on the floor. 'There you are. Take the weight off. Want a coffee?'

Briefly he hesitated, wondering how clean the cup was likely to be, then decided to risk it. Accepting hospitality made him more acceptable himself, in his experience. The public was always more forthcoming to someone they had fed or given a drink to. 'Thanks.'

'Black or white?'

'Black, please.'

She vanished into a tiny kitchenette; he heard her clinking and banging about, then she came back with two mugs of black coffee.

He accepted one, saying, 'Thanks', again, and noting with relief that the mug looked perfectly clean. She sat down on a bean-bag shaped like a bright yellow banana, nursing her own mug, staring at him with those big, panda-like, mascara-ringed eyes. Her skin had an improbable tan, certainly not gained naturally – it probably came from a bottle, thought Neil.

'So, tell me about your missing friend. When did you last see her?'

'Last Sunday. She was up early, for once, Tracy don't get up in the mornings much, but she had a lunch date, she was all dolled up for it, must have took her hours just to do her make-up, and she woke me up to borrow a few quid for fares, selfish cow, although she knew I'd been out late on the Saturday night. I only had a ten-quid note, so she took that, and promised to give it back that evening. Said she would get it off Sean.'

'Sean?'

'Finnigan. Tracy's been going with him for a month or two.'

'You're sure of that? Have you seen them together? You've met him?'

'Once or twice he come here to pick her up. Not my type, mind. Oh, looks good, got some great clothes — but I like older men, men with a bit of character.' She fluttered her lashes in Neil's direction but he was not flattered. He wasn't even middle-aged yet — what did she mean, older men? 'But he's loaded, his dad runs some business, computers, Tracy said, and Sean's his only kid.'

'Was it Sean she was meeting for lunch?'

'Yeah, or why would she say he'd give her a few quid when she asked him? Said he owed her. But she never come back and I never got my money, did I?'

'What did she mean, he owed her?'

'How the hell do I know? Tracy said he was going to have to pay for his fun, whatever that meant. She's nice enough, but she can be a tough little cow. Needs to be, like all of us. The world's always trying to get us, we have to be tough to survive.'

'What about her family? Have you contacted them?'

'She ain't got a family. There's her dad, but he's in a home you can't get any sense out of him, Tracy says. He doesn't know who he is, let alone who you are. Nobody's at home, OK?'

'And her mother?'

'Died of cancer while we was at school. Real cut up, Tracy was. Loved her mum. I guess that toughened her up. The social took her away from her dad; he tried it on with her. He was losing it, even then.'

'Have you got a photo of Tracy? What's her full name?'

'There's this picture of her and me at Brighton a month ago, that suit you?'

They looked very similar, much the same height and make-up, with dyed blonde hair and bright, knowing, eyes. They wore the same sort of clothes, too. Tracy was wearing a lacy top through which you could catch glimpses of her smooth, pale skin; a straw hat with the words Kiss Me Quick printed around a red satin ribbon.

The lacy blouse gave her sexiness; the cheap hat made her look like a schoolgirl; very young and pathetic, perhaps because, mused Neil, the hindsight of suspecting she was dead altered the way you thought of her.

'Her name's Tracy Morgan, she said her family came from Wales,' said Delphine. 'I've known her since school. We both lived around here all our lives.'

He glanced out of the window at the ugly greyness of the streets. A life lived here must be depressing.

'Anything else you can tell me about her, or the young man she was seeing?'

'Yeah. She was too good for him, and you can

quote me. She was OK, was Tracy. D'you think something's happened to her? Or has she just gone off with her bloke?'

'At the moment, I've no idea.'

The next time Miranda woke up she was in bed in a quiet, softly lit hospital ward. There was a bed on either side of her, both occupied, the women in them sleeping, the bedcovers pulled up to their necks. There were another three occupied beds across an expanse of polished wooden flooring. The windows had beige blinds drawn down over them. It was night, she realised. Somewhere somebody coughed. Quiet, steady footsteps came from outside.

She had spent so much time in hospital three years ago that this was all very familiar. Almost comforting. In here, she felt safe.

The pain she had been in had diminished, ebbed away. She felt calm and heavy. Miranda knew what that meant. They had drugged her. She recognised this lethargic state, the woolliness inside her head. She was unworried, unafraid, because she was tranquillised.

She carefully moved to see what injuries she had. Her right leg was in plaster, her right arm was bandaged, and there were bandages on her head.

The right must have been the side of her body that was hit by the car. Her left side seemed quite undamaged. She could move her left arm and leg freely, without pain, tentatively fingering the bandages on the other side of her body, investigating what had happened to her.

She wasn't dead, she wasn't even dying, she realised. The angel of death had missed again.

At least this time she had not woken up to find him in the room with her, waiting for her to die.

A nurse came over to her bed, smiling brightly, whispered, 'Back with us again? That's great. How do you feel?'

'I'll live,' she said, and laughed, although it wasn't really funny.

'Well, you sound cheerful! That's good. My name's Sally, Nurse Embry. Can you tell me your name? Then we can get in touch with your relatives or friends, or whoever you want us to ring.'

'I'm Miranda Grey. You'd better tell my mother, but don't ring her until morning, I don't want her woken up in the middle of the night and scared to death.'

The nurse scribbled on the chart hanging from the end of her bed. Miranda watched her, noticing her pallor and deep-set eyes. She looked tired, and no wonder, working all night. Miranda would have hated the job, could never have coped with the long hours or low pay, not to mention the sheer horror of what nurses had to cope with, broken bodies, blood, death.

'We'll need your mother's telephone number and address.'

Miranda whispered them and the nurse wrote them down with long, elegant fingers.

'Dorset? That's a long way off. Is that where you grew up?'

'No, she moved there when she retired.'

Mum had decided, in Miranda's last year at school, to sell their London home and move out to the country. She looked for somewhere special for months without success. At last she fell in love with, and bought, a beautiful, thatched cottage in a village set way off the beaten track within miles of the sea at Lyme Regis. There were only two small, rather poky bedrooms, a huge bathroom, a big, country kitchen, a cosy sitting room. It was ideally a house for one or two people at most.

But the garden was what made Fern Cottage a wonderful home. Her mother spent hours in it, every day – pruning, weeding, mowing the lawn, deadheading roses in the busy cottage garden. Warm, pink, climbing roses sprawled across the front of the cottage every summer, twining around golden honeysuckle whose scent on summer evenings was paradisal.

When she had time, her mother loved to sit out there as long as the light lasted, reading or doing embroidery, under the tiny porch which framed the front door.

But she was always very busy. In fact, her social life was positively hectic. Far more crowded than Miranda's and certainly more crowded than her life in London had been. Country people seemed to take more trouble over their social lives. There were fetes in summer, at the church hall, jumble sales every month or so, flower shows, film shows, gymkhanas and pet shows. Every Saturday, throughout the year, there was a dance at the village hall – country dancing, old time dancing, square dancing, line dancing. Something different every week. The band was the same and not wonderful; they all lived locally and had other jobs but lived for Saturday nights. They had a following locally, people thought a lot of them. When you didn't have much entertainment, except TV or radio, you enjoyed anything that came along.

Her blonde hair might have turned silvery but Dorothy still had sex appeal although she didn't work at it. It was simply something she had been born with; men reacted to it on sight, picked up the vibes she gave out, the dazzling come-hither of her smile, the glint in her eye, the sheer liveliness of the way she talked and moved and laughed. Watching men's faces as they talked to her mother, Miranda could see that to them she seemed almost to glitter like the star on top of a Christmas tree. Men queued up to take her out and she enjoyed their company, but although she kept getting marriage proposals she always turned them down.

'I don't fancy being married, again, and tied down to one man. I'm having too much fun,' she once said. 'I like them all, but there isn't one of them I could be serious about. I just want a partner to go dancing with, have dinner with – and I like to ring the changes. Once you really know them, there's nothing new to learn and it gets tedious.'

'You're a wicked woman,' Miranda had said, laughing. 'As you get older, you'll need companionship, somebody else around night and day. Surely?'

'Maybe, but I haven't got to that stage yet. You won't have realised it, yet, Miranda, but life is one stage after another. When you're young you want to have fun, then you start yearning to get married, to have babies, all that. The biological clock starts ticking. I remember feeling that way. Been there, got the t-shirt. Now I'm on another level. I've been through that stage and come out the other side. I've discovered freedom and being responsible for yourself. I love running my own life. I don't want a man around full time. They're bossy. They can't help it. It's the testosterone. They always want to run things, tell people what to do. They feel that that's their role in life. Well, I won't put up with it. At the moment I'm free to make my own decisions, and I want to go on doing so. I don't want some man around all the time, trying to run my life, giving me orders, telling me what I can and cannot do.'

Miranda had stared at her, absorbing what she said, and her mother had grinned teasingly. She still had all her own teeth, small, neat, whitish, just as she had the same trim, healthy figure she had had all Miranda's life. Dorothy took care of herself; ate a lot of fruit and vegetables, drank the odd glass of wine, walked a lot, swam, was always busy working either in her small house, or out in the garden.

'Am I right, or am I wrong?' Mum had demanded.

'It's your life,' Miranda had shrugged. 'How do I know if you're right or wrong?'

'Oh, I'm right. To paraphrase Jean Jacques Rousseau, women are born free and everywhere they are in chains. Even worse, they seem to like it that way. Well, not me. I've been married. I don't want to put the chains back on again.'

'But you loved Dad, didn't you? I don't remember him as some sort of tyrant.'

'No, of course not, but I was still a prisoner, of you as much as your dad. Duty is the worst prison of them all, don't forget that. When you have a husband and children, you're never free. But now I can get up when I like, go to bed when I like, do what I like.'

'What are you smiling at?' Nurse Embry asked as she tidied the coverlet on the bed.

'Something my mother once said to me.'

'She lives alone? Your dad ...'

'Died. You haven't told me yet exactly what my injuries are.'

'Your right ankle is broken, that's why it's in plaster. That will take a while to heal, I'm afraid. You've strained your right wrist, that must have been when you fell, you would have put your hand out to stop yourself. You've got superficial cuts and bruises to your head, hence the bandages – but you haven't got concussion or any serious injury.'

Frowning, Miranda said, 'Well, that doesn't sound too bad – I thought it might be worse.'

'You sound almost disappointed!' Nurse Embry grinned at her. 'It's bad enough, surely!'

Miranda smiled back at her. 'I'm relieved, believe me!'

A woman in a bed on the other side of the ward raised her head and called, 'Nurse ... nurse ... I feel sick!'

Nurse Embry hurried over there. Miranda closed her eyes and drifted away into a dream about the Dorset garden; the clove-like scent of old-fashioned, frilly petalled pinks, a thrush picking up a snail and smashing it down on the rockery, the sound of the wind in the lime tree, and her mother wandering about clipping and weeding.

At lunchtime next day she was eating a small chicken salad when a man walked up to her bed, drew up a chair and sat down. The other women in the ward watched curiously. One of them bridled and said pointedly, 'This isn't visiting time, you know.'

The man ignored the comment. One of the nurses came into the ward and the other patients all watched avidly as she went over to Miranda's bed, expecting the visitor to be turned out. Instead the nurse drew the curtains around Miranda's bed and murmured, 'Now, I told you, you can only stay for a little while.'

Miranda stared at the visitor who smiled.

'Hello,' he said. 'You remember me, don't you? Sergeant Maddrell, Neil Maddrell. I interviewed you a couple of days ago.'

She flinched back against her pillows, reminded sharply of what she only wanted to forget. She had barely taken in what he looked like, but now she realised she did remember him. What was he doing here? Had he come to give her another chilly warning about wasting police time?

'I'm sorry to hear about your accident. I've talked to your doctor and heard about your injuries. I'm afraid you'll be stuck in bed for a while. That will be boring for you, but at least you're being well looked after and you can have a good rest in here. You look as if you need one.'

His face was angular, a sculptured mask, the skin pulled tight over the bones and framed in straight, dark hair. His eyes were sharp and intelligent, bright hazel. He wasn't good-looking, yet he was attractive, she liked looking at him. Perhaps it was that calm, cool expression he always wore? You felt you could trust him. She should have remembered him. He had a memorable face.

'How did it happen?' he asked her.

Nervously she whispered, 'I don't remember much, just that I was crossing a road when a car hit me.'

She remembered his quiet, level voice very well, she found; the patient technique with which he questioned, water dropping on a stone, repeating every query until he was convinced he had got a final answer. He took her through her accident now in the same way.

'Did you notice the make of car?'

'No; just that it was black.'

'Had you ever seen the car before?'

'Not that I remember.' She was puzzled by the question – why should she have seen the car before? What was he implying? Filaments of doubt began twining through her mind. Why was he here, anyway? Why would a detective follow up a perfectly ordinary traffic accident? Surely they didn't suspect her of inventing it?

'Did you see anything of the driver?'

She shook her head. 'It all happened too fast.' Defiantly, angrily, she said, 'There were plenty of people around. I'm not inventing it.'

He considered her soberly, his head on one side, then crisply told her, 'I know you're not. We have statements from a number of people who saw it happen, including an eye witness who says the car deliberately swerved towards you after you had moved out of its path.'

'Deliberately …' Miranda looked at him with startled incredulity and he nodded.

'You seem surprised – that hadn't occurred to you? Our witness said the driver drove straight at you.'

She remembered with sudden, shocking intensity the way the car had been driven at her, had hit her twice. 'He meant to hit me?'

'You didn't get that impression at the time, or since?'

She had to be honest. 'No. Never.' She wished it hadn't entered her mind now, she did not want to think that somebody had deliberately tried to kill her. A shudder ran down her spine.

Sergeant Maddrell stared fixedly, those hazel eyes wide and clear. 'Try to remember exactly what happened, how the car came towards you – and think about it. Could the driver have meant to hit you?'

'I don't know, how can I tell? I heard the car behind me and looked round.' Her memory sharpened. 'No, wait a minute . . . the driver sounded his horn, to warn me he was there. Yes, that was what happened. I heard his horn and looked round – surely he wouldn't have warned me if he wanted to hit me?'

'Maybe not,' agreed Neil. 'You hadn't been aware of a car behind you until then?'

'No, it was the horn sounding that made me realise there was a car right behind me. When I saw it, I tried to get out of the way but it swerved at the same time, and hit me. And . . . anyway . . . why on earth should anyone try to kill me?'

A little silence fell while they stared at each other. A coldness crept through her bones at something in his eyes, a thought which leapt from him to her.

'You can't think of anyone who might?' His voice

held no particular inflection, yet she knew what he was hinting.

She slowly shook her head, refusing to believe what she realised he was suggesting.

'Someone couldn't be trying to silence you?' he persisted.

'Terry wouldn't do something like that,' she burst out. 'No. The idea's ridiculous. Terry's not a murderer.'

'But you believed his son killed that girl.'

She bit her lip, remembering those sounds in the bathroom. Sean was so young, a boy with fresh, apple-blossom skin and clear eyes — it was hard to think of him as a cold-blooded killer. If he had killed his pregnant girlfriend it must have been in a fit of crazy rage. He wouldn't kill again, Sean wasn't a natural killer; she couldn't believe he would try to kill her.

'You didn't believe a word I said!' she accused and saw his eyes flicker. Suddenly she began to realise there was something behind his visit, something he had not yet told her. 'Why have you really come to see me, Sergeant?'

He hesitated, then reluctantly said, 'We have had some further information. A girl has been reported missing. She shared a flat with another girl, who went into a local police station yesterday to report her missing. She went out on Sunday morning, and has not been seen since. I saw the report and went to see the flatmate who told me that her friend had been seeing Sean Finnigan for a few months.'

Her eyes were stretched wide in shock and a strange sort of relief because she could see at once that the police no longer thought she was crazy and had imagined the whole thing.

'So you believe me now!'

He didn't say yes or no, he simply shrugged. 'When I heard a car had tried to run you down I was concerned, obviously. It seemed a big coincidence, and we had several witnesses too, who seemed sure the car had driven straight at you, hit you, then gone on without stopping or even slowing. In fact, it seems the car accelerated after hitting you. A pity you didn't see who was driving it.'

'I told you, it happened too quickly.'

'Yes. But if you had seen the driver . . .' He broke off, seeing her face tense. 'What is it? Have you remembered something? Did you see someone?'

'Not in the car,' she said huskily, shivering. 'But before . . . and afterwards, after I was knocked down. I was conscious for a while. There were people all round me and one of them . . .' She swallowed convulsively.

'Yes?'

'One of them was a man I recognised. I saw him first outside my apartment building, standing on the other side of the road. In fact, that was why I ran round the corner. He scares me, I didn't like the way he was staring at me. And then when I was lying in the road I saw him again, among the crowd.'

'Who was he? Does he know the Finnigans?'

'He's a Greek ...'

'A Greek?' the policeman interrupted sharply.

'Yes, he's called Alexandros Manoussi, and he's a client.'

'Of the Finnigan firm?'

'Yes, we ... they ... make the navigational computers he puts into his boats. He's a boat builder, back in Greece.'

'And you saw him outside your flat before the accident?'

'Yes.'

'And again, after you were knocked down?'

She nodded, remembering her foreboding the minute she set eyes on him after the accident, the strong sense she had had that she was about to die. She did not tell Sergeant Maddrell her fears. Or that she had always called Alexandros Manoussi the Angel of Death – he would look at her incredulously, then revert to his first belief that she was crazy.

Miranda knew how it would sound. She also knew

85

for certain that she wasn't mad, or even irrational. The way the Greek showed up just before something terrible happened was more than just coincidence. She didn't really know what it was, only that she was terrified whenever she saw him.

Strange how she remembered so distinctly seeing that picture of the Angel of Death in her childhood. It had petrified her; the stern, dark eyes, the commanding hand beckoning, the black armour, those wings. Her grandfather had told her the Angel of Death came for children, maybe that had disturbed her? She had never seen the picture again, yet she recalled every detail as if she had seen it yesterday. But then childhood memories were like that. If they sank into your mind at all, they stayed there, unchanged, year after year.

'But you only know him through the firm? There's no personal relationship?'

'None at all. I've only met him twice, in fact – the first time three years ago. His firm owned the boat Terry chartered.'

Sergeant Maddrell watched her as she broke off. 'The boat you and your husband were on, the one that was wrecked?'

She nodded.

'And the second time you met him?'

'At the party for Sean's engagement.'

The policeman's eyes narrowed thoughtfully. 'Now that is an odd coincidence — that you met him first just before your husband was drowned, and then again, just before you heard a girl drowning in the office block.'

Miranda didn't answer. Sergeant Maddrell was intelligent enough to seize upon the coincidence, but she still could not tell him that she called the Greek the Angel of Death.

'Have you talked to Terry and Sean since the girl was reported missing?' she asked.

'We're going down to their country house this afternoon.'

The reply surprised her. 'Wasn't Terry at work this morning?'

'Yes, he was, but we preferred to interview them in the country. I want to get an idea of the ground around it.'

Were they going to search it for the girl's body? Where would Sean have hidden it? It must be buried somewhere, you couldn't just leave a dead body lying about. But there was plenty of room to hide it in the grounds of Terry's country house.

That would suggest, though, that he knew his son had killed the girl. Sean could surely not have buried a body near the house without his father knowing?

The nurse came along with a trolley of rattling

medicine containers, pulled back her curtains and nodded to Neil Maddrell in a friendly, bossy way. 'Sorry, officer, but I'm afraid you're going to have to leave now. It's time for the patients to have their treatments and they won't want an audience. You can come back tomorrow if you need to ask her any more questions.'

He stood up immediately. 'I may do that. I hope you're feeling better by tomorrow, Mrs Grey.'

He walked out of the ward watched by seven pairs of female eyes. 'Now he's nice,' the nurse said, and Miranda agreed with her.

Later, the woman in the bed next to her asked, 'Was that really a policeman visiting you? Was he asking questions about your accident? It was a hit and run driver wasn't it? Have they caught him?'

How did such gossip get around? Presumably they had asked the nurse.

'Not yet, but they have had some information, and they wanted to check it with me.' Miranda was on medication that left her drowsy and peaceful, and finding out that the police now believed her about Sean was very comforting. The tension had drained out of her. She felt safe, her body heavy and limp.

'Well, let's hope they get him soon. They want locking up, driving like that. He could have killed you.'

Had he intended to? that was the question, but Miranda was not going to discuss that with the other woman.

'I'm Joan Patterson, by the way. Your name's Miranda, isn't it? I heard the nurse talking to you. You don't mind me using first names? Call me Joan.'

She was much older, about fifty, with a thin, flushed face and sharp, curious eyes.

Miranda made a polite response, but her heart sank as she realised the other woman was one of the sort who talks non-stop, barely pausing to give you a chance to reply.

Her mother arrived that evening, along with the other visitors streaming into the ward with bunches of flowers, bags of fruit and boxes of sweets. The patients were all sitting up against banked pillows, beds very tidy, their hair brushed and most of them wearing make-up which they had spent the last half-hour applying slowly and intently.

Miranda had not expected a visitor and was surprised to see her mother, wearing a flowered scarf flowing round her neck, coming along the ward towards her, clutching flowers.

'Now what have you been up to?' she asked, dropping the brown-paper-wrapped flowers on to the bedside table and leaning down to kiss Miranda's cheek. 'Getting yourself run over! Silly girl.'

'Hello, Mum.' Miranda was suddenly surrounded by her mother's perfume; a home-made essence of lavender Dorothy made every year. She made rose water, too, from the flood of roses which appeared in her garden each spring and summer. On shelves in her kitchen the glass bottles of perfume stood in rows. The sun shone through them and made an impressionistic wash of pink and mauve on the green walls.

'What on earth were you doing, to get yourself into this state, darling?'

'I couldn't help it, a car ran into me from behind. Good of you to come all this way. I know you hate leaving home, especially at such short notice. You must stay in my flat – I'll give you the keys if you pass me my handbag.'

Mrs Knox looked around. 'Where is it, then?'

'In the cupboard down there.' Miranda pointed and her mother bent to open the small cupboard under the bedside table top.

'Oh, I see it.' Mrs Knox brought out the brown, yellow and navy-blue harlequin patchwork leather shoulder bag which Miranda had bought at a trade fair in Dublin last year during a short trip there with Terry on business. Miranda opened the zip compartment inside it and found her keys. 'Here you are, Mum. Don't forget to give them back to me, I have only this set.'

'Why don't I have another set made for you while I'm here. You ought to have a spare set, you know, in case you lose these.'

'I suppose you're right. Thanks, good idea.'

Putting them into her own bag, Mrs Knox pulled up the chair which was pushed under Miranda's bed at the far end, and sat, smoothing down her brown velvet skirt. She was wearing shades of yellow and brown, today; a sweater as vivid as the feathers of a canary, toffee-coloured suede shoes, that rich, silky skirt. Miranda felt people staring. Her mother had always made people stare. As a young woman she had been beautiful. As an old woman she was still lovely, in a different way. She glowed with life and other people watched her with admiration and envy, wishing they felt as obviously happy as she did.

Some people were so dull, so traumatised by their humdrum lives that they trudged along without lifting their heads, merely straining to get through each day. Dorothy Knox almost danced through her life.

It must be her genes, Miranda thought. But I inherited them, too, so why don't I look like her, give off that radiant self-assurance, that laughing certainty? I inherited genes from my father, too, of course, a completely different set. Impossible to untwine them all, decipher the secrets of my own biology.

How many genes were there? Hundreds? No,

thousands, if not millions. The ones that dictate your colouring, height, tendency to put on weight, your ability to draw, or sing, or dance? The ones that make you good-tempered or irritable, that give you the talent to cook brilliantly, or shape wood into amazing reality? It was like a card game where you never knew what sort of hand you would draw, you just had to play it the best you could.

Was there a gene for luck? Were some people born fortunate? Some who habitually won a prize in raffles, or a bet on a horse race? While others inherited bad luck.

She was sure she wasn't lucky. When Tom died, that had been bad luck — but had it been her genes or Tom's dictating that outcome? And when she saw Sean in that bathroom, whose bad luck had caused that? Surely, Sean's. Yet she felt as if it were she who had unlucky genes. If there was such a thing.

'Tell me about the accident,' her mother said, taking a plum from the bowl of fruit on Miranda's bedside table. She peeled it delicately, dropping the dark red skin into a paper handkerchief, before putting the fruit into her mouth with a sighing sensuality.

'I was crossing a road near my flat. A car came round the corner, very fast, and hit me.'

Dorothy swallowed the fruit in her mouth. 'And didn't stop, so the police told me!'

'No, it was a hit and run driver.'

Miranda was getting sick of telling the story, this was the third time today, she had the words off pat and muttered them in a cross voice.

'Feeling fed up?' her mother guessed shrewdly. 'A bit tart, those plums, not quite ripe enough for me.' But she took another one and began peeling that. She loved fruit, perhaps she was so healthy because she ate well, lots of fruit and salad and vegetables. She grew a good deal of what she ate, saving money, too. She had green fingers; she could persuade the most difficult plants to grow for her.

'I don't feel too good.' Miranda admitted.

'I don't suppose you do.' Dorothy eyed her thoughtfully. 'You don't look good, either. Are they looking after you well?'

'The nurses are very kind.'

'I hate hospitals, myself. If you're ill, they make you worse. If you aren't, you soon catch something with all these germs buzzing around. As soon as the doctors allow you to leave here you must come home with me. You need some fresh air and good country living.'

'I'd like that, thanks, Mum,' she said gratefully. It would be wonderful to get away from London. Especially at the moment.

Her mother finished her second plum and wiped

her fingers on another paper hankerchief. 'I suppose you've let your firm know you're in hospital?'

'I left there. I haven't got another job yet.' Miranda didn't want to explain the whole story to her mother, she didn't feel well enough to talk about Sean and the girl, and what she had heard and seen.

Dorothy Knox looked surprised. 'I thought you liked working there.'

'I did, once. It's too complicated to explain, I'll tell you all about it later. I'm not up to talking much just now.'

Her mother stayed another ten minutes, then, seeing Miranda's eyes half-closed, her body limp, left, kissing her.

'I'll be back tomorrow. Anything I can bring you?'

'No, I'm fine, thanks, Mum.'

'Well, eat some fruit – it will do you more good than any of the medication they're giving you in here. You're so pale, I worry about you. You need lots of vitamins and anti-oxidants.'

When she had gone, Miranda slid into sleep and the old dream about Tom and the sea and the angel of death. She had endured it so often, yet it was always as frightening; her own emotions as powerful as the rush and violence of the dark green waters.

She woke up with a start to find the ward in silence.

All the visitors had gone; the other women lay in their beds, staring at her in a strange way.

The woman next to her, Joan Patterson, leaned over and said, 'Having a nightmare, weren't you, dear?' She had made up carefully before visiting time; the yellow foundation and bright red lipstick looked bizarre on a woman lying in bed, in a hospital-issue nightdress, made her clownish, ridiculous, but her face was serious and concerned.

'What?'

'You were making pretty scary noises. Sounded as if you were crying in your sleep.'

Desperately embarrassed, Miranda flushed, knowing all the other women were listening, but somehow forcing a smile. 'I must have been dreaming about hospital food.'

Mrs Patterson laughed obligingly. 'Ugh ... don't even talk about it! I hope to God we don't have that stew again, it was disgusting. I'd swear it was dog meat.'

The others all joined in, then, with comments of their own about the food they were given, making it possible for Miranda to shut her eyes again. She would give anything to go home soon, she hated living in public, cheek by jowl with strangers, who could watch her when she was in pain or dreaming or even just thinking. There was no privacy in here. Even if you had treatment and the curtains were drawn the others could all hear what was going on.

Sergeant Neil Maddrell slowed down as he drove through the gates of Blue Gables, Terry Finnigan's big house in Sussex, ten miles from Horsham.

He gave a low whistle. 'Not bad! A bit flash for my taste, but spacious and the gardens are gorgeous.'

Detective Constable Haddon made a face. 'Bet he had it built – it doesn't look that old. It must have cost a fortune, too. He could have bought an Elizabethan mansion for what this must have cost him.'

'Some people prefer new houses.'

'Some people have no taste. If I was as rich as Finnigan I'd buy something old.'

They parked on the gravelled terrace outside the front door. A girl in a dark blue dress with white cuffs and collar opened the door and invited them inside.

'Do you have an appointment?'

'We rang to tell Mr Finnigan that we would be coming.'

'Please wait here, I'll tell him you've arrived.'

Jim Haddon walked around, inspecting the gilt-framed sporting prints hanging on the wall. 'Bought down Hoxton Market,' he muttered.

'No, actually I got them from Sotheby's, they're the real thing,' Terry Finnigan said behind him.

Jim Haddon went red, mumbling, 'Oh ... sorry ... I'm no art expert.'

'They're boxing prints over here. Very early ones. Worth quite a bit.'

The three men solemnly inspected the four prints of naked-chested men squaring up to each other in pairs.

'No gloves, notice,' Terry said. 'In the eighteenth century fighters didn't wear them. They fought bare-knuckled, and there were often nasty injuries to the face, which was why boxing was banned at times.'

Neil pointedly glanced at his watch. 'Sorry to hurry you, Mr Finnigan, but we have to get back to town by six. Can we talk somewhere private? Is your son here?'

Terry's face stiffened. 'Yes, come into my office. Would you like something to drink? Tea, coffee, or something stronger?'

'Tea would be nice, thank you.'

Sean was standing by the window in the square room they went into. He turned to nod coolly.

'Sit down, officers,' Terry said, gave his son a look. 'And you, Sean.' He picked up the phone. 'Ellen? Tea for four, in my office.'

Sean sat down, but fidgeted restlessly. 'I've a lot

to do today. Can we get on? You keep asking stupid questions day after day.' He gave Neil a sullen stare, his face mutinous. 'I have better things to do with my time.'

'Do you know a girl called Tracy Morgan?'

The question knocked Sean backwards. He opened and shut his mouth like a fish out of water, making wordless noises.

Terry froze in his chair, watching his son anxiously.

Sean swallowed, finally said hoarsely, 'Tracy? Yes, I know her. I've met her, that is. I don't know her well.'

'I've been told you have been dating her for weeks.'

'Who told you that? Miranda Grey, I suppose! They ought to move her into a psychiatric ward. They shouldn't ever let her out.'

'They will, she's quite sane.'

'They're letting her go home? When?'

'Never mind Miranda. It was not her who told me about you dating Tracy Morgan. That's true, isn't it? You have been seeing her quite often for several months.'

'No! It's a lie, a dirty lie.' Sean was almost desperate with fury, his face darkly flushed, his eyes glittering.

He hesitated, muttered, 'Well, maybe I took her out once or twice, that's all. I don't call that dating.'

'You saw her more often than that, I think. And now she's vanished. She went missing the day Mrs Grey says she witnessed a scene in the bathroom of your flat. A big coincidence, isn't it?'

Sean blundered to his feet, glaring like an angry bull. 'You can't prove I did anything! You can't prove she's dead. Stop badgering me or I'll get my solicitor to deal with you.'

'I think you are going to need your solicitor, sir, when we find the body.'

'Find it before you come here again, harassing me!'

Dorothy Knox stopped off en route to the flat to buy herself a few groceries. Heaven knew what sort of larder Miranda kept. Dorothy did not have a very high opinion of her daughter's housekeeping. Oh, the flat would be tidy enough, no doubt, Miranda was fastidious about where she lived, but she would eat her lunch out every day when she was working, and probably ate a very small breakfast, some cereal, at most, and in the evenings would eat out of the fridge, snacking on microwave food the way young people did these days.

She did not look well, and that wasn't simply because of her injuries. Dorothy had noticed a deep-seated malaise in her daughter's eyes. But the misery had been there for a long time, ever since Tom died.

They had been so happy together. Dorothy had rarely seen a couple who were so perfectly suited. His death had blighted Miranda's life. She had always been a very affectionate child. She was not one of those cool, self-contained people who do not appear to need people. Miranda was open and loving with her family and friends.

On her wedding day she had been a radiant bride; her happiness visible, even in the photos Dorothy kept on her mantelpiece at home. It had been a wonderful occasion; everyone who had been there had been uplifted by seeing such a joyful bride and groom.

The tragedy of losing Tom in such a terrifying way had shadowed the child's life ever since, though. Dorothy sensed that her daughter had not recovered even now.

She needed to spend some time somewhere very quiet and peaceful, especially now, after this accident. Dorothy was determined to take her back to the country; force-feed her, if necessary, see that she went to bed early, make her take walks in God's good air, spend time in the garden, let nature work its miracle. She believed in nature's power to heal.

In her capacious shopping bag, Dorthy had packed some of her own produce; a box of freshly laid eggs, a bag of mixed, washed vegetables; tomatoes, courgettes, onions, cauliflower, potatoes. Another bag of fruit; gooseberries, raspberries. But she would need other items; staples like rice, spaghetti, salt and pepper, flour and olive oil.

She was heavily laden by the time she put the key into the front door of Miranda's flat. Putting down her bags she pushed the door shut behind her then groped for the light switch.

Stupid woman, you should have put that on first, she thought. Now, where is it? While she was feeling along the wall with one hand, she was taken aback by a sound, and then the faint rustle of a movement.

She realised with a gulp of shock that there was somebody else in here, in the dark, with her. Somebody trying to breathe quietly.

'Who's that?' she cried, trying to see in the shadows, but only glimpsing a solid bulk in front of her.

It ran at her a second later. Dorothy shrank back with a gasp, but could not get out of the way. Blows began to shower on to her head.

Chapter Four

Miranda was sipping milky coffee during the mid-morning break next day when Sergeant Maddrell arrived, marching without hesitation along the ward under the close scrutiny of the other women, who stirred and began to whisper, recognising him from yesterday.

'Your young man's back,' Joan Patterson whispered to her. 'He looks like a policeman – is he?'

Was she a witch, wondered Miranda, or had she asked Nurse Embry? Gossip went round the ward like wildfire; everyone seemed to know what was wrong with everyone else, all about their marital status and relationships, their jobs and personal problems.

'Good morning, Miranda,' Neil said, apparently oblivious to the stares and murmurs, drawing the curtains round her bed before he pulled out her chair and sat down. 'How are you today?'

'Fine,' she said, although she was in some discomfort all the time, with her arm and her leg, not to mention the dull ache in her head. There was no real pain involved, but at the same time she never felt really well and the drugs she was being given to keep her pain under control made her feel vaguely depressed and lethargic.

He hesitated, studying her, and she tensed, watching his face, certain suddenly that he was going to give her bad news.

'What is it? Something's wrong, I can feel it. What's happened?'

'Now, don't get upset, this isn't anything terrible,' he quickly said. 'Be calm, please.'

'Tell me, just tell me!' Easy for him to ask her to be calm, when his very expression made her heart beat fiercely, and made it hard to breathe.

'Your mother . . .' he began and she gave a sharp cry, her eyes wide.

'Mum! Oh, God, what's happened to her?'

'She's OK, I promise you,' he soothed, taking her hand and patting it as if she were a child. 'But she won't be visiting you today because she's in here, herself . . .'

'She was run down by a car, too!' Guilt and

worry made her voice high and shaky. Neil patted her hand again, stroked it softly, watching her with concerned eyes.

'No, no, it wasn't that.' He paused, said in a careful voice, 'She was going to be staying in your flat last night, wasn't she?'

'Yes, I didn't want her having to pay for a hotel.' Miranda's mind raced with alarm, trying to guess what had happened. 'Get on with it, tell me what's happened to her. Are you trying to frighten the life out of me? Just tell me.'

'She walked in on what was probably a burglary,' he said flatly.

'Oh, God.' Miranda's lip trembled and she bit down on it. 'They attacked her? Was she badly hurt?'

'No, no. He knocked her out, but as I said it isn't serious. They're only keeping her in here for a night to make sure she hasn't got concussion. And because there would be nobody to look after her if she was sent home while she was a little groggy.'

'Have you seen her?'

'Yes, and I promise you, she is OK. She talked to me quite rationally. All that was wrong with her were some bruises and a headache. Maybe the nurse will arrange for you to visit her in her ward, so you can see for yourself. They could take you along in a wheelchair.'

'I'll ask Nurse Embry.' Miranda was thinking hard, her brow furrowed. 'Do you think the burglary was mere coincidence? Or is it part and parcel of what's been happening? The murder, the hit and run driver . . . is it all connected? It must be, mustn't it?'

'We aren't sure, but it could be. He certainly ransacked your flat, I'm afraid. We won't know if anything was taken until you've been able to check the flat yourself, but we have a feeling nothing at all is missing. The obvious things are all still there – the television, the microwave, the musical equipment. Burglars usually take stuff like that. Easy to carry, and then to sell.'

'Did Mum see him?'

'Apparently not. She opened the front door but before she could switch on the light somebody started hitting her on the head.'

'Oh, poor Mum! She must have been terrified. I shouldn't have suggested she should go to my flat. That was stupid of me, but I didn't think . . . it never entered my head that she could be in danger.'

'Obviously, why should it? But she was lucky – he left the front door open and one of your neighbours walked past and saw her, and called the emergency service. A Miss Neville?'

'Oh, Janet, yes,' Miranda said absently. 'We aren't friends, but we do say hello, and talk about the weather, now and then.'

'Well, your mother may owe a big debt to Miss Neville. Had she lain there all night she might have developed hypothermia. Older people do, even in warm weather, especially with a head wound. Miss Neville didn't recognise her, and, knowing you were in hospital she had no idea what your mother was doing in your flat, so as well as asking for an ambulance she talked to us, and since I'm dealing with your case the word reached me. I didn't want to disturb your sleep in the middle of the night, which is why I'm here now.'

'You've seen my mother?'

'I've just come from seeing her. And she seems fine to me. But I don't think she should return to your flat. I've advised her to go home, to Dorset, in fact. That would be wisest.'

Miranda took a sharp breath. 'You think she might be attacked again?'

'Highly unlikely, but it is better to be safe than sorry.'

Closing her eyes, she asked, 'Have you found ... anything, yet?'

'In your flat? I told you, it had been thoroughly searched – he had been through all the drawers and cupboards and thrown stuff about, I'm afraid, all over the floor. Deliberate destruction, I'd say, there's no reason to make such a mess, but he might be trying to scare you off, warn you against talking to us.'

'I didn't mean my flat — I meant have you found ... her, yet?'

He grimaced. 'Not yet, but then — where do we look? She could be buried anywhere. We're still searching his father's place, but we haven't found anything, and it's my opinion that that's the last place he would put her, knowing you witnessed what happened.'

She nodded. 'I see what you mean. Yes. And it would mean that Terry knew, was involved — which I can't believe. You don't know him, but he's really a very nice man, I simply can't imagine him getting mixed up with murder and ...' Her voice trailed away.

They stared at each other. Neil nodded slowly. 'And these attacks on you and your mother? You don't believe Terry Finnigan would do anything like that?'

'No. Do you?'

He didn't answer. 'I must go. I'll keep in touch. Oh, and I'll ask the ward sister if you can visit your mother this morning.' Drawing back the curtains he walked away. She saw him go into the ward sister's glass-walled office at the far end of the ward, watched them talking, saw the sister nodding.

Half an hour later Nurse Embry came along with a wheelchair and helped her climb out of bed.

'Going for an x-ray?' Joan Patterson asked, eyes glinting with curiosity.

'No,' the nurse said, amused, deftly enfolding Miranda into a dressing gown before putting a much-washed hospital rug over her knees.

'She isn't going home, is she?'

'No.' Nurse Embry began wheeling Miranda towards the swing doors, leaving Joan Patterson seething with frustration.

'What ward is my mother on?' Miranda asked as they turned into the corridor.

'Mary Leeman. It's an observation ward, mostly head injuries; patients don't stay long, they're only in for a night or two but they need to be watched carefully so there are always plenty of nurses on the ward. I worked on it myself last winter. I didn't like it much. You don't get to know the patients – they come in and go out like on a conveyor belt.'

She pushed the wheelchair along another corridor and through more swing doors into a glass-walled waiting room.

'I'll leave you here for a minute while I check with Sister that they're ready for you. She's a tartar. She'll bite my head off if I just barge in there without warning.' She picked up a few magazines from the table in the middle of the room and dropped them on to Miranda's lap. 'Here you are, these will keep you occupied while I'm gone.'

The only other occupant of the waiting room was a man; out of the corner of her eye Miranda noted that he was expensively dressed; a beautifully cut suit, a crisp white shirt, a dark red silk tie and what she suspected were handmade shoes on his feet. He turned his head to glance at her and Miranda hurriedly looked down, embarrassed at being caught staring; she began to turn the pages of the top magazine, a glossy monthly which she saw was a year old. Odd how reading out-of-date magazines was somehow more riveting than reading the latest editions. She soon became absorbed in an article, which was why she didn't notice the other magazines sliding slowly floorwards.

By the time she did realise what was happening it was too late. The magazines plummeted, pages fluttering.

The other occupant of the waiting room got up and came to help her.

'Sorry, stupid of me,' Miranda mumbled, very

flushed. He might think she had dropped them deliberately, to get his attention.

He put the magazines back on her lap, then sat down on a chair right next to her and smiled. He had dazzling white teeth, a golden tan, which looked wonderful with his thick, curly, blond hair and bright blue eyes.

'Which ward are you in?'

She couldn't remember the name and made flustered noises, finally saying, 'I'm visiting my mother in Mary Leeman ward.'

'What is she in here for?'

'A head injury, but they say she'll be OK. Are you visiting someone?'

'My wife.' He sighed. 'She's pregnant, but has to be very careful. She's had two miscarriages already. So she's in here for observation. The same ward as your mother. I'm worried about Pan; she gets so scared, afraid she's going to lose this baby, too. They would like her to spend the next six months in bed here, but I've just started a new job, at a hotel in Greece, I can't stay on in London, and Pan won't stay here without me.'

'There must be good hospitals in Greece, though, where she can be taken care of?'

'Yes, of course. But Pan wants to be in her own home.'

CHARLOTTE LAMB

'I can sympathise with her. I'm sure I would feel the same. She has an unusual name – Pan. Is it short for something?'

'Pandora.' He smiled at her. 'Her father had a weird sense of humour. He always said, women cause most of the trouble in the world. Greece is still very much a male-orientated country although some women have gained more freedoms over the past twenty years. There's an old Greek story about how trouble first got into the world. It tells you a lot about the way Greek men think. Trouble is supposed to have been shut up in a box. It was released by a woman, called Pandora.'

'Yes, I've heard that story, but it's just a myth, isn't it?'

'Greek men take it seriously. Even Socrates had a nagging wife, you know.'

'Did he? Maybe that's why he was always out of the house talking to young men! Does your wife like her name?'

'She laughs about it, but she prefers to be called Pan. It's shorter, and sounds quite modern, although, of course, it was also the name of one of the Greek gods. Pan, the god of nature.'

'Are you Greek?' He certainly didn't sound it, and his colouring made her suspect he wasn't Greek but he obviously knew a lot about the country.

'No, I'm English.' He held out his hand. 'Charles Leigh.'

Miranda took his hand, saying her name.

'Miranda,' he repeated. 'Now that is a lovely name, and *The Tempest* is my favourite Shakespearean play. Of course, my wife is Greek, although she speaks English. She spent several years at an English school.'

'Why was that?'

'Her father wanted her to speak good English – it helps in their business. He owned the hotel I'm going to run, and a majority of their guests are English. I met my wife when she was over here, on a training course, run by the hotel chain I work for.'

'But she's delicate?'

'No, on the contrary. She plays a lot of sport, is very active. She's a perfectly healthy girl, she just has a problem staying pregnant.'

Sympathetically, Miranda said, 'What a pity, it must be very worrying for both of you.'

'That's an understatement. It's a nightmare. I'd be happy to adopt, I hate to watch her going through this, but she wants to have a baby of her own.' He grimaced. 'Sorry, I don't know why I'm burdening you with all this – there's something about hospitals that gets you talking about things you wouldn't normally mention!'

Nurse Embry came bustling back. 'Ward sister

says she's ready for you, now.' She smiled at the man. 'Mr Leigh?'

'Yes.'

'Sister asked me to tell you to come in, too.'

She began to wheel Miranda out into the corridor and Charles Leigh followed them.

'Well, I hope you find your mother well, Miranda,' he said, holding open the ward door for them.

'Thanks, and I hope your wife is fine, too.'

He was a very attractive man, but under that smooth tan she saw pallor and his eyes had a veiled desperation in them. She was sorry for him, and his wife. How did anyone cope with such a situation?

They were in a far worse plight than she was, despite the fear she felt all the time. She couldn't imagine how you coped with their problem. The grief and apprehension must be overwhelming.

Nurse Embry pushed her over to a bed at the far end, by a high window, in which her mother lay, her head bandaged and her face very pale.

'Mum.' Miranda was stricken, staring at her, feeling very guilty. It was all her fault. If she hadn't sent her mother to stay at the flat it wouldn't have happened. It should have occurred to her that whoever had tried to kill her might go to her flat and try again.

'It looks worse than it is,' Dorothy quickly said,

seeing her expression. 'Now, don't be taking any notice of these bandages, the nurses were just practising on me, that's my opinion. I haven't any serious injuries, just a few grazes and bruises. And a great big lump like an egg! They've x-rayed my head but they said there was no brain damage, no internal injuries. They're only keeping me in for a night in case I turn out to have concussion.'

'But you're having headaches, Nurse Embry told me.'

'Well, I suppose that's only natural, after being thumped on the head. But a headache won't kill me.' Dorothy searched her face anxiously. 'Miranda, that nice policeman says I should go home when they let me out, not go back to your flat.'

'Yes, he's right, I think you should, too.'

Her mother burst out, 'What is going on here, Miranda? Why did someone burgle your flat? What's this all about? You haven't told me the whole story, have you? There's something behind all this.'

Miranda sighed. 'Yes. You see, I ... saw ... something, somebody was killed, and I was the only witness. And the murderer is trying to kill me, well, the police think so, and it is beginning to look like that.'

'The hit and run ... that was deliberate? He wanted to kill you?' Dorothy looked aghast.

'Yes, Neil thinks so. Sergeant Maddrell, that is. Some witnesses thought he drove straight at me. Of course, it could all be a mistake, but after you walked in on this burglary I don't think so. It's too much of a coincidence.'

Her mother groaned. 'Miranda, you can't go back to that flat, either. I must have been attacked in mistake for you – and next time it could be you walking in and being beaten over the head, and that time you could die. You could come to me, but the police think he searched my bag, so now he'll know my address. It might not be safe for you to come down to Dorset.'

'It might not be safe for you, either. Maybe you shouldn't go back there. They might know your address, might come looking for you.'

'Why should they? I don't know a thing; it wasn't me who saw a murder.' Dorothy paused, staring at her. 'What exactly did you see?'

Miranda hesitated. 'It might be better if I don't tell you. What you don't know, you can't be forced to tell them.'

'Maybe you're right. But I'm going home anyway. I'll feel safer in my own home. And I'll get someone to stay with me.' Dorothy chewed her little finger thoughtfully, then her face cleared. 'Freddy. He's a retired policeman – you know, you met him last time you came. A big chap with a ginger moustache. The funny thing is, the hair on his head is brown, not ginger. Odd that. But I'll feel safe having him in the house. Tough as shoe leather, he'll make sure nothing happens to me.'

'Isn't he the one who proposed at Christmas?'

'And a couple of times since! I like him a lot, but I'm still not ready to give up my independence. I'll ring him before I leave here, make sure he can come. But I'm still worried about you. You can't stay in London, or at my house. You can't stay indoors all the time, can you? But if you go out you'll be vulnerable. He might get hold of a gun next time. If he's serious about killing you. Do you really think he is?'

Miranda nodded. 'It is beginning to look like it. I'll have to think of somewhere to go.'

'Abroad would be safest, and don't tell anyone where you're going! Not even me!'

Miranda let her gaze wander around the ward at the other patients. 'Abroad, yes – but where, that's the question?'

On the other side of the ward she noted Charles Leigh sitting beside a bed in which a really beautiful girl lay. A girl with hair like black silk, a smooth, golden skin and slanting dark eyes.

Dorothy saw her looking at them and said quietly,

'She's in here for tests. Poor girl, she keeps losing her babies and they're trying to find out why. I had a long chat while we were both in the x-ray department. She's foreign, I couldn't make out whether she had said her name was Pam or ... well, it sounded like Pan but that's ridiculous.'

'No, it really is Pan – short for Pandora. I just met her husband, in the waiting room. He's English, but she's Greek.'

'She's a lovely girl, seems very cheerful but I could feel how sad she was underneath.'

'And she's so beautiful.'

'Very,' her mother agreed, but her voice was vague. 'How about Italy?'

Miranda blinked at her, bewildered. 'What?'

'You could go to Italy, get a job there.'

'I don't speak Italian.'

'You don't speak any languages.'

'I know a little French.'

'A very little,' her mother said drily. 'I suppose you could go to France, though.'

'I was thinking of America or Canada – at least they speak English.'

'Or Australia,' Dorothy suggested with enthusiasm. 'You can cook and use a computer – I'm sure you could get a job there.'

'It's an idea,' Miranda agreed. 'I've often thought

of having a holiday in Australia and working there would be fun.'

Ten minutes later Nurse Embry arrived to wheel her back to her own ward.

'I'm sorry to break up your chat, but a consultant is expected soon and visitors cannot litter the wards while he's here. He'd be outraged. He likes a tidy ward.'

'He's one of the older generation,' Dorothy tartly explained to her daughter. 'Thinks the world revolves around him, treats patients like dolls, not human beings.'

As she pushed Miranda back to their own ward, Nurse Embry said with a chuckle, 'Your mother is very funny. I wonder how she gets on with Sister? She is one of the old-fashioned variety, runs her ward as a military operation. These days hospitals are very different, they aren't as strict and nurses won't put up with being snapped at and bullied. Nor will patients.'

'My mother certainly won't.'

'I could see that.'

They passed the waiting room where Miranda had sat for a while talking to Charles Leigh. There was someone else in there now. Another man whose profile seemed familiar, unless she was becoming paranoid. Miranda turned to glance at him and felt her heart crash inside her ribs.

'What's wrong?' Nurse Embry asked, bending over her. 'Hey, you're hyperventilating. What is it?'

'Don't stop,' Miranda gasped. 'Go on, take me back to the ward, please.'

Nurse Embry hurried her along the corridor. 'Can't you tell me what's wrong? Are you in pain?'

'No, just . . .' Miranda took one quick look backwards as they turned the corner but he wasn't in sight, he hadn't followed them. Perhaps he hadn't seen them.

'Upset? About your mother?'

'Yes,' she lied, because she couldn't tell the nurse the truth. Had he really been there, in the waiting room? In a black leather jacket and a black shirt with no tie, casually relaxed. Didn't he ever wear any other colour?

Had she simply imagined seeing him? What would he be doing in the hospital? Who could he be visiting? Whatever the truth, it was another of these unbelievable coincidences which kept happening to her. Her life, her world, had become chaotic with them.

Was he going to come to her ward? Her ears beat with the sound of her own blood. Her blood pressure must be sky high. What would she do if he walked in here? Every time she set eyes on him something terrible happened. When she was a child, her mother had often told her she had a guardian angel looking after her, night and day. She had never told her the Angel of Death was likely to follow her around, haunt her.

Nurse Embry put her back to bed then insisted on taking her pulse, her temperature, her blood pressure, looking concerned as she took that.

'Your pulse is a bit fast, but it's your BP that bothers me. It's far too high. You know, there's no need to worry about your mother. She's going to be fine. She'll be going home tomorrow.'

And I'll be left alone here, thought Miranda. What if he comes tomorrow, after she has gone? She grasped wildly at a way out.

What if she spoke to Neil Maddrell? Told him she was afraid of having visitors, apart from him, got him to ring the ward and insist that she had no visitors without warning, without the staff asking her if she wanted to see whoever had come.

'Can I have the phone brought over?' she asked Nurse Embry who looked uncertain, but finally agreed and went away and came back wheeling the portable phone. Neil had given her his number at the police station.

'Sergeant Maddrell isn't here at the moment,' she was told. 'He'll be back later today. Can I take a message?'

She tried to think but her mind was in such a tangle she couldn't work out what to say.

'Hello?' the operator at the police station asked.

Pulling herself together, she hurriedly said, 'Yes, would you tell him Miranda would like him to ring her at the hospital?'

She hung up. When Nurse Embry came to take the phone away Miranda said, 'I'm tired, I think I'll have a sleep. Don't let any visitors in, will you? Except the police. And if I get a phone call from Sergeant Maddrell will you bring the phone over to me?'

'Are you OK?' The nurse hesitated, looking anxious.

'I'm fine, just sleepy.' She kept her eyes shut and after a moment heard the phone rattling away. She hadn't expected to sleep, it had just been an excuse, a way of making sure she had no unwanted visitors. But as she kept her eyes shut and refused to listen to the desultory chat going on in the ward, from one bed to another, she slowly slid into a light doze.

Neil Maddrell rang hours later when she was eating her light supper. It wasn't disgusting, but on the other hand she would rather have had something else than this salad with tinned tuna followed by a tinned pear with tinned cream.

'I saw that man, here in the hospital,' she broke out

in a shaky whisper, afraid somebody might overhear. The other patients always eavesdropped on phone conversations. 'You know, the man who I told you about, who is a customer of Finnigan's, the boat builder, the one who I saw just before my accident and afterwards, among the crowd around me. He was sitting in a waiting room. I was being wheeled back to the ward. I don't think he saw me, but I don't want him visiting me – can you talk to the ward sister, leave instructions to make sure they don't let him in?'

The policeman was reassuring. 'Of course, don't worry, I'll make sure they keep him out, but ... tell me, why do you find him so frightening?'

She couldn't tell him; it would sound so stupid. 'I don't know.'

It was true, in a way. Whenever she tried to think about him her mind became confused, muddled, with different emotions churning inside her. 'I just don't want him near me,' she insisted.

'I'll take care of it. Is that all?'

'Yes.' She couldn't tell him that she had felt safe here, in the hospital, but now she didn't. Would she feel safe anywhere in future?

'How did you find your mother?'

'She seems OK. Well enough to go back to Dorset tomorrow, she says.'

'What are you going to do when you get out of hospital? Have you decided yet?'

'Well, I can't go back to my flat, obviously, and I don't want to put my mother into danger by going to her house, in case they follow me down to Dorset and have another try at . . .' She didn't want to finish that sentence or contemplate what 'they' might do next. She plunged on huskily. 'I may go abroad, I'm trying to decide where. My mother suggested Australia.'

'Rather a long flight, especially for someone who has recently been ill. These long-haul flights are tiring. Also, we may need you to come back at any time. I would rather you stayed in Europe, where you can get back here quickly.'

She didn't really care where she went. 'I'll bear that in mind,' she promised.

He rang off a moment later and she finished her salad, then ate some of the pear, which tasted tinny.

'Why can't they use fresh ones?' she complained when the nurse came round to remove the trays.

'Tinned ones are cheaper and quicker. I had them – I thought they were quite nice. Nobody else said anything,'

I bet my mother did, thought Miranda. She would have said a great deal. Her mother had a pear tree in the garden, dropping snowy white petals in spring before the fruit began to develop. Dorothy bottled most of the pears and ate them through the rest of the year, just as she preserved raspberries, blackcurrants, apples, and other fruit. She led a very busy life in many ways.

Last year she had won prizes for her preserves, for the tomato chutney she made and for strawberry jam, thick with whole fruit, meltingly delicious on bread and butter, or on thick brown toast. Her mother made her own bread too, which always tasted far better than shop bought. When they lived in London, Dorothy hadn't made bread or bottled fruit; all that had entered her life only when she left the city, as though that part of her had been liberated by her new life.

Once her mother had told her, 'I used to dream about living in the country, lots of times, it was a fantasy, you know, like daydreaming about winning the lottery. It wasn't really possible because I had to have a job and there was you, I wanted you to go to a good school and then maybe university, so I stayed on in London. We didn't have room, either, for growing things. Once I was sure you were settled, I could afford to move out into the country. I would only have cramped your style by then, so I didn't feel guilty. I knew you would need to be independent, free to live however you liked. I've been very lucky, I've achieved my dream, I've got the garden, and the life, I always wanted.'

Mum was so lucky. Miranda wished she knew what she wanted, but she had no dreams, no ambitions. In fact, at the moment she had only fears, they darkened her horizon, were between her and the sun. She could think of nothing else, most of the time.

That night she woke up in the shadowy ward to hear footsteps. Sleepily she raised her head and there he was – the Angel of Death – walking towards her. In a state of panic she climbed out of bed, running towards the ward sister's office, where the two night nurses sat drinking tea not looking in her direction.

One minute he was behind her, and the next he was between her and the nurses. She saw him too late to stop or evade him. She ran right into his arms which closed around her. Miranda looked up at him, eyes wide, barely able to breathe.

He gave her a strange slow smile, then his head began to descend towards her.

In terrified shock she realised he was going to kiss her.

His mouth was beautifully moulded, she thought, staring at it. A full lower lip, parting from the firm-cut upper one, a warm pinkish colour, his white teeth just visible.

She wanted him to kiss her. Yet she was appalled by the thought.

Miranda closed her eyes, afraid to watch.

At once she was back in bed, in the dark, with the dizzying abruptness of nightmare.

Was that what this was?

She leaned up on her elbow, out of breath, trembling – and there he was again, walking towards her down the ward.

God, what was going on?

She pulled back the bedclothes and climbed out, began to run and found him confronting her once more, his arms going round her, his head coming down.

This time Miranda closed her eyes without looking at him at all, and in the same strange, dreamlike way was back in bed. She lay still, listening, her eyes tight shut. This time she wasn't looking at him if she heard him.

But the ward was still. Nobody moved. All she heard was the heavy breathing of the other patients, the sonorous tick-tick of the round-faced white clock on the wall, the distant sound of traffic somewhere in the streets round the hospital. She wouldn't risk opening her eyes, though – she might see him again.

In the morning, as she faced her boiled egg and toast, she wondered if she had ever been awake in the night. Had she dreamt the whole thing?

Why had she dreamt of him kissing her? What

did a kiss from death mean? But she would rather not know.

Later that morning her mother came to see her before she went home. To Miranda's surprise she was not alone. The beautiful, black-haired girl walked with her. They were leaning on each other, moving slowly and carefully.

'Miranda, this is Pandora Leigh, we've both been discharged – I gather you met her husband yesterday?'

The other girl smiled at her. 'Hello.'

Shyly, Miranda said, 'Hello,' thinking how ravishing she was, what wonderful skin and hair, what luminous eyes.

'Her husband has offered me a lift in their car, to get my train,' said Dorothy. 'I'm off back home right away. I'll ring you tomorrow, maybe you'll have news for me? Is there anything I can do for you? Book a flight, or a hotel somewhere?'

'I haven't made up my mind yet. The police don't want me to go too far, I'm to stay in Europe, not go to Australia. In case they need me quickly.'

Pandora Leigh was sitting beside the bed, too. 'Dorothy has explained your problem to me.'

'You don't mind, do you, Miranda?' her mother interrupted placatingly. 'We were chatting and it came out.'

Miranda gave them both a polite smile. 'No, of course not, but I'd rather you didn't mention it to anyone else, either of you.'

Pandora nodded. 'Of course not. But ... well, I wondered ... we could offer you a job and somewhere to live, out of Britain, if you're interested. I was going to be working as translator and courier, at our hotel, but the doctors want me to stay in bed as much as possible from now on, so we'll have to get someone else to do my work. Does the idea of working in a hotel appeal to you?'

Miranda was surprised and uncertain. 'Didn't your husband say your hotel was in Greece?'

'Yes, not on the mainland, though. On a small island. Delephores, in the Cyclades – the little group of islands between the mainland of Greece and Crete. It's beautiful, you'll love it.'

'But I don't speak Greek, I'm afraid, I couldn't translate or talk to Greek people.'

'That wouldn't be important at first – you would be dealing with English tourists staying in the hotel, you see; and there will be plenty of Greek speakers in the hotel, who would help if you had a problem. You could have Greek lessons, too, I'm sure you would soon pick up enough to get by with. You would share a bungalow in the grounds with other members of staff, and you would have one whole day free every week, for whatever you wanted to do.'

'It sounds wonderful, I'd love it, but I don't even know how long I could stay – the police may want me to come back to London, any time, at short notice. And I have a broken ankle. My wrist is sprained, but it seems to be improving a little every day, I expect it will heal completely soon. But I wouldn't be much use to you with a broken ankle.'

'I expect we could find a way round that, you would mostly be working in an office, not needing to walk anywhere – but I don't want to try to push you into it. Here's a phone number you can reach me at until we fly back to Greece.' Pandora pushed a little piece of paper into her hand. 'Let me know if you decide you would like to come. The job will be open for the next two weeks. After that, we'll have to find someone else.'

Her mother leaned over to kiss her cheek. 'I think it's a chance in a million. Be good, but above all be careful. I'll ring you.'

Chapter Five

Terry Finnigan cradled the phone on his shoulder while he ran an eye down the order form in front of him on the desk, then spoke into the phone again. 'That's marvellous, Alex. We'll be despatching them within a fortnight – they should be in Piraeus within a couple of weeks after that. I hope that date is acceptable to you?'

At the other end of the line Alex Manoussi nodded, sunlight glinting on his hair, giving the thick black strands a blue shimmer. 'Yes, that should work out very well. We won't complete the contract before the end of next month so we won't need the electrical equipment before then.'

'Good, good. We haven't got enough stock to despatch them any earlier, we shall have to make part of the order. I'll see to it that it's processed with speed. When do you go back?'

'Soon, I haven't fixed a date, I have some unfinished business here. My manager has everything under control in Piraeus, so no problem there.'

'And I'm sure Mrs Manoussi is taking good care of your home. She's such a wonderful cook, too. I've never forgotten that barbecue she made for us when our sales team were over in Greece. Out in your lovely garden on such a gorgeous day, and your views are breathtaking. But what I remember most is that amazing lamb dish, with the aubergines and rice, I've never eaten anything like it.'

'One of the best dishes she cooks,' Alex agreed. 'How is your boy?'

'Sean.' Terry stopped smiling, his eyes sombre as they moved to stare out of the window at the grey-blue sky and the roofs stretching into the distance; high office blocks with dark glass windows between the smaller buildings. It was the view he looked at every day during the week; he barely saw it any more. 'He's OK, thanks. You haven't got a son, have you?'

'No.'

'Well, don't be in too much of a hurry to get one. They give you a lot of grief. You want children, you get them, and while they're small you think they're magic. Then one day they turn into adults and you start having heartache. Thank God I've only got one. I wouldn't survive having a couple of them.'

'In Greece it is the daughters who give trouble. You have to take care of them day and night. The minute they are in their teens the young men appear, like bees around a honey pot. A nightmare for fathers.'

'Have you got a daughter?'

'Not yet, and I dread it. It was bad enough when I had to watch out for my sisters! My parents never stopped telling me to keep an eye on them. It ruined my own social life. I could never relax.'

Terry laughed. 'I remember how I was at that age! Always ready to try my luck with a bird.'

'A bird?' Alex frowned.

'A girl.'

'Oh, yes, a girl. Of course, I knew that, I had forgotten it for a moment. Well, I must ring off, I'm afraid, I have a lot to do.'

'Of course, I know how busy you are.'

'I shouldn't complain, it's better to be busy than to have nothing to do. Well, Terry, I look forward to getting my order in due course and my cheque will be in the post.'

After hanging up, Terry said to his secretary, 'You know the really worrying thing about Greeks? They shake their heads and say 'Ne' when they mean yes, and nod when they mean no. You're never really sure what they are thinking.'

She nodded and looked vague. 'I know what you mean.' But she clearly didn't.

And what was going on behind those black Greek eyes? thought Terry, picking up the phone. Alex Manoussi was an enigma.

He rang the hospital, spoke to the ward sister, avoided giving his name. 'I'm just a friend – I wondered how she was today?'

'As well as can be expected.'

The standard reply, telling you nothing – what did it mean? Whatever they wanted it to mean.

'When are you letting her out?'

'I really couldn't say – the doctor will make that decision. Not yet, anyway. Can I give her a message?'

'No, I'll come in and see her sometime. Or maybe I'll see her at home. Is she going back to her flat, do you know? Or going to stay with her mother in the country?'

'I have no idea.' The sister was getting starchy; her tone cold and distant.

Terry ended the call, then rang home on his mobile. The housekeeper put him through to Sean's room. Sean answered, sounding thick-headed and sleepy. Angry blood rushed to Terry's head.

'Were you out drinking again last night? How many times do I have to tell you – you should stay off the booze until this is all over. The police could come any time. You're going to need to keep a clear head, you don't want to make any stupid slips.'

Sean snarled. 'Stop nagging, will you? I'm perfectly clear-headed. Now, did you want something? Or did you only ring me up to scream at me?'

'I just rang the hospital; she's still there but her mother has been discharged. Don't go near her flat. Do you hear?'

'I'm not deaf.'

'No, but you are stupid. Now, get up, take a shower, and do something useful. Go jogging, play golf – anything that gets you out into the fresh air. But stay out of trouble. And don't chase girls. Why don't you ring Nicola and arrange to have lunch with her?'

'OK, OK. I'll do that. Finished now?'

'Yes.' Terry hung up, feeling defeated. The boy was hopeless. Who would ever have thought that that adorable baby, with tight little blond curls, big saucer-like eyes and a sudden, enormous grin, would have turned into this sulky, selfish, indifferent man?

His childhood had given no hint that he would end up the way he was now. At eight years old Sean had been so funny; always grinning, making very bad jokes, chucking himself about.

He had been a solid, boisterous boy who loved football and watching TV, went around in a crowd of other boys, nudging and shoving each other, giggling in class, driving his teachers wild.

When had he changed? In his teens? Yes, that was when he began to get into trouble.

When his hormones began to riot and he started chasing girls!

No, they had chased him in the beginning, remembered Terry. Sean had been a beautiful boy at fifteen. Girls had swarmed around him, he could have his pick. And did, no doubt. Terry had been amused by it at the time; now he saw that Sean had been spoilt by all that attention, had started to take his sexual power for granted, had come to despise girls. He had had them too easily.

Or had it been the abandonment of his mother that made him the way he was? He had adored Sandra. She had been a very loving mother. When she went off like that it must have hurt Sean badly.

The new PR girl came into the room as if on tiptoe. Terry looked blankly at her. He could never remember her name. She was older than Miranda, and not as pretty. Far too thin, with short brown hair and a bony neck. She wore a sort of office uniform; black skirt, white blouse, with flat black shoes. So far he had not seen her in anything else.

'Yes?' he demanded impatiently. Why had he chosen her? Perhaps because she was everything Miranda had not been, or perhaps because he saw at a glance that he could awe her into doing whatever he demanded.

'The police are downstairs.' She was breathless, anxious. 'Should I deal with them? They say they want to see you.'

Not again! What did they want now? They had asked a thousand questions, visited him at home, and here – why did they keep coming back? Terry's hands clenched into fists on his knees, out of sight, but he fought to look calm and unbothered.

'I'll see them, tell my secretary to show them in!'

There were the same two of them. Sergeant Maddrell and a six-foot tall constable with pink cheeks, curly hair and a notebook in one hand, ready to make notes.

'What can I do for you today, Sergeant?' Trying to make them feel stupid – maybe they would stop coming if they realised how ridiculous their questions were.

'Do you have a private plane, sir?' the Sergeant asked, watching him intently.

Terry's face went blank. How had they got on to that? It wasn't something he talked about to his friends. He didn't want them asking him to take them up.

'Yes, I do, as it happens — a light aircraft, a four seater. I've had it for a few years but I rarely take it up lately, I'm too busy.'

Miranda must have told them about it — he should have realised she would. Yet, why should she? How had it come up in the conversation?

'Where do you keep it?'

He mentioned the name of the airfield a few miles from his house in the country. They probably knew it anyway, if Miranda had told them about the plane she would have told them which airfield he used. He had been a member there for years, had learnt to fly with an instructor there.

'We would like to take a look at it.'

'What are you hoping to find?' Terry snapped. 'Bloodstains? I can assure you, you won't.'

The sergeant looked bland. 'She was drowned, we wouldn't expect to find bloodstains.'

The expression on his face made Terry so angry he wanted to punch the smug bastard.

'My son did not drown anyone! You aren't still listening to that crazy girl? Haven't you talked to the psychiatrists at the hospital? Seen her records?

She's obsessed with people drowning. She imagined the whole thing.'

Ignoring all that, the sergeant asked him, 'Does your son fly?'

'He doesn't have a licence. But he has just begun to have lessons.'

'At the airfield where you keep your plane?'

'Yes, but he isn't allowed to go up without a qualified pilot. He has only had a couple of lessons.'

The two policemen looked at each other, then got up. 'Thank you for your co-operation, sir,' Sergeant Maddrell said politely.

When they had left the office Terry reached for the phone, began to dial, then changed his mind and slammed the phone down again. It would be a mistake to ring the airfield and tell them not to talk to the police. What would they think, if he did?

He ran his hands over his face and groaned softly. For years he had been free of this tension, this permanent anxiety, needing to watch everything he said, did.

He had thought it was all behind him, he would never have to live with feelings like that again. But here they were once more. He was living in a minefield; before he took a single step he had to test the ground around him, and even then something could set off an explosion which might blow his whole world away.

He had tried so hard, moving away from everything he knew, distancing himself from all his old friends, even from his family, transforming his life in every way. Sean didn't remember how it had been. The boy had no idea what he had achieved, how hard he had fought. He took for granted everything they owned, the house, the cars, the money.

Maybe it was time to tell him, but Terry wasn't ready to do that yet. There was a tightness in his chest, a coldness round his heart. He was afraid that Sean would be excited, fascinated, rather than alarmed or frightened. The boy was drawn to that dark side of life, to clubs and cheap women, to fast cars and gambling. It wasn't his fault, though, Terry knew very well. It was in his blood. It was their genes, their fate.

Terry was afraid for him. Sean was all he had, his hope for the future. He couldn't see him destroyed without trying to save him, even if it meant fighting Sean himself.

He would talk to that girl again. It was a risk, but one worth taking, with so much at stake. Maybe now she would listen. She had come close to death. That always made you think, made you realise hard facts, harder choices.

* * *

Miranda was being allowed to walk, well, hobble, round the ward now. She had a stick to lean on, to help her balance, her plastered ankle lifted off the ground. Not being in bed made everything look brighter. She could talk to the other patients, sit down beside their beds, chat to them, then move on to someone else. She could go to the bathroom alone.

'You'll be home any day now,' Nurse Embry said, smiling. 'Will you go to your mother?'

It was decision time. Miranda could not risk her mother's life by involving her. Nor did she want to go back to her flat, after the burglary. But what should she do? Where should she go?

She rang the number Pandora Leigh had given her. A man answered, his voice deep and foreign. Yet strangely familiar.

'Who's that?' she asked, knowing it wasn't Pandora's husband. Charles was English, she would recognise his voice. She guessed that this man was Greek.

He did not answer the question, simply asked, 'To whom do you wish to speak?'

'Mrs Leigh, Pandora, please.'

'Who wishes to speak to her?'

'My name's Miranda Grey.'

'Please wait.'

A moment later Pandora said, 'Hello? Miranda? How are you?'

'I'm better, thank you. What about you? How are you feeling?'

'I have to rest for hours every day, which is a bore, but I'm watching TV and videos and reading, and Charles and I play Scrabble most days. I like to sew and knit, but I'm afraid to make baby clothes in case it brings me bad luck.'

'Oh, I'm sorry,' Miranda said inadequately, feeling a pang of sympathy. Poor girl. She had heard the old superstition that it is not wise to make clothes for an expected baby, or buy prams or blankets, until very close to the birth, but she did not believe it. Yet in Pandora's situation, having already lost other babies, it was easy to understand this reluctance to tempt fate.

'I hope the fact that you've rung means you've thought about coming to work for us and decided to come?' Pandora said brightly.

'Well, I'm walking, with a stick, and in another couple of weeks I may be able to walk unaided, I hope. So, if the job is still open I thought . . .'

'It is! Oh, I'm so pleased. I'm sure we're going to get on. The minute I saw you I liked you, and it will be so nice to have someone English to chat to. Oh, I have Greek friends, girls I knew as a child, but I always feel half-English, because I came to school here. Look, we shall be leaving in a few days –

would you be able to fly with us? Or must you stay in hospital for a while?'

'I'm not sure. I'll speak to the doctor when he makes his rounds later today, and ring you again tomorrow to let you know.'

'Don't forget you'll need your passport.'

'Of course, it is up to date, don't worry.'

'Charles will draw up a contract for you to sign before we leave. And we'll need some references — just a couple, from your bank, your doctor, simply personal references. Is that OK?'

'I'll get that done when I get out of here,' Miranda promised and, while she waited to speak to the doctor, made a list of what she would need to take with her. It would mean going to the flat, which made her nervous.

Neil Maddrell came to see her an hour later and she told him her problem.

'I'll pick you up and take you to the flat to pack a suitcase and find your passport,' he offered. 'Until you go to Greece I suggest you stay at a hotel. I'll book that for you.'

'You're so kind,' she said, deeply relieved. 'Do you think it's a good idea for me to go to Greece?'

'I do, yes. Just don't tell people that that is where you're going. We don't want anyone flying out to Greece to find you and do you a mischief.'

She shuddered. 'No. No, we don't. I'll only tell my mother.' Changing the subject hastily, she asked, 'Why did you come? Is there any news?'

'I just wanted to ask you a few more questions. Do you know how long Sean has been having flying lessons?'

Blankly she shook her head. 'I only remember Terry mentioning it once, a month or so ago; he was paying for Sean to train as a pilot.'

'You know Finnigan senior has a plane?'

'Yes. I know he flies, too, and I believe he's quite good, or that's what I've heard. I don't know anything about flying. I've never been up in a private plane. He pilots himself about all over the place.'

Neil nodded. 'Yes, we've been to the airfield where he keeps his plane. Tell me, after you fainted in your office that day – you told us you started to drive home, then parked to think, and drove back to ring us and report what you had heard. How long would you say all that took? How long were you away from the office before you actually rang us?'

'I'm not sure. I wasn't looking at my watch. Not long. Half an hour, maybe? But then it took the police some time to arrive, it must have been three-quarters of an hour later. Maybe even an hour. I don't know.'

'Quite a long time, anyway?'

She nodded.

'Long enough for Sean to have time to tidy up the bathroom, dry the bath, carry the body down to his car and put it in the boot ... maybe wrapped in the damp towels he had used? Along with the girl's clothes?'

'It would not have taken him longer than half an hour,' she agreed.

'And by the time the first police arrived on the scene it must have been an hour since you thought you heard the girl drowning?'

'I didn't *think* I heard that. I did hear it!' she said fiercely.

Neil nodded. 'OK, I believe you. So it must have been around an hour later that the police actually got there?'

'I'd say so.'

'By which time the bathroom was pristine, no sign of anyone having had a bath in it.'

'Yes.' What was he getting at? She watched him doubtfully. 'Are you hinting that I might have made a mistake? Might have imagined it? Because I know I didn't.'

'I'm sure you didn't. But we have been searching for a body for days without success. So we're looking for alternative ways of disposing of the corpse.'

She was baffled. What did he mean by that?

Did he suspect Sean of having flown the body somewhere before burying it in a remote district far from London?

He got up. 'Well, thank you for helping. Let me know when you're being discharged and I'll come to drive you to your flat.'

He was very thoughtful. She felt better for knowing he would be with her when she went home.

'And as soon as I know which nights you'll be in London before you go to Greece, I'll book a hotel for you. That way, nobody will have a clue where you're going to be.'

He was as good as his word. Two days later he collected her from the hospital in the morning, drove her to her flat and waited while she packed her case, then took her to a quiet hotel in a leafy street in Kensington.

'There's only one entrance and exit – nobody can escape being noticed by the staff on duty in the foyer,' he reassured her.

They took the small lift upstairs to her room, overlooking the back of the hotel. They didn't pass a soul in the corridor, nor hear a sound from any other room.

'You'll be safe here, but keep the security chain on the door and check visitors through the peephole before you let them in. There's also a closed circuit

TV system recording everyone who comes in and goes out of the hotel, day and night.' He grinned at her. 'Hurry up and unpack, then I'll take you to lunch downstairs.'

They ate Italian, she chose minestrone soup, he ate Parma ham and sliced melon, then they both had grilled salmon with lime sauce, boiled potatoes and green beans, followed by icecream with hot chocolate sauce.

'After hospital food that was brilliant,' Miranda sighed. 'Now I feel too full to move, though.'

Neil escorted her back up to her room and left her there. 'Have a siesta, Italian-style,' he advised, smiling.

As he turned to leave she caught his sleeve. 'Before you go — any news about the body?'

He shook his head. 'But if our theories are correct we should have news before too long.'

'What theories?' she asked and he grimaced.

'I can't tell you that. Sorry.'

He left and she locked herself in her hotel room, and went to the window to stare out. It was pouring with rain outside, the green branches of trees lining the street whipped by a savage wind, the view one of endless grey streets. London in this weather could be depressing.

She turned towards the bed, kicking off her shoes.

Turning back the duvet she lay down, pulling the duvet over her. Minutes later she was asleep, and did not wake for several hours. Her body wasn't accustomed to exercise following her long stay in hospital. She had had a very busy, tiring morning and then eaten rich, heavy food. She needed this long rest.

Two days later she drove to Heathrow with the Leighs and caught a plane to Athens. As they drove she noticed a black Ford with smoked glass windows following them; it stayed there, right behind them, all the way to the airport.

'What's wrong?' asked Pandora, noticing that she kept turning her head to look back.

Miranda didn't admit what was worrying her. A lot of this traffic would be going to Heathrow. She was becoming paranoid.

Nevertheless, as they got out of the taxi she looked around for the black car and spotted it parking not far behind them. Nobody got out, but she felt the hair rise on the back of her head as she saw a front window slide down a little, wide enough for something to show.

Sunlight glinted on what looked like the muzzle of a gun.

Chapter Six

A scream curdled in her throat, her eyes clouded with terror, and then her sight cleared and she saw that it was not a gun being pointed at her. It was the long lens of a very professional-looking camera.

Charles and Pandora were unaware of her reactions, too busy supervising the unloading of their luggage on to an airport porter's trolley. They had their backs to the other car, she realised they were unaware of being photographed.

'Ready, Miranda?' Charles said, turning his wife's wheelchair towards the entrance. 'Sure you don't want a wheelchair?'

'I can manage,' she said, and would have told them about the camera then, but Charles walked away, pushing his wife in front of him, and she had to follow them at her slow hobble, leaning on her stick or she would have lost sight of them. By the time she had caught up with them at the check-in desk she had decided not to mention the photographer. His camera had been pointing towards them, but perhaps he had been taking a picture of someone else, someone she had not noticed.

By the time they had checked in and gone through into the departure lounge they still had over an hour to kill. They had some tea, bought magazines to read on the plane, then sat down to wait.

'How far is the hotel from Athens?' she asked them.

They looked at each other. Charles laughed. 'Didn't we explain? The hotel isn't on the mainland, it is on an island called Delephores, in the Cyclades, several hours from Athens.'

She remembered then that Pandora had told her all that when she first offered her a job.

'We get there by boat,' Charles added.

'A ferry?'

'There is one, yes, but the hotel has its own boat, to make the trip easier for guests. It will be waiting for us at Piraeus, where all the cruise ships tie up. Our boat has a cabin with comfortable seats, and another tiny cabin with a couple of bunks, for people who get sea-sick and prefer to lie down. You don't get sea-sick, do you, Miranda?'

'I never have before, but then I haven't sailed much.'

'Well, let's hope you are a good sailor.'

'I don't ever remember a problem.'

'Good. The boat is well equipped. There's a bathroom and a tiny galley — a kitchen, so we can have tea or coffee on the way.'

'It sounds fun.'

Four hours later they were approaching Greece. Miranda was sitting by the window, leaving the aisle seats free for Charles and his wife, if Pandora needed to go to the lavatory en route. Leaning her face against the cold glass Miranda stared down at the brilliant, blue sea beneath them, at tiny, grey and green islands scattered across it and then at the indented coast of the Greek mainland, frilled like the neck of a lizard.

'We should be landing soon,' Charles told her as the plane dropped suddenly, leaving her stomach churning. From the air Athens appeared to be a sea of white buildings with flat roofs and the occasional tower or spire.

What nobody had warned her about, what she had not expected, was the violent heat.

As she came down the steps from the plane the sun beat on the back of her neck like a brazen gong.

'It's so hot!' she said, only just able to breathe.

Charles looked surprised. 'Didn't you realise it would be? It is usually around ninety or a hundred degrees here in summer.'

'Usually?' she gasped and he laughed.

'You'll get used to it.'

She wished she could walk faster, to get out of the sun, but she could only scuttle along on her crutch like a crab. By the time she was inside the airport building her skin was so hot it felt as if it was blistering. How could anyone get used to this temperature?

They somehow made their way through the crowded terminal, collected their luggage from the carousel and managed to find a porter to push it outside for them.

A long, black limousine was waiting for them. The chauffeur took charge of their luggage while she and Pandora got into the back of the car. To her enormous relief it had air-conditioning and was blissfully cool.

Ten minutes later they were driving through the Athens suburbs on their way to the coast. Miranda stared out of the window, fascinated. The buildings, set in gardens full of trees and shrubs, were mostly white and often had a strangely unfinished look, with wire sticking up out of the top floor.

'There's a tax on finished buildings,' explained Charles. 'So builders leave them not quite finished, to avoid paying the tax. Also people often plan to add another floor, when they have more money, so it is cheaper to do that if there is no roof.'

She wished she had had a chance to see the city — to visit the Acropolis or the great museum Pandora had told her about as they were flying here, where the gold of Troy could be seen, the mask of Agamemnon, the necklaces of Helen, and marvellous bronze statues of the Greek gods.

When she said so Charles regretfully said, 'We still have quite a distance to travel, there's no time for sight-seeing, I'm afraid. You'll have to tour Athens on your way home.'

'Why do so many houses have a gap under them?' she asked.

'They're built on stilts, for earthquake protection – this is an earthquake area, although in fact they rarely have quakes in Athens. Two or three times a century, maybe.'

'That's often enough for me!' she said, surprised and horrified.

'And for the Greeks.'

'I remember the last one,' Pandora said. 'I was in Athens at the time. The house shook violently, and a wall split from ceiling to floor. Everyone began screaming and running out into the street, away from buildings. I've never forgotten.'

The sky was a startling, vivid, cloudless blue. The sun burned in it, gold and round and dangerous to look at; she did not dare to try, already half-blind with the sunlight. They pulled up at traffic lights and she stared at a garden in which grew a tree she had never seen before, bark peeling from the trunk to show a strange orange-brown skin underneath.

'What's that?'

'A strawberry tree.'

She began to laugh. 'You're kidding! It grows strawberries?'

'It has a berry, you can see some developing, but they aren't really strawberries although from a distance they look like them once they've ripened and turned red.'

Most of the trees and plants were familiar, but here and there she noticed something she had never seen before. So much of the suburbs seemed to be new, recently built, there were very few older houses and many blocks of flats. Perhaps that was the result of earthquakes?

Pandora leaned back and closed her eyes. Miranda watched her anxiously. She was pale and sweat dewed her forehead. The journey must be tiring for her.

'Is she suffering with this heat?' she whispered to Charles who smiled and shook his head.

'She's used to it. Don't forget, this is her country.

But travelling is exhausting, even if you're healthy. I shall get her to lie down as soon as we get on the boat. She could sleep for a couple of hours.'

A few moments later she saw masts against the skyline and caught sight of the sea on the horizon. They must be near the coast.

'Piraeus,' Charles confirmed and then they turned into a road running into the port, which was crowded with vessels.

With people, too. Crowds flowed along outside rows of tavernas; girls in shorts and t-shirts, with straw hats on their heads, young men in jeans and sleeveless tops, children pulling along balloons. People sat at tables under fluttering umbrellas, eating grilled meat, fruit, locally caught fish, drinking glasses of corn-coloured retsina which filled the air with the strong scent of resin.

Artists sat in front of easels, painting views of the boats and ocean-going cruise ships, while the crowds jostled around to watch.

'It looks like a film I once saw about St Tropez,' Miranda murmured.

'No, no,' protested Charles. 'Piraeus is a working port. St Tropez is a playground now, whatever it was before Brigitte Bardot made it famous.'

The hotel's boat was moored right at the end of the quayside. They parked beside it and Miranda saw black Greek lettering painted on the white hull. That must be the name of the hotel. Pandora stirred, opening her eyes.

'Are we here?'

'Yes.' Charles got out and came round to help her out of the car.

The chauffeur got out too and began unloading their luggage. A young man in a white shirt and shorts appeared and carried the cases away. Miranda warily followed Charles and Pandora down a gangplank into the sleek white vessel bobbing on the water.

Half an hour later they were heading away, out into a blue, blue sea. Miranda sat on deck, under a striped red and green awning, on a matching lounger, dazzled by the blinding light. There was a strange exhilaration in feeling it fill your eyes. The crewman in white had brought her a tray bearing a jug of iced fresh lemonade, a couple of bottles of spring water, and some glasses.

Charles came up to join her and sat down too, to sip a glass, sighing in relief.

'That's better, I was dying of thirst.'

'So was I,' she said, her own glass still in her hand, her throat full of the taste of lemons. 'Does it get cooler in the evening?'

'A little, but just a little. When I first came out here in the summer I used to sleep in the swimming pool, on a floating lilo. It was the only way I could get cool enough to sleep. But now there is air conditioning in the hotel life will be much easier.'

'How big is the hotel?'

'We can sleep a hundred guests – it isn't one of those gigantic hotels, thank God.'

The passage of the boat churned up white spray which blew over her, cooling her face and body deliciously. Suddenly she saw something silver glint among the waves and sat erect, pointing.

'Oh. What's that?'

The silvery sleekness cut through the water and leapt up in a glittering arc. Four of them, in a line, great fish with a familiar outline although she had never set eyes on them before.

'Dolphins,' Charles said casually, and no doubt he was blasé about them, had often seen them before, but she was entranced by the thought of the beautiful creatures. 'You see them quite often out here.'

Breathlessly, she got up and leaned on the side. 'They're coming closer!' The fish were so marvellous she could have cried. She would have loved to touch them, swim with them.

'They're very friendly creatures,' Charles told her. 'They seem to enjoy human company and they're very curious about ships.'

The dolphins swam beside the boat for some time,

leaping and curvetting, turning wide, curling grins upwards to them, so much like smiles of greeting and friendliness that her delight grew even stronger.

When, tiring of their game, they vanished down into the blue waters again Miranda was very sad to see them go. There was something wonderful, almost godlike, about the great, silver-blue fish.

Charles went down to check on his wife and Miranda lay under the awning, her eyes closing in the drowsy heat. When she woke up Charles was back, leaning on the side, staring ahead.

As she stirred he looked down at her, smiling. 'We're nearly there.'

Yawning, she asked, 'Was I asleep for long?'

'A couple of hours at least. You must have been tired. Pandora has been sleeping, too. I must go and wake her up soon. We should dock in an hour.'

She slid off the lounger and joined him. Ahead of them in the distance, rising out of the sea, was a small island, its indented coast rocky and wild.

The centre was green and mountainous, steep sides climbing from the shore, with few signs of habitation.

'It looks deserted. Do many people live there? Where's the hotel?'

'There are a few hundred inhabitants, that's all. The hotel is a short drive from the harbour, but you can't see it because it's surrounded by trees. As we get closer you may catch a glimpse of white walls and red roofs. The hotel building is one storey; it isn't very big because the guests live in bungalows scattered through the grounds. It gives them more privacy. They can cook and eat in their bungalow, or walk up to the hotel to eat.'

As they drew closer, a rough, powerful scent blew towards them on the wind. She distinguished pine, herbs, lavender, and other smells she couldn't identify.

'What an amazing scent!' she said to Charles who nodded.

'The French call it the maquis; it's the smell of the plants and shrubs that grow all over the island. There's a lot of gorse, heathers, wild olives, pine trees.'

'I can smell those!' She could make them out, tall, gaunt, leaning in the wind's path, and even see the olive trees now, their silvery green leaves tossing and fluttering. 'Is yours the only hotel on the island?'

'Yes. There aren't many roads, and those there are really aren't suitable for motor traffic. You need a four-wheel-drive vehicle to get about. There are no towns, just a few villages scattered around the coast. The main industries are fishing and farming. This is still an unspoilt island, tourism hasn't had much of an impact.'

'But somebody built the hotel!'

'Not exactly. It was a private house, built around the turn of the century, and not that big – there were six bedrooms in the beginning. When it came up for sale, Pandora's father bought it, to turn into a hotel, but decided not to build on to it. It would have spoilt the appearance. Hence the bungalows in the grounds. Pandora's brother designed them – they're adobe style, very plain, rough-cast white plaster on the walls inside and out. Some have just one bedroom, some have two and there are a couple with three bedrooms. They have shower rooms and a tiny kitchenette in one end of the sitting room. The decor is pretty; each is furnished in just one or two colours. There are televisions but mostly so that guests can watch videos. We have a video library in the hotel. There are several pools. The bungalows are set around them so that guests can swim in privacy if they wish, only using their pool if nobody else is in it.'

'And they're mostly British, the guests?'

'We get people from all over Europe and America, actually, but the majority speak English. He turned away. 'I'd better go and wake Pan.'

They were close enough to the shore now for her

to make out the harbour, white-walled, set round with small white houses, a church bell tower here and there in the back streets, fishing boats moored at the jetty, and along the sea wall a few tavernas, with fluttering awnings in blue or yellow. Further along there was a narrow beach with half a dozen children playing on it.

As they moored at the jetty she jumped, seeing a couple of pelicans clacking their beaks and making squawking noises of affront.

Pandora laughed behind her. 'They're the island's watchdogs. Don't go too close, they sometimes push people off the jetty into the sea.'

'I've never seen them outside a zoo. Are there many of them on the island?'

'A few. There were far more, once, I think, but now there are just a handful. The fishermen don't like them because they eat fish, but I don't think they persecute them, they are too popular with everyone else. I'm not sure why the population dwindled.'

'They're so funny!' Miranda watched them stalking back and forth, their beaks constantly opening and shutting. 'A couple of clowns! Where do they nest?'

'On the beach somewhere. People keep away but tourists sometimes go down to take pictures, which upsets the pelicans. In the spring the storks nest on the church tower; everyone complains about the noise they make, but it's charming to watch them sit up and spread their big wings and clack their beaks, when they're disturbed. They do it every time the priest rings the bell. But tourists can't get up there to take their everlasting photographs, so the birds keep coming.'

Charles leaned over the side, pointing. 'Here comes the car.'

It was not a limousine this time, but a large, black four-wheel-drive. Charles and the young crewman helped Miranda and Pandora up the ladder to the top of the jetty and the driver of the vehicle came to give them a hand into the back seat. Then he and the other two men shifted the luggage into the spacious boot before they slowly backed off the jetty on to the narrow road running along the sea front.

Miranda wished she had her camera to take pictures of the tavernas, the pelicans, the brightly coloured boats, some of them painted with an eye or an open hand, on the side. But she had packed it, and from Pandora's tone when she talked about tourists taking photos it was probably just as well.

'Why are there those signs painted on the boats, Pandora?'

'They're ancient symbols against evil and bad luck.'

The eyes were slanting, black, with a faintly sinister

look in Miranda's opinion; the hands were small, fingers spread wide, outlined in frilly black and red. She couldn't guess what they symbolised.

The road out of the fishing port deteriorated within minutes. Despite the excellent springs on the four-wheel-drive they began bouncing and rocking to and fro as they drove along. Charles looked anxiously at his wife. Pandora was holding on to the strap on the window beside her; Miranda saw her knuckles whiten and her face took on a greenish tinge.

'You aren't going to be sick, are you?' she asked and Pandora grimaced.

'I hope not. Luckily, it isn't far.'

Ten minutes later they turned off the unmade, rocky road on to tarmac which wound between trees; through them Miranda saw white walls from time to time. They must be some of the hotel's bungalows, she realised, seeing one of them clearly. A girl in a dark blue swimsuit was lying on a lounger under an umbrella on a balcony. She glanced down at them through sunglasses. Her skin was smoothly tanned, her figure slim and healthy.

Turning sharp left they came in sight of what was obviously the hotel, a long, low, one-storey building with a veranda running along in front of it. The driver parked in front of the entrance and Pandora sighed in relief. Charles came round to help her down, his arm around her thickening waist.

'OK, darling?'

She nodded, leaning on him. 'But I'd like to go to bed right away. I need to lie down where it doesn't rock about or bump.'

He smiled. 'I'll take you now. Miranda, for tonight you'll be staying in the hotel, too. Tomorrow we'll sort out a bungalow for you.'

A man came forward from the reception desk in the lobby, smiling warmly. 'Miss Pandora – it is good to have you back home with us. How are you?'

Although he asked a question Miranda saw his black eyes quickly, shrewdly, running over Pandora, watched his brows twitch together, his smile first fade, then come back, stronger, yet no longer so genuine. He could see how Pandora was and it made him unhappy.

He put a hand on her shoulder, very lightly, almost a caress, a touch of sympathy.

'You are home now, we will take care of you.'

'Hello, Milo.' She smiled at him with obvious affection. 'How is everything?'

He raised his thin shoulders in a shrug, lifted a hand and moved it from side to side gracefully in a gesture which was easy to interpret, wordlessly saying that one day everything was up, the next it was down.

Pandora laughed. 'As normal, then!'

'The French say: *comme d'habitude!*'

'You know my French isn't good! I am useless at languages.' She turned to Miranda. 'This is Milo, who has worked for us for years. He really runs the hotel, hires and fires staff, keeps an eye on things for us, I don't know what we would do without him.'

He was not very tall, his hair thinning slightly, but very black and shiny. He had olive skin, very weatherbeaten, a big nose, big ears, a face which was not goodlooking, slightly comic, in fact.

How old was he? Fifty? Older? Hard to tell. But he was very likeable.

'Milo, this is Miranda, who has come to work for us, doing my job.'

He bent his head forward at the neck in a sort of bow. 'Welcome to Delephores. I hope you will be happy here.' His English was very good; she was impressed and felt stupid, knowing no Greek.

She shook hands, shy and flushed. 'Thank you. How do you do? I'm hoping to have some Greek lessons while I'm here – can you recommend anyone?'

'Me,' Pandora said, laughing.

Milo gave her a sideways smile, his eyes very warm, then turned towards Charles. 'Mr Leigh, welcome back. I hope you are well.' The formal note told her that he did not know Charles very well, and was keeping him at a distance although there was no hostility in face or voice. Simply a coolness, a wariness – didn't he trust Charles? Or was he jealous of him? Clearly Milo was deeply attached to Pandora – he may well have resented her marriage to an Englishman.

Charles was polite, too, but brisk. 'I'm fine, but I want to get my wife into bed immediately. Could you deal with the luggage, Milo, while I take her to the room?'

'Of course.'

Remembering Miranda, Charles added, 'Will you show Miranda to one of the rooms? She is going to translate for us, and work in the office. Tonight, she can stay here, then she is to move into a bungalow, tomorrow.'

Milo gave her a brief, measuring glance, half-smiling politely, nodded.

'I will take care of her.'

He watched Charles steer Pandora towards a door behind the reception desk, then turned to a young man waiting for orders, spoke in Greek to him. The younger man nodded. He brought forward a luggage trolley on to which he piled the various cases which had been brought in from the car.

'Which is your luggage, miss?' asked Milo and Miranda pointed. Milo picked up her case.

'This way, miss.'

They walked along a quiet, red-carpeted corridor, Milo setting a slow pace she could keep up with, leaning on her stick. He stopped at last, at a door. 'Here you are, miss, this will be your room for tonight.'

He produced an electronic key card, and unlocked the door, standing back to let her enter, then laid the key on the bed.

'I'll leave you the key. If you lose it, come to reception and we will make you a new one. I had this ready for you.'

So he had known she was coming – she had wondered if he had been informed.

He explained the contents of the room to her. 'You have a mini-fridge, which contains bottled water and soft drinks, only. There will be no charge, of course. There is a telephone so that you can talk to reception, or other rooms. Dinner is at eight; the dining room is off reception.' He put her case down. 'If there is anything you need, please telephone me. The air-conditioning is set low, but you can turn it up if it isn't cool enough for you. I can have some tea or coffee sent along, if you want it.'

'Thank you, but I will be quite happy with the cold water,' she said, adding rather shyly because she wasn't sure how he would react, 'Please, call me Miranda.'

He smiled; she saw gold gleam among his white teeth and was startled. She had heard that some people had gold false teeth but she couldn't remember ever seeing it before.

'I hope you will enjoy working here, Miranda.' He whisked out of the room, closing the door almost silently.

She stood, looking around her curiously. The room was small, but well furnished. There was a neat, narrow bed covered with a white cotton cover; lime-green curtains, a small white wardrobe, a white counter with a mirror above it, and a chair pushed under it, and a polished hardwood floor on which lay one lime-green cotton rug. The effect was springlike, cheerful.

She walked over to look out of the window. Outside a tree moved, throwing shadows on the white wall, trembling leaf patterns in black. Gardens stretched in front of the hotel; smooth, manicured turf, small beds of roses hedged with lavender, the elegant sway of silver birch trees and hazel, the sun shining down through them, and behind them the white bungalows, half-hidden by leaves.

Miranda's heart lifted. She began to feel happy. But despite the air-conditioning she was very hot after that drive and she would die for a bath.

She investigated her en-suite bathroom, which was

the size of a cupboard; there was no bath, just a shower and toilet. Stripping off, she took a long, refreshing shower, put on white shorts and a pink t-shirt, and lay down on top of the bed. Within minutes she was asleep.

When she woke up there were shadows in the room, but outside it was still bright, the sun had not yet gone down. She changed into a thin summer dress; a blue-and-white tunic just covering her knees, slid her bare feet into white sandals, and went out to explore the gardens before dinner.

As she came out of the hotel she saw Milo walking very fast through the trees, carrying a covered tray; and idly followed in the same direction. Was he delivering room service to one of the bungalows? she wondered.

The air was mild and slightly salty, a faint breeze blowing off the sea ruffled her hair and whipped her dress against her warm body as she set off with her stick, swinging her plastered foot.

There was another scent, too, less identifiable — herbal, pungent. Thyme, marjoram, mint, and was that basil? Charles had said it grew wild here and that smell was unmistakable.

The tall birches gave her a strangely pied appearance, arms and legs now black, now white, her dress chequered like a chessboard, the shadows shifting over her as she moved. At least it was cool under the leafy trees.

She walked past bungalows and heard voices, splashes in a pool beside one, saw people moving about inside the buildings. The she was back among trees, thicker, now, closer set. Ahead of her from time to time she caught another glimpse of Milo, like the White Rabbit, hurrying along with his tray. Where was he going? They had left the bungalows behind now, and the carefully tended gardens. They were in wilder territory, bushes, trees, long, rough yellowish grass, like over-ripe corn, which rustled as she walked through it, the bearded stems rasping her bare legs.

She was some distance behind Milo when she saw him entering a house. Not a bungalow, a rather elegant house built in something akin to a Georgian style, with well-proportioned windows and a small portico, resting on two white pillars, above the dark wooden front door.

Miranda hesitated — should she turn back now, before Milo returned and caught her, realised she had been following him?

Well, she hadn't, really — why should she? He had merely been a marker for her to follow in her exploration. Where he could go she had assumed she could safely go.

She was curious, though — who lived in that house? Pandora's father, who owned the hotel? Or perhaps this was accommodation for richer guests who did not wish to stay in a bungalow and who demanded privacy, set apart from everyone else. She could see the blue gleam of a pool to one side, and they were near the sea out here on the furthest extent of the hotel grounds.

But she couldn't hover here, staring. Inside the house Milo or whoever was staying there might be watching her, in turn, wondering what on earth she was doing.

Turning back among the trees she wandered back to the hotel and went to her room for half an hour to do her make-up and brush her hair, before making her way to the dining room.

Milo met her as she entered it, bowing slightly. 'Are you more rested, Miss Miranda?'

'Yes, thank you.'

'Good, good. I'm afraid you will be alone at dinner. Miss Pandora is too tired to get up, and her husband is staying with her. They will be having room service tonight.'

'I'm not surprised. It was a long journey and Pandora hasn't been at all well.'

He sighed. 'It is very sad, she and her husband long to have a child, as I am sure you know. Let us hope she will carry this one to a birth. We must take great care of her now.'

'You must have known her for many years,' Miranda said, liking him very much. He had a steely centre, she realised, but he was a kind and sensitive man, his smile was gentle and sympathetic.

'Since she was a child,' he agreed. 'Would you like a table by the window looking out into the garden? It won't be dark for several hours. You'll have a wonderful view while you eat.'

She followed him to a small table and sat down, glancing out of the open window at a bed of dark red roses whose perfume drifted into the room. There was a fine-meshed net stretched across the window.

'What is that there for?' asked Miranda.

'Mosquitoes – you have been warned to be careful to keep your doors and windows shut? This is not a malarial area, thank heavens; but if you get bitten it could still cause problems. The itching is a nuisance, and if you scratch, you can get blisters, or even worse, it could lead to blood-poisoning. Walking around the gardens after dusk isn't a good idea.'

'I saw you coming out of the hotel with a tray, earlier, and walking in among the trees,' she said, watching him. 'Don't you get bitten?'

'Very rarely. They prefer to bite women, especially

fair-skinned women. Our skin is tougher, our blood full of garlic.'

'Like vampires!' she said, laughing.

'Exactly. Garlic is good for keeping insects at bay.'

Casually, she asked him, 'Were you taking room service to someone?'

She saw his black eyes flicker, his face stiffen, there was the briefest pause, then Milo said blandly, 'Yes, I was delivering food to one of the bungalows. Would you care for an aperitif, Miss Miranda?'

'Just some sparkling mineral water, thank you. I drink very little wine or alcohol.'

'A glass of wine is good for you with your dinner. Helps you sleep, is excellent for your blood. But I will send water to your table right away.' Milo gave another of his little bows and smoothly glided away. She stared after him, brow wrinkled.

He had lied to her. But why?

Chapter Seven

It was raining heavily as Terry Finnigan went to the hospital with a very expensive bouquet of flowers only to discover he was a day too late.

'She left yesterday,' a nurse briskly told him, hovering obviously to get back to whatever she had been doing when he interrupted.

'Where did she go?' he asked and got an impatient look.

'No idea. Ask the hospital administrator. Excuse me. I've got a lot to do.'

He went straight to Miranda's flat, got no answer there and started knocking on doors in the building. Most people seemed to be out, but at last he found a young woman in a dressing gown with sleepy eyes and the pink nose of someone who has a cold. She told him that Miranda was away.

'I saw her yesterday, when I was on my way to see my doctor. She was going out with a suitcase. She was on crutches, poor girl. She'd had an accident. I expect she's gone somewhere to convalesce.'

'She didn't say where she was going?'

The woman shook her head. 'Maybe she went down to stay with her mother, in the country? Her mother was staying here and disturbed a burglar who attacked her. So she went back home, but I don't know where she lives.'

Terry took the flowers back to the office and gave them to one of the typists who was expecting her first baby without benefit of a husband or even the boyfriend she had had but who had vanished the minute she spoke the dreaded word 'baby'. Flushed and startled, she held them cradled in her arms as if rehearsing for motherhood.

'Ooh . . . they're lovely, thank you, Mr Finnigan.'

'All men aren't rats, Sharon,' he said paternally.

The other girls in the office exchanged looks, raised eyebrows. Could the baby be Sean's? they wondered, not for the first time, since Sean had had a go at all of them, with varying rates of success. Or was Terry simply a very kind and generous man?

In truth, he had not known what to do with the flowers, but, seeing Sharon's swelling figure as he walked by her desk he was hit by a sudden inspiration and acted on it at once. He felt sorry for her, poor girl.

He was too busy to have time to leave London for a few days, but the following weekend he drove into Dorset, took a room at a pub in Dorchester, and waited until Sunday morning to drive over to Miranda's mother's cottage.

He found her in the garden pruning and weeding, wearing old blue denim dungarees and a t-shirt. She managed somehow to make them look like the very highest fashion.

Terry was programmed to buy women flowers or chocolates when he visited them, so he had bought flowers again, en route, a great polythene-wrapped spray of red roses, but looking around the garden he could see he had brought coals to Newcastle. Dorothy Knox lived surrounded with flowers, like a princess in a fairy tale in an enchanted bower.

She paused, flushed and breathing fast, to stare at him as he pushed open the gate, which whined and creaked like an old dog.

'Mrs Knox?'

She nodded, pushing a lock of fine-spun silvery hair back from her forehead.

She was amazingly attractive for a woman of her age, he thought, staring at the brightness of her eyes, the warm tones of her skin, her slim, active figure.

Terry hesitated to tell her his own name. He had no idea how much Miranda, or the police, would have told her.

'Is Miranda here?'

'No,' she said and suddenly there was frost on her voice. 'Who are you?'

He couldn't refuse to answer. 'Terry Finnigan, I was Miranda's boss.' He held out the flowers in what he felt, himself, to be a pathetic attempt to placate her. 'I happened to be down in the west, so I thought I would look her up, see how she was, and I brought her these.'

Dorothy Knox made no move to take them. Her face had become cold, hostile. 'Well, she isn't here, and before you ask, I don't know where she is. If I did, I wouldn't tell you. I know about you and your son.' She put a hand up to her head. 'I still have the scars to remind me.'

Terry ground his teeth. He had forgotten what had happened to her. 'Look, I'm sorry for what happened to Miranda, and to you, too, but I wasn't responsible, I assure you. I haven't done anything to either of you.'

'Your son did! If you have any decency, you'll stay away from my daughter. The police won't be too pleased to hear that you've been here, looking for her. And I will tell them, don't worry. She's under police protection, so don't bother searching for her. Even if you found her you wouldn't get near her. Now, I'm very busy, so please go away and don't come back.'

Flustered, he protested, 'Look, I'm sorry, honestly, that you got hurt. I just want a chance to . . .'

She lifted the hoe she was using, poised to use it if he came any nearer. 'Clear off. I don't want you here.'

A car was progressing along the country road towards them. Dorothy glanced at it, her face lighting up. 'Here's my friend. He's a policeman, he'll soon deal with you.'

Terry looked round as the battered red car stopped at the gate. The man getting out was in his sixties but he had a wiry, faintly belligerent look that would, recognised Terry, make him something of a problem in a struggle.

'Go on, get out,' Dorothy said. 'Before Freddy throws you out. He's a lot tougher than you think you are, believe me.' Her eyes were contemptuous.

Terry didn't try to argue or plead; he just slunk away, passing Freddy at the gate without meeting his stare.

'Who's he?' he heard Freddy ask.

Terry dived into his car and drove off before Freddy could catch up with him. He wasn't afraid of the man, simply reluctant to get into a fight and perhaps attract police attention.

Back home, he found Sean lying on a sofa in a towelling robe, his hair wet from a swim in the pool, listening to deafening rock while he cut his toenails. Terry looked at him with a mixture of despair and disgust, then walked over and turned the music off.

'Hey!' Sean began then stopped at the glare he got. 'What's the matter with you now? You're always on my case these days. This is the weekend. Don't I deserve a bit of peace on a Sunday morning?'

'Have you seen Nicola this weekend?'

'Yes, we had dinner and went on to a club last night, then I drove her home at midnight. Her dad insists she's in by then, old-fashioned git. Where were you last night? Don't tell me you picked up a woman?'

'I was doing what you should have done. Looking for Miranda,' his father bit out with scorn. 'She's out of hospital, but she's gone underground, and I'm told she has police protection. I went down to Dorset to find her mother and got warned off.' He was still burning over the way Dorothy Knox had spoken to him.

Sean ran a hand through his springy, wet, blond hair. 'Maybe a chick would find out more – why don't I get one of my birds to look around? Chat people up. Even the filth get friendly with a pretty girl.'

Terry frowned. 'What the hell d'yer mean, one of

your birds! Don't you ever learn? You're supposed to be engaged to Nicola. You shouldn't be seeing any other women. You don't have any common sense, do yer? Grow up, for God's sake.'

Even his accent was deteriorating and his son noticed it, giving him a startled look.

'OK, OK – but shall I get someone to ask around, or not?'

Terry didn't even answer. He was staring out of the window, thinking hard, facing facts.

Sean had mentioned the police and that was a source that could be tapped, although not by Sean, who wouldn't know how. Or by Terry himself. He dared not risk approaching them. He was going to have to talk to some of his old friends. He had not seen them for years, had stayed well clear of them not wanting to be tarred by that particular brush, but Sean was forcing him to get involved again. They were men who had contacts he no longer had. They had friends in the police force. Friends who were on the payroll and who could be persuaded or blackmailed into finding out information.

Somehow he had to find Miranda, get to her. She was dangerous to him, and to Sean. She had to be silenced. Whatever the cost.

*   *   *

'*Kaleemera!*' Miranda said to the waitress at breakfast next day and was given a smiling 'Good morning!' back in English.

As she sat down at the table she had sat at last night the girl asked her: '*O kafes?* American? *Eleeneeko?*'

She dimly understood the question. 'American, please.' Greek coffee was great after dinner, but far too strong and far too small at breakfast.

A basket of rolls and croissants stood in the middle of the table with a tray of butter, jam, marmalade and honey. The waitress indicated a buffet table and rattled off some more Greek. Miranda didn't grasp a single word of it, but she got the general drift, and went to the buffet table to investigate the choices. It all looked delicious.

Fruit juices – grape, orange, cranberry. Lots of fresh fruit; grapes, peaches, berries, piled high. Yoghurts in a chilled cabinet. A covered hot dish in which she found scrambled egg and crispy bacon. Cheeses of various kinds, including a very soft white one over which she noticed another guest trickling smoky, golden Greek honey.

She took some cranberry juice, grapes and yoghurt and returned to her table. The coffee arrived, but it was not the waitress who brought it.

'*Kaleemera!*' Milo said, smiling at her in that paternalistic way of his. 'I hear you already speak Greek.'

Going pink, she shook her head. 'I picked up a couple of words from my phrase book.'

'I suspected as much. But you impressed Sophie. She's now convinced you speak fluent Greek.'

'Oh, dear,' groaned Miranda. 'Will you explain for me?'

'Yes, but, remember, a journey of a thousand miles begins with the first step. If you learn a few words a day you'll soon be speaking Greek like a native.'

'I intend to learn as much as I can, while I'm here. Have you heard how Pandora is this morning?'

'She and her husband had their breakfast in their room half an hour ago. Pandora would like you to go and see her after you've eaten your own breakfast. You'll be moving into a bungalow today, but there's no need to start work yet. We have only a handful of English-speaking guests at the moment. Pandora will talk to you about the work.' He looked at the table. 'Is there anything you need? Anything I can get you?'

She shook her head. 'No, thank you, Milo.'

'Then I will leave you to enjoy your breakfast in peace.'

She ate an unhurried meal, aware of Milo moving about the room, greeting guests, escorting them to tables, checking that every detail was correct, talking to the other staff. Seeing that she had finished, he came back, raising his fine black brows, asking her: '*Kala?*'

Miranda looked blankly at him.

'That means good,' he explained. 'Was your breakfast good? *Kala?*'

'*Ne,*' she said, remembering to shake her head, not nod. 'I enjoyed it very much.'

'The Greek for that is *"moo a resse para polee",*' he translated.

She repeated the phrase, then got a notebook out of her handbag and wrote it down while Milo spelt it.

He smiled at her approvingly. 'You will soon be speaking Greek, I can see that. Now, I will take you to see Pandora.'

It was a much larger room than her own, with several windows, very bright and sunny. Pandora was lying on a cushioned lounger, reading a book, while music played. There was no sign of Charles – no doubt he had gone to his manager's office.

Lifting a smile to greet Miranda, Pan said, 'Did you sleep well?'

'Very well – how about you? You look better.'

'I am. I've barely moved a muscle since we arrived. Come and sit down. Milo, can we have some more coffee, please?'

'Of course.' He withdrew and Miranda sat down facing the window and the view over the gardens.

The window was open, the warm, rose-and-lavender-scented air softly blew into the room.

'I gather I have the rest of the week off, starting work on Monday,' Miranda said.

'Yes. We have a party of Americans arriving this Sunday, though, so you may be called upon to translate for them. But Milo's English is fluent, and so long as he isn't otherwise occupied, he can cope with any problems that come up.'

'He seems to do a dozen jobs! Watching him this morning I felt I should be starting work at once, not taking the rest of the week off.'

Pan laughed. 'No need! Milo could run this place single-handed if he needed to. He has worked here for years and has done almost every job — even the cooking! If we're short of staff in one job Milo can take over if necessary. He's wonderful.'

'How old is he? It's difficult to tell.'

'He's in his fifties, but, as you say, he carries his age very well.'

'Is he married?'

'He was, once, to a lovely woman, I can still remember her smile and her great big eyes, she was always so kind — but Silvana died when I was about ten. She worked here, too. They had a staff bungalow in the grounds. Milo still lives there.'

'Did they have children?'

'Yes, two boys — one of them is in medical school in New York, and the other is an athlete. He's in America, too, training at some sports camp.'

'Milo must miss them.'

'Yes, but he is ambitious for them, he wants them to be very successful and that means leaving home. He's very logical, he accepts that they have to go away.'

'He's promised to help me learn Greek.'

Pandora laughed. 'He has amazing patience. He trained me to work here, I have the highest respect for him. Milo is one of our family.'

'Really? Related to you?'

'Not in blood, but in every other way. He was my father's best friend, and now he's very close to my . . .' She stopped abruptly, looking out of the window. 'Oh! Who's that?'

Miranda looked out, too, but could only see some children running ahead of an elegant woman in a black bikini over which she wore a black and poppy-red pareo, floating and filmy, falling to her mid-thigh.

'That woman? I've no idea. She must be a guest.'

'Yes — beautiful, isn't she? I'm sure she's an actress, I think I've seen her in Greek films.'

'Does Greece have a big film industry?' asked Miranda, rather surprised.

'Not really, but nobody else makes films in Greek

so we have to make some ourselves. We have American films, with subtitles, or dubbed into Greek, of course. And a lot of Greeks can speak pretty good English.'

Pandora pulled a sheet of paper down from the table next to her bed. 'This is a list of what you'll have to do in the office. Read it and then ask me about anything you're worried about.'

Miranda ran her eye down the list. 'No, it all seems pretty straightforward.'

Pandora leaned back, yawning. 'I'm sorry, I'm still sleepy, despite having slept so much since we arrived.'

'That's probably a good idea. Travelling is exhausting.'

'Yes, I was beginning to get worried about feeling so weak.' A brightness showed in her eyes, the brilliance of unshed tears. 'I'm terrified of losing this baby, the way I did the others, of course.'

'Of course,' said Miranda, watching her with sympathy. It must be a nightmare to be in that position.

'Charles and I want children so badly. It's unfair that I can't have them as easily as other women do. Every time I lose one I feel so useless. No, it's more than that – I feel cursed.'

Miranda didn't know what to say. How did you comfort someone you barely knew? Huskily, she muttered, 'Well, if you stay in bed this time, with any luck everything will be fine.'

Giving herself a little shake, Pandora said, 'Oh, yes, sure. Take no notice of my moaning. What are you going to do today? Would you like Milo to arrange a tour of the island for you after lunch?'

Lighting up, Miranda said, 'I'd love it, that's exactly what I'd like to do. But maybe I could sit with you and keep you company?'

'That's very kind of you, but I have to sleep a lot of the time. The doctor gave me tranquillisers to keep me sleepy. You go and find Milo. You'll find him in the dining room, supervising the layout of the buffet lunch. We have a buffet lunch every day, it saves on staff and is cheaper and easier than serving at the tables.'

On her way to the door, Miranda tentatively said, 'I promised to ring my mother, to reassure her that I'm safe – I'll pay for the call. Do I ask the operator to give me a bill?'

'No need to do that. If you make private calls they will be deducted from your salary at the end of each month. Make your call after eight o'clock, it will be cheaper.'

It was only as she walked towards the dining room that Miranda wondered what Pandora had been about to say when she suddenly stopped and changed the subject. She had mentioned her father, who had been Milo's best friend, then added something about Milo now being the best friend of someone else. 'My ...' she had begun then halted.

Had she been going to say Milo was her husband's best friend? No, Miranda was sure Milo was no friend to Charles. She had noticed a coldness in his face, in his voice, whenever he spoke to Pandora's husband.

Who had Pandora been thinking about? Herself? How close was her relationship with Milo? Was he jealous of her husband because he was deeply attached to her? But that was ridiculous. Milo was twice her age, old enough to be her father.

Reaching the dining room, she sat down to wait to have a word with Milo, who was watching the staff clearing the breakfast things away before beginning to lay the buffet table for lunch. He amiably promised to arrange a tour at three o'clock that afternoon.

'Would you like to see your office now? I have half an hour free.'

It was a large room, spacious and light-filled, but with grey louvre blinds fitted at the windows. 'If you lower them it makes the room cooler in the afternoons,' Milo explained.

There were two Greek girls working in the room. Milo introduced them to her and they smiled and shook hands, but obviously did not speak much English.

'Letha has just got engaged to Melanie's brother,

Philo,' Milo told Miranda. 'I told you, this is very much a family firm!' He turned to the other girls and spoke in Greek.

They laughed, nodding. Letha was tall and willowy, with long black hair, a beautiful, golden-skinned girl with a wide, full mouth. Melanie was short and slightly plumper, with brown hair and big, bright hazel eyes. It was obvious they were very good friends.

'They will help you with your Greek, too,' promised Milo. 'And you will help them with English,' he added, again translating his comment into Greek, and both girls nodded enthusiastically.

'Yes, yes, please. We do English at school but . . .' They shrugged their meaning. 'Not good.'

'I'd be delighted,' promised Miranda.

A telephone rang, Letha answered it and began to chatter away in Greek.

Milo pointed to the third desk in the room. 'This will be yours. You do know how to use a word processor, don't you?'

Faintly surprised, she recognised the machine on the desk. 'Yes. In fact, this model is the one I used in London. My firm made them.'

'Ah, yes, of course.' Milo steered her out of the room. 'I'm sure you will enjoy working here. I'll arrange that tour at once. What are you going to be doing for the rest of the morning?'

'I thought I might walk down to the sea.'

'Take care on the beach. There are rocks and pebbles as well as sand. We don't want you to fall and break your other leg, do we?'

'No, we don't,' she fervently agreed.

She set off ten minutes later, moving slowly, enjoying the morning sunshine. It was not yet hot enough to be uncomfortable. It took longer to reach the sea than she had expected. The gardens tailed off, then she was in that rough, wild territory she had found last night when she followed Milo. This time she did not glimpse the house. She was following a well-marked track through the long, sun-bleached grass and gorse. Hotel guests often went down to the beach, Milo had told her. Especially those with children.

She heard the sea before she saw it, tumbling up on to the sand, then falling back with a hoarse whisper, and smelt the cool, salty breeze as it blew her hair back.

Suddenly she wanted to walk in the water, paddle like a child, remembering other times when she had, when she had been three, six, nine, young enough to find the sea enchanting, to love playing in it.

She sat down and took off her sandals, then began a slow descent over pebbles and sand, leaning on her crutch. She hadn't reached the curling waves when she heard somebody else walking on the beach.

Between her and the clear, blue horizon she saw a tall, dark shape.

Her heart seemed to stop.

It was him. The Angel of Death. Walking along the edge of the sea, through the shallows, towards her. He was naked, to the waist; wore just brief black swimming shorts.

Her eyes widened painfully; she stared at his shimmering golden body, the broad shoulders, deep muscled chest, the powerful arms, the slim waist, the long, bare legs, the feet moving gracefully through opaque blue water.

My God, he was beautiful.

Her heart was beating now, so fast it was frightening. She knew this feeling, the hot, sweet surge rushing through her. Desire so strong it made her lightheaded. She had not felt like this since Tom died.

She had never felt like this about Tom.

Guilt overwhelmed her. She swayed, staggered, missed her footing on shifting pebbles and began to fall to her knees. Somehow she clung on to her crutch and stopped herself from falling.

When she was standing upright again she looked towards where he had been, but he was gone.

She blinked incredulously, looked in every direction, along the beach, across the rough grassland, into the trees, but there was no sign of him anywhere.

He couldn't have vanished so fast. There was no cover in which he could hide which was not some distance from the sea; the rustling forest of bamboo, the long, sun-bleached grass.

What was going on here? Had she imagined seeing him? What strange, perverse instinct had made her conjure up his almost naked body, had sent that wave of passion running through her?

When she had recovered she walked down and stood in the sea, kicking the cool water with her unhurt foot, swinging the other one above the waves while she stared into the brilliant blue distance, eyes dazzled by sunlight. She had dreamt about him for years. But now she was beginning to see him when she was awake and she was forced to recognise that her feelings about him were not what she had thought they were.

She had been afraid of him, she had feared him, she had hated him.

None of those reactions had been what she felt, seeing him, just now.

Her mouth had gone dry, she had been on fire. Those dreams of him had not been of death — she had not been having a premonition, a warning, that she was going to die.

She had dreamt of him passionately, wanted him, so badly that it had been like dying.

Her love for Tom could not protect her from such raging, voracious feelings. Tom had been her friend for years before they got married. She had known him most of her life. They had been at school together, played, as children, grown up together.

Tom was a quiet, gentle boy and had not changed when he became a man. Nor had her feelings for him changed. Or his for her.

Oh, she had loved him, but without urgency or need, no hot desire, no flow of burning lava rushing through her body. Tom touched her deeply because he needed her. His own mother had died when he was a boy. Miranda had taken her place, protected him, cherished him.

That was the measure of their love – they were family, as well as friends – and Tom trusted her to take care of him.

But she had not been able to save him from drowning.

It made her guilt heavier to know that just before Tom drowned she had met Alex and instantly wanted him with all the violent necessity she had never felt for Tom.

She could not bear to think about it. She never had been able to.

She walked out of the sea and went back to put her sandals on, then returned slowly to the hotel.

Milo met her at the door of the dining room and showed her to her table with all the courtesy, reverence and attention he offered to guests with fortunes at their disposal. You would never have guessed she was only here to work, was a junior employee compared to him.

She liked him more every time she met him, and wished she dared confide in him, ask him for advice, but she could not talk to anyone about what had just happened.

'Did you walk to the sea?' he asked her as she sat down.

'Yes. I paddled,' she confessed, forcing a smile, trying to sound light-hearted. 'Like a child.'

'It is good to be a child sometimes. We all need to go back to our childhood now and then.' He poured her a glass of chilled water from a bottle.

She looked past him. 'What's the procedure with lunch? Do I just go to the buffet table and make my own selection?'

'You can, if you wish, but why not let me bring you some food? It would be easier than for you to stand in line to select your own food . . .'

'That's very kind of you, thank you.'

'Is there anything you don't like?'

'Squid,' she said, grimacing. 'And I don't much care for lobster, either.'

He bowed and went over to the buffet table, came back a moment later with a tray holding a glass of pink grapefruit juice, a roll with sesame seeds sprinkled on the top and a platter of hors d'oeuvres.

'I chose taramasalata,' Milo explained. 'That's this, pink smoked cod's roe marinaded in olive oil and lemon, you may have eaten it in London, it is very popular there, I know, but this is the real thing. It isn't made with mashed potato, which is the easier version, but with breadcrumbs, the texture is much lighter. And I've given you some caviar to go with it. This tiny triangle of filo pastry is called tiropitta, it has a cheese and spinach filling. There are some prawns, a little crab and some melidzanosalata, which is a purée of baked aubergines, with onion, tomato, garlic and olive oil.'

'It all sounds very interesting.'

His long finger flicked at something green. 'This is dolmadhakia – vine leaves wrapped around minced meat and rice.'

She had recognised it. 'I've eaten that in London, I liked it. I shall never manage a main course after all this! But it looks delicious. You're so kind, Milo.'

'Entirely my pleasure,' he smiled. 'I'll come back later to see how you are getting on. Will you take wine with your lunch? Something white and cold? I'll send some over.'

She ate slowly, enjoying the new tastes, sipped at her glass of white Greek wine and stared round at the guests laughing and talking as they ate or went back to the buffet for a second helping of lobster or caviar.

A young waiter came by her table later and took her empty plate away, then Milo brought her another platter which held a skewer of charcoal-grilled lamb, tomatoes, green pepper and onion, with some green salad, boiled rice and sliced, charcoal-grilled pitta bread in slices on the side.

She managed most of it, but refused a dessert and just had some coffee to finish with.

'I like Greek food, it isn't too rich. Maybe I'll lose weight eating like this!'

'You don't need to lose weight,' Milo scolded. 'By the way, I've arranged for you to join a small coach of guests going on a tour of the island at three o'clock this afternoon.'

'Thank you, that's wonderful.' She felt weird, living here in a little enclave, surrounded by an island she had not seen. Once she had orientated herself she would feel easier.

The driver was also the guide, and spoke very good English. A thin, dark young man he wore glasses and was, he told them, a university student home for the summer vacation. The rest of the year he lived in Athens and studied at the university there.

The island was beautiful, but a little wild; there were the tavernas she had noticed down at the port where they had docked yesterday, a few detached villas on the outskirts of the port, some others scattered here and there around the rest of the island but no tourist development anywhere else.

They stopped in the port for a glass of freshly squeezed orange juice, grown, they were assured, on the island's own trees, which were grown everywhere, as were lemon trees.

Afterwards they were given time to go shopping. Miranda bought herself a straw hat with a wide brim with a vivid cotton handkerchief wrapped round it, the ends fluttering on her nape, some rope-soled espadrilles she could wear on the beach, and a little lacquered fan made in Hong Kong which would fit into her handbag and would be very useful in this hot weather.

Piling back on to the coach, they drove away from the port, turning up into the mountain which dominated the centre of the island, along a dusty, roughly surfaced road full of bumps and ruts. Olive groves ran along the terraced slopes, the fruit showing through those narrow, flickering silvery leaves. Beneath the dimpled, rugged boles were black shadows which

Miranda found very inviting; it would be delicious to lie down in that coolness and sleep.

A lizard lay basking on a low stone wall, in full sun, for all the world like one of the olive-tree leaves whose shape and colour it resembled, until the noise of the coach made it run for cover, diving out of sight into the darkness of the wall's interior.

The air was warmly scented with eucalyptus and pine, which grew on the higher slopes of the mountain, but they saw no flowers.

'The island is full of flowers in the spring,' the guide told them. 'But by July it is too hot here for flowers to survive.'

Miranda grew sleepy, her skin hot with the sun although she had put on the hat she bought at the harbour. She woke with a start as the coach came to a stop on a stony layby high on the mountain. Everyone got off and stood about, gazing down into the valley far below; terraced fields, marked out by stone walls and the odd cypress tree, a dark green flame against the hot, white glare of villages.

'Behind us stands the ruins of a Byzantine castle and the early Christian church of St John. It is inaccessible to the coach, there is only a rough path which you have to follow on foot and which is too close to the edge of the mountain. If you want to visit it, I will be happy to guide you some other day, by prior arrangement, but I must warn you that it is dangerous and difficult. You need to be very fit and active to get to the top. When you do, the views are spectacular.'

None of the guests seemed disposed to find out. The guide gave them a quick account of the castle's history, then they all climbed back on to the coach again to set off down the other side of the mountain.

They stopped again at a village in the valley; a huddle of the usual white-painted houses, set around a blue-domed church, which they visited, escorted by the black-robed priest, who spoke very little English, and the guide, who interpreted for him.

Coming out of the sun they were half blind, at first seeing nothing in the darkness of the interior of the church; then their eyes became accustomed to the shadows and they gasped at the dazzle of silver and gold on the walls, on the altar. Icons of favourite Greek saints – St Basil, St John and St Michael the Archangel – hung on all sides, the dark Byzantine faces with their sombre, brooding gaze and olive, high-cheekboned austerity set against the shimmer of a metallic setting.

The ceilings were painted with visions of heaven; angels with gilded wings, the virgin and child, serious and intent on each other, Christ as a man, floating on white clouds, hand stretched out in blessing.

They spent fifteen minutes in there and stumbled out into the bright sunshine, blinking.

The trees were stirring, beginning to bend and sway, and the guide looked up into the sky, frowning.

'I hope that is not the *meltemi* coming. You know about the wind? The *meltemi*, a dry, north wind which blows across the islands in summer and blows sand in your face, makes doors and shutters bang, drives people crazy.'

'Like the sirocco, the French summer wind,' said an American woman.

'Exactly, but the Greeks do not allow the wind to be used as a legal excuse for killing your wife, as the French do,' the guide said, laughing.

They arrived back at the hotel half an hour later and Miranda hurried off to her room. The shutters were closed against the afternoon heat; the room was cool and shadowy. She drank a bottle of iced water from the mini fridge, stripped off and took a quick, refreshing shower, put on her towelling robe and lay down on her bed. Within about five minutes she was fast asleep.

When she woke up, it was almost dinner time. She rang her mother before she got dressed.

'How are you?' Dorothy asked in concern.

'Fine – this is a really lovely place. I haven't started work yet, but I'm looking forward to it.'

'Good.' A pause, then Dorothy told her, 'That boss of yours came down here, looking for you.'

Miranda stiffened. 'Terry?'

'Finnigan himself. Yes. Don't worry, I didn't tell him anything.'

'He didn't threaten you?'

'No, and anyway, I've got Freddy here, taking care of me. You needn't fret about me. Just take care of yourself. How's Pandora?'

'She was very tired after the journey, but she's been in bed ever since we got here.'

'Poor girl. I hope she manages to keep this baby inside her. She's so desperate to have a child. You take care of her, OK? Keep her company if she has to stay in bed. It must be very boring lying down all day.'

'I will, don't worry. I like her very much, I'll do what I can.'

Ringing off a few minutes later, Miranda slowly got dressed, hearing a strong wind raking the trees outside, tossing them to and fro, tearing off their leaves, rattling the windows and banging the shutters. Somewhere in the hotel doors slammed. How long did the *meltemi* go on blowing?

Looking in the mirror she saw the feverish bright-ness of her eyes and knew she was frightened. So Terry was still looking for her? Well, what did she expect? Her mother might not tell him where she had gone, but Terry would not give up looking.

He loved his son too much. He would want to silence her, forever. He would do anything for Sean.

Another realisation hit her, she bit her lip, shud-dering.

What if she had not been imagining it when she thought she saw Alex Manoussi? What if he was staying here?

If he caught sight of her he might pass the news on to Terry. They were in business together, and often talked on the phone. And they were good friends. He probably knew nothing about what was going on; Terry was hardly likely to tell him. It would be perfectly natural for him to say: did you know that girl who did your PR is here in Greece?

How could he guess what might happen if he told Terry she was here?

If he did, this time he really would be the Angel of Death, for her.

Chapter Eight

Next day she moved into a staff bungalow, one of a row of four set apart from those used for hotel guests. Hers was single storey, roughly plastered, whitewashed, with a terracotta tiled roof. There was a bedroom, with a bathroom off it, a small sitting room with a kitchenette at one end, and a balcony overlooking the sea at the other.

'I hope you will be comfortable,' Milo said, watching her walk out on to the balcony and gaze over the dazzling blue sky, the even bluer sea, whipped into white caps by the *meltemi*, which had been blowing now for nearly twenty hours. The force of it was diminishing, but the trees still lashed to and fro and the sound of it had an eerie, disturbing whistle.

'I'm sure I shall — it's delightful. I shall enjoy eating

out here, too.' Her gaze was fixed on the sea, where she had yesterday thought she saw Alex.

Had she imagined it? Or had he really been there?

It wasn't so impossible, after all. He was Greek. He had said he lived at Piraeus, where he had his boat-building business, but why shouldn't he come over to the island for a holiday? He sailed, didn't he? He could come here on one of his own boats, anchor in the harbour. It would be perfectly natural for him to visit the hotel, even stay here.

Or was she looking for an excuse, trying to convince herself she wasn't going out of her mind?

She turned back into the sitting room, smiling at Milo. 'Are you sure you don't want me to start work at once?'

He shook his head. 'Acclimatise yourself first. The heat here can be exhausting, you'll have realised that by now. In a few days you'll be used to these temperatures, you'll find it easier to work all day. And if we need you to interpret for us with any guests we know where to find you! If I'm in the hotel, I can do it. If I'm out you may get a call asking you to come and help. OK?'

She smiled, nodding. 'I'll be happy to do what I can. That's what I'm here for, after all.'

Milo left her to unpack again and explore her new domain. She put her clothes away in the built-in wardrobe then wandered around to look at the prints hanging on the walls. One was a watercolour of nineteenth-century Athens, a view with the Parthenon to the fore. Round it stood thickly painted trees, white Georgian-style houses a little below that and in the far distance an emblematic sketching of the sea; blue waves, a boat, masts. There were other watercolours of the island; she recognised the harbour, with its clutter of tavernas and houses, painted dark brown, blue and red. Beside it hung a painting of a blue-domed church. It must be the one they had visited yesterday.

Even more interesting to her was an old map of the Cyclades. She studied it closely, orientating herself. There was the sacred island of Delos which was the centre of the islands. There was Mykonos. Nearby was another little island, called Syros. Where was Delephores? She couldn't read some of the print, it was too small, and there seemed to be dozens of tiny islands scattered over the brightly painted blue sea.

While the morning air was still cool enough she decided to go for a walk. First, she had to make sure the bungalow was safely locked up, the shutters down over the windows.

She wished she could go swimming but she couldn't risk getting her plaster wet. But she decided to walk to the sea again, by another route, past guest bungalows and swimming pools, some of which held people, splashing about, swimming lazily. And today the beach had a number of children on it, running in and out of the waves, playing beach ball, lying down on towels on the yellow sands where their parents sunbathed under umbrellas. The dry north wind, the *meltemi*, was still blowing in sharp little flurries.

It seemed unbelievable that she was here, not in London. That was another world, far away.

Terry Finnigan wasn't in London, either. He was in Manchester, having driven up there overnight and taken a room in the Hilton. When he had settled in, he poured himself a shot of whisky from one of the miniatures in the fridge, before getting a number from directory enquiries, then dialling.

A voice he instantly recognised, despite the many years since they had met, answered cheerfully. 'Hello?'

'Irene?'

'Yeah. Who's this?'

Clearly *she* did not recognise his voice.

'Terry.'

'Terry who?'

'Finnigan,' he said and heard her intake of breath.

'You're kidding! Terry Finnigan? My God, we never thought we'd hear from you again. Where've you been all these years?'

'London. How're you, Irene?'

'Fine – how are you?'

'I'm in a bit of trouble.'

'And now you need help, so you thought of Bernie?' There was a touch of cynicism in her tone, which didn't surprise him. Irene had always been blunt, and he could hardly deny the truth of what she had said, could he?

'That's about the size of it,' he admitted.

'Come up here and talk to him, then. Whatever it is, he can't do it over the phone. Come to Manchester.'

'I'm here, staying at the Hilton.'

'Well, jump in a taxi and come over. We still live at the same address. You remember it? Greeby Road? Number six. Have you had your tea yet? We haven't. Have it with us. I've made a lovely hotpot, that was always your favourite.'

'Wonderful,' he said, remembering vividly the golden circles of potato fitting on top, the deep dish of lamb and onions and carrots. You could smell it the minute you walked through the front door. 'Thanks, Irene. I'll be there in half an hour.'

He drove there in his Jaguar, not merely covering the distance in miles but in time, back to his youth, in these grey, huddled streets. Why had Bernie and Irene stayed here? They had money, they could have moved out, as so many rich Mancunians did, to Cheshire or

Shropshire, to the beautiful countryside so close to Manchester.

Instead they had stayed here, in their grey-brick, tiled house ten minutes away from Old Trafford, the sacred ground on which Manchester United played. Bernie wasn't simply a fan; he was a fanatic. To him the team were gods and Old Trafford was Mount Olympus. He was there whenever they played at home, and would travel round the country to cheer them on when they played elsewhere.

Irene opened the door to him. She had grown old – what was she now, fifty-five? A few years older than him. She had never been very slim, even as a girl, but now she had really put on weight; her peroxide hair was as unreal and gold as a fairground ride, her skin heavily powdered, her mouth as red and ripe as a strawberry.

They stared at each other and he wondered how he looked to her. Had he aged as much?

'Hello, Terry, she said in her husky, whisky-thickened voice. Glancing past him at his car, she added, 'Like the Jag. So it's not money that's your problem?'

Without answering he leaned forward to kiss her cheek and she enfolded him in both arms, gave him a hug that almost squeezed the breath out of him, kissing his mouth at the same time.

'Bernie's waiting for you in the conservatory,' she said, letting go of him, and led the way, her wide hips rolling as she moved. 'How's the boy?' she asked over her shoulder. 'We read in the papers about him getting engaged to that rich bird. Did Sandra go to the party?'

'No.' Sandra had always got on well with Irene. They were two of a kind, in some ways, although Irene was more of a home-maker, devoted to her four children and her husband.

'That's a shame – she doted on that boy of yours. Does he visit her?'

'No.'

That got him a shrewd look. 'Won't you let him?'

'I'd never stop the boy seeing his mother, but Sandra's too busy having fun to be bothered. When she's over here she drops in to see him, but she rarely asks him over to Spain.'

Irene sighed. 'That's too bad.'

They were walking through a long sitting room which took up most of the ground floor of the house, full of what Terry thought of as brothel furniture: chairs with gilded legs, onyx occasional tables, gold velvet floor-length curtains with gold fringes, ornaments on every surface, a huge television.

It was a grey evening, cloudy and threatening rain, but ahead of them he saw a brightness which resolved itself into a glass conservatory designed in Victorian fashion. It was ablaze with electric lights.

'Here he is!' Irene said to the man sitting in a comfortable armchair, facing them.

That was when Terry had a shock. Bernie had been in his forties when they last met. Not a big man but very muscular, powerful, although he was already bald.

Now he seemed to have shrunk, withered. Under his expensive suit his body was frail.

'Hello, Terry,' he said, holding out his hand. 'Excuse me not getting up. Did Irene tell you what happened to me? A bit of turf war a few years back; one of the black gangs trying to muscle in on our territory. I got shot in the back. I was in hospital for months. And I still can't walk.'

'That's too bad, Bernie. I'm very sorry to hear that.' Terry shook the hand held out, noticing how thin and limp it was. The life force seemed to have gone out of the man.

'Sit down, have a drink,' Bernie said.

Irene poured him a whisky, then said, 'Excuse me, I have a lot to do, I'll be dishing up in half an hour.'

'Hotpot,' Bernie told him contentedly.

'Yes, she said, I can't wait to taste it again, Irene always made the best hotpot. How are your kids?'

'They're fine, Irene will tell you over dinner. She

says you've got a problem you hoped I could deal with – tell me about that.'

'Are you still in the business?' Terry said doubtfully.

'Me and my boy Andy – remember him? The youngest one. The others make their money strictly legit. Matt's a lawyer, and a good one. Jim's a builder, makes a fortune, building estates all over the north west. Now, tell me about your problem.'

'Sean, my boy, is in trouble.'

'We were reading about him in the gossip columns only last week. Isn't he marrying some rich banker's daughter? Lucky boy.'

'Yes, but he ... well, he's always after other women.'

'Can't keep his flies zipped? Takes after his mother, not you, then. Sandra was always chasing men.'

Terry had never known until the end when she went off with one of them. He felt stupid. Had everyone known? Why hadn't someone drawn him a diagram?

'Yeah, well, one of Sean's girls got herself up the spout and threatened to tell Nicola – the fiancée – and Sean panicked and ...' He took a deep breath, then forced the words out, 'And killed her.'

Bernie whistled softly. 'So he's in prison, waiting to be tried? Funny, we missed that story.'

'He got rid of the body. The police know what

happened but they can't prove it, without the body.' He quickly explained the background, how his publicity girl had overheard the murder, called the police and how he and Sean had been trying to silence her. 'Now she's vanished, and we haven't a clue where she is — we think the police have her in a safe house somewhere. We must find her. The information has to be in the police computer, but how do we tap into that? Do you still have friends in the force?'

Bernie's fingers tapped thoughtfully. 'You want me to ask my friends in the police to find out where she is?'

Terry nodded. 'Please. I'd be eternally grateful. We have to find this girl, deal with her, before she destroys my boy.'

Miranda turned east along the sea shore. After another five minutes she came in sight of the house Milo had visited. This morning the shutters were closed. Whoever was living there must have gone out.

She went right up to the house, slowly made her way all round both front and back. Had this been the original building on the site? Was it eighteenth-century, or had it been built more recently, in the style of two centuries ago?

She could imagine Lord Byron living in it, swimming naked in the sea below these windows, making love to some beautiful Greek girl in fluttering white muslin, by moonlight.

A plane tree grew close to the back of the house; the dappled, grey and pinky cream bark peeling in strips, the round green spiky fruit still hanging among the deep-lobed leaves. Miranda stood in its cooling shade for a while, gazing over the hotel grounds and orientating herself.

It was so pleasant there that she was reluctant to move, to walk back, to her bungalow, or the hotel. A quick look at her watch told her it was gone mid-day. Lunchtime. She could eat at the hotel today, but soon she must go to a shop and buy food she could cook herself in her bungalow.

She would get lots of salad and vegetables, some eggs, maybe a chicken she could put into the little fridge in her kitchen. The hotel staff were entitled to eat in the hotel, but she would prefer to make her own meals.

Setting off at a brisk pace she found lunch being served when she arrived at the restaurant. She queued at the buffet table and selected chicken soup from the great urn. As she turned to go she collided with another woman in the queue, spilling a drink the woman held in one hand.

'Oh, I am sorry, stammered Miranda, uncomfortably observing the red stain the wine had made on the woman's elegant peacock-blue dress.

She received a glacial, angry stare from black eyes. 'Why don't you look where you're going?' The words were English, but the accent was a peculiar mix of American and Greek.

Flushed, Miranda said sorry again. 'Of course, I will pay the cleaning bill. Tell them at reception – my name is Miranda – they'll see I get the bill.'

She hurried away, not daring to meet Milo's watchful gaze, and sat down at a table to begin to eat. The soup was delicious; light and fragrant with what she thought must be lemon.

As she collected her main course – grilled sardines and salad – she noticed Milo talking to the woman she had bumped into. Was he apologising for her? Her job here was supposed to be liaising with guests – that had not been a good start.

After lunch she visited Pandora, whom she found in bed, drinking green tea.

'Do you like that?' asked Miranda.

'It's OK. I'm not supposed to touch coffee – they say caffeine is bad for me. But I'm suffering from withdrawal symptoms.'

There were stains on her upper cheeks; Miranda

could see she had been crying. 'Is something wrong? What has upset you?'

'Nothing!' Pandora denied, unconvincingly, then yawned, deliberately. 'I think I'll have a nap now.'

Miranda left; knowing she was not wanted. Pandora did not want to talk about whatever was worrying her. The baby? Or was something else on her mind?

Walking back through the gardens she paused, mid-step, hearing Charles' voice. 'You shouldn't be here, you know that very well, Elena. There will be hell to pay if he hears about it.'

The wind stirred the leaves; one detached itself and floated down, turning in mid-air and fell almost at her feet. She shifted sideways, staring through the trees. Charles stood a few feet away, his back to her. Facing her, but all her attention fixed on Charles, was the woman in the peacock-blue dress.

Who was she? Did her appearance at the hotel explain Pandora's tear-stained face and distress just now? And what did Charles mean — there will be hell to pay? If he hears about it? Or had he said: if *she* hears about it?

'He doesn't scare me. This is a hotel. I've a perfect right to be here.' The woman's voice warmed, grew sensual. 'How are you, Charles? You look wonderful. You haven't given me a kiss yet.'

Miranda moved again, in shock in time to see the

woman leaning closer, her slender arm going round Charles' neck. There was the sound of a kiss; their mouths together.

Had they been lovers? Was it over? Or was the woman Elena refusing to let him go?

She was so disturbed by her own thoughts that she crept back the way she had come and took another route to her bungalow, but she could not shake off what she had seen. If Pandora found out about her husband and that woman, it could bring on another miscarriage.

She skipped dinner that evening and stayed in her bungalow learning some more Greek, listening to an audio tape Milo had lent her.

Next morning she went out for a walk to the sea after an early breakfast. Fetching up near the isolated house again she stopped to stare, wondering again who lived there. While she was staring she heard a footstep, the sharp snap of a twig someone had stood upon, the rustle of grass parting as a body came through it.

Miranda turned in the direction of the sounds. A man in black shorts and a white t-shirt was only a few feet away, walking briskly towards her. She recognised him with a painful twist of the heart.

She could barely breath. It was him. On the beach two days ago, she had not been imagining things or hallucinating. It had been Alex Manoussi walking at the edge of the sea.

He saw her a second later and stopped moving, staring at her, then he came on in a calm, unhurried fashion, his long, bare brown legs gleaming in the sunlight, and gave her a polite bow of the head.

'Mrs Grey. Good morning.'

'What are you doing here?' she whispered, then, before he could answer hysteria swept through her. 'Did you follow me here? Are you stalking me? I suppose you've already told Terry where to find me so that he can send someone to kill me? Or has he asked you to do it?'

His hand came up and clamped over her mouth, his long, slim fingers cool.

'You're hysterical. Try to be calm.'

She tried to bite him but could only mumble at his palm, voice muffled by the flesh pushing down against her teeth. 'You . . . bastard . . .'

'Ssh . . .' he murmured. 'You don't need to be frightened of me! I did not follow you here. I didn't need to, I was already here.'

Then he let his hand drop away from her mouth. She took one long, unimpeded breath.

'You expect me to believe that?'

'It's true. This is my hotel. I own it,' he expanded. 'Pan is my sister.'

A tide of disillusion and hurt swept over her. 'She set me up? It was all a plot to get me here? She lied to me?' She had liked Pandora and her husband the minute she met them, had never suspected for an instant that they might not be straight with her. Why should she?

While she had been busy feeling sorry for Pandora, worrying about her, trying to help her, Pandora had been conspiring with Alex Manoussi to lure her here.

Alex shook his head. 'No, Pan didn't tell you any lies. Everything she told you was the truth. Except . . .'

'Except what she left out!' Miranda said with fierce contempt. 'She didn't mention you, for instance, didn't tell me you were her brother, or say she knew Terry Finnigan. I know he visited your home and met your family, he told me so. So she knew all about me!'

He sighed. 'I did talk to her about you, and I asked her not to mention me, but I didn't tell her anything about Terry. What she knows about that she heard from your mother. I simply said that you might not come if you knew I would be here.'

'I don't believe you. How can I trust a word you say?' She moved sideways to get away, but he put both hands on the trunk of the plane tree and fenced her between them, leaning towards her, his body very close yet not actually touching hers, merely reminding her how much more powerful his body was than her own. Her senses rioted. She had never been so aware of any man.

His expression was very serious, even brooding. 'Don't you know my sister better than to believe she would conspire against you? She likes you. And she needs help; if she doesn't carry this baby full-term I'm afraid she may crack up. She really needs you, Miranda. Don't turn against her because of me.'

'Of course it was a pure coincidence that she was in the hospital at the same time as me!' she said with biting sarcasm.

'She had been asked to spend a few days having tests to check that the baby was still OK but she hadn't arranged a date. When I heard you were in that hospital I admit I asked her to ring up and book herself in at the same time. As a foreigner, she was a private patient anyway, so it wasn't difficult.'

She was breathing in the scent of his skin, faintly salty, and smelling of pine – aftershave or shower gel? she thought inconsequentially, so disturbed by her reactions to him that she leaned away, her head back and touching the tree trunk. He was far too close.

'Why lie to me, though? Why didn't she tell me the truth?'

'Because I asked her not to! I've explained that.'

'You haven't explained why you didn't want me to know!'

'If she had told you she was my sister would you have come?'

She looked away, very conscious of his long fingers only inches from her cheek. 'I don't know.'

'I do. You would have refused.'

'I wanted to find somewhere safe, to hide from the Finnigans. Now I know you own this hotel I know I'm not safe here. I shall have to leave.'

'No! You can't go. You've signed a contract, promised to do this job, I won't let you leave!'

Terror leapt inside her, she felt all the colour rush out of her face and was suddenly very cold, despite the increasing heat of noon.

'You can't force me to stay!'

'You have a legal obligation to stay for three months — that was the term specified in the contract, wasn't it?'

She couldn't even remember. She had signed the contract after one brief glance at the terms.

'You already owe us a considerable amount,' he added.

She was shaken by that, her voice thready and weak. 'Owe you? What do you mean? I don't owe you anything.'

'Did you read that contract you signed? If you leave

before the three months is up you must refund the cost of your fare out here.'

'I don't remember that.'

'Well, check your own copy of the contract.'

She looked down, her breathing fast and uneven, trying to think, to work out what to do. 'Have you told Terry I'm here?'

'No.'

Her eyes lifted incredulously, stared into his dark ones. They had midnight's blackness, the round pupils like dangerous mirrors, reflecting her own face, very small. 'But you are going to tell him?'

He shrugged those wide shoulders, his face impassive. 'No, why should I? I'm one of Terry Finnigan's clients, I'm not a friend of his. I won't speak to him again for months, unless there's a problem with the shipment he'll be sending me shortly.'

She searched his eyes. 'You know about the murder, though, don't you?'

'Yes,' he said flatly.

'You know he sacked me for telling the police I overheard his son with the girl?'

He nodded. 'And I know about the hit and run driver who ran you down in the street. I have talked to the police, I was one of the witnesses who was interviewed after your accident. I saw what happened.'

'Oh.' That astonished her. 'You were really there?'

She had not imagined that she saw him among the crowd surrounding her while she lay on the road.

One of his black brows lifted in sardonic mockery. 'Did you think you were seeing things?'

'I suppose I was concussed. I wasn't sure what I was seeing.' She caught sight of his gold watch, realised time had flashed past. 'Oh, I must go, it's lunchtime.'

'No, come in and eat with me,' he ordered in an autocratic tone that she resented.

'Don't order me around!'

'We have a lot to talk about, don't we? I've only heard the police version of what happened. I haven't discussed it with Terry. I'd like to hear the story from you.'

His face was sober, his gaze direct; she stared back at him uncertainly, biting her inner lip. Could she believe him? Did she dare trust him, this man who had haunted her nightmares for years?

Chapter Nine

If she was honest with herself, she was curious to see
the interior of the house, and curious, too, about Alex
Manoussi. She knew so little about him or his family.
Even what she had thought she knew, had heard from
Pandora and Charles, from Milo, was obviously not
entirely true. They had left Alex out of the stories
they told, and that made what they had said flawed,
unreliable, as well as making her uneasy about them.
As they had lied to her by omission, they were no
longer the people she had believed they were.

'Come along,' he said softly, coaxingly, and took
her elbow.

She could have pulled away, but she didn't. She
let him lead her into the house, although she was
trembling inside, her head swimming with doubt and
uncertainty.

He unlocked the front door and took her into a hall from which a flight of beautifully polished stairs rose into a shadowy first floor. There was a scent of summer flowers; roses and lavender mingled. A large green glass bowl of them stood on a heavy oak table by a fireplace whose blackened chimney bore witness to years of fires. Charles had said it was cold here in the winter; snow often lay on the ground for days, which was why the hotel now had central heating, although Pandora had laughingly said that in her childhood before the central heating was installed they had had huge fires of wood, perfumed by pine cones from the pines in their grounds.

Had she really meant the hotel, or had she been talking about this house?

'Is the house old?' she asked Alex, as they entered a large sitting room leading off the hall.

Alex let go of her and walked through the shadowy light to the windows, pressed a button which operated the shutters.

'By English standards, no. It was built in eighteen sixty-one; Greece had a King, then, King Otto. He was driven out in eighteen sixty-two, just a year after this house was built.'

'Did your family build the house?'

'My great great grandfather, Philip built it.' He pointed to a brightly coloured painting hanging on one wall. 'That is him.' She studied the proud, weather-beaten, hawk-nosed face.

'I can see a resemblance.'

Alex laughed. 'Thank you. He was fifty when he built this house. He had just married for the third time, a girl of eighteen called Helena. His first wife and child were killed in an earthquake in Athens. He married again, but that wife died in childbirth. Medicine was very primitive here in that era. It was bad luck. But he tried again, with my great great grandmother, and she had four children – two boys, two girls.' He gestured to another painting of a similar-looking man with the same black hair, black eyes, flashing stare. 'My great grandfather, Constantine, was the eldest. He was married at twenty, but his wife didn't have a child for ten years, and then only had one, my grandfather, Basil. That's him, that photograph over there.'

Miranda went over to look at the faded, monochrome photograph standing on a highly polished sideboard. The resemblance to Alex was striking; the family face was oddly uniform, they all looked much the same.

'That was a very early photograph. Apparently my grandfather was a keen amateur photographer. He was too busy constructing his boat-building yard to get married. He finally chose a girl whose father was well-to-do; one of grandfather's customers. My grandmother was beautiful, but we don't have any photos or paintings of her here. There are photos taken by my grandfather, but a cousin of mine has those, in Athens.'

'What was her name?'

'Sophie. When she had a daughter first, she gave her the same name. My father was her third child and first son. She had seven children in all, but several of them died in infancy, which was not uncommon in those days.'

'Did they live in Piraeus, near the boat yard, or here?'

'Sometimes here, sometimes in Piraeus. Once children started to arrive, my grandmother chose to live here. I spent my childhood here, with my mother, while my father lived on the mainland and came over here at weekends.'

'It must have been a difficult life for your mother.'

'Yes, she missed my father when he was away, but she was a good wife and accepted the way of life he wanted.' He turned to look down at her, his dark eyes glinting mischievously. 'Greek women were very submissive then.'

'Not now?'

'We have feminists now. Life is not so easy for men as it used to be. Women argue back more than they did.'

'Good,' she said, chin lifted, and his mouth went crooked, half in amusement, half in derision.

'Home life was much more peaceful in those bad old days, though.'

'For the men — I wonder if women liked their lives much?'

'They had their children, and their home to run. They were not powerless, not in their own homes.'

'And you would like to go back to those times, I suppose?'

He considered her drily, then shook his head. 'I don't believe you can ever turn the clock back. No, I'm perfectly happy with the way things are now.' He walked over to a drinks tray and lifted a glass. 'What would you like to drink? White wine, retsina?'

'White wine, please. Retsina is interesting but it is an acquired taste, a glass of it now and then is OK, but I wouldn't want to drink too much of it.'

'Nor would I,' he agreed, pouring them both white wine.

Taking her glass she sat down. The furniture was mainly golden oak, the armchairs covered in dark blue velvet which matched the curtains hanging at the windows. She got an impression of tranquillity; the room was cool and elegant. The walls were painted a soft eggshell blue; on them hung family portraits and watercolours of the Greek landscape.

A face caught her attention; younger and softer but familiar all the same, and very beautiful. The woman she had seen with Charles – Elena. Was she a member of the Manoussi family, then?

Watching her, Alex said, 'Shall I order lunch from room service, or shall we make our own?'

'Well . . . have you got anything here?'

'Plenty of salad in the fridge. Would you like fish or lamb with that? I've got some lamb chops and some sea bream, or squid.'

'Sea bream would be lovely.' She wrinkled her nose. 'I'm a bit dubious about squid, I'm afraid.'

'We'll have to teach you to love it. It tastes like chicken, you know.'

'I've been told that, but I can't get over those tentacles, and the horrible little suckers. When I see squid I keep thinking it is going to slither off the plate and grab me by the throat.'

He laughed. 'You're letting your imagination run away with you! By the time it turns up on a plate, it's dead and has been cooked.'

She shuddered. 'Maybe, but I still don't like the look of it. Can I help with the cooking?'

'Would you make the salad and the dressing while I cook the fish?'

'Of course.'

'Well, come through to the kitchen.'

She was still staring at the portrait of Elena. Should she ask Alex about her? Slowly she turned to follow him.

The kitchen was an ultra modern room with high windows through which the sun streamed once Alex had opened the shutters.

The cabinets were made of golden pine, there was a bright yellow range and a tall refrigerator on top of which sat a tabby cat with a huge, bushy, stripy tail. It stood up, yawning widely, showing sharp little white teeth.

'Oh, isn't he sweet? Is it a he?'

'Yes, but he is not sweet, nor would he want to be if he understood what you were saying. His name is Attila, and his occupation is mostly murder. He prowls through the grounds and kills everything he can catch; mice, rats, shrews, birds. Red in tooth and claw, I'm afraid. Not sweet at all.'

She stood on tiptoe to stroke the cat's silky head. 'You're not an assassin, are you?' she whispered. It narrowed its eyes to a slit and humped its back, making a growling noise.

'Careful, he bites and scratches, for no reason at all,' Alex warned.

A second later the cat launched itself on to her stroking hand, dug its very sharp claws into her and bit her at the same time.

'Ow,' she squawked, jumping away.

'I warned you,' Alex said, taking her hand and looking with concern at the red marks scarring the smooth surface of her skin. 'Does it hurt? I'll find some cream for it.'

'No, don't bother. It isn't serious.'

His long fingers were caressing her hand, sending shivers down her back. She pulled free and he gave her a quick, upward glance but said nothing.

Moving away, he opened the fridge, got out a plate on which lay a shiny, silver-scaled sea bream. Then he got out a large plastic bowl of salad; lettuce, cucumber, green peppers, tomatoes.

He put the salad on the kitchen table, took the fish over to the sink and began preparing it, holding it under a running tap and scraping off the scales with a knife into a bowl. When he had finished he put the bream on a wooden board and neatly gutted it while she watched.

'Cutlery is in the table drawer right next to you,' he told Miranda. 'Vinegar, olive oil, pepper, to make a dressing, you'll find on the shelf over here.'

She walked over to the shelf and took down the condiments. Alex got a copper frying pan down from the wall, poured a little olive oil into it and set it on top of the range.

Then he began chopping onions, which he dropped

into the smoking oil before crushing some garlic and slicing tomatoes, which he added to the pan. When they were all cooked he cleared a space in the pan for the bream. The kitchen filled with the fresh scent of cooking fish.

Miranda put the ingredients for the salad dressing into a glass bowl and beat them lightly, added some smoky Greek honey and a few spoonfuls of orange juice. In the fridge she found some feta cheese, the white goat's cheese you found everywhere in Greece, and with which she was already very familiar from eating it in the hotel. She chopped it into cubes and sprinkled them over the salad before pouring the dressing over it, adding a handful of stoned black Kalamata olives and a few capers.

'There's some fresh bread in the wicker bin here,' Alex told her over his shoulder.

She got the domed golden-brown bread out. The smell was delicious, she felt as if she had never smelt bread before. By the time she had cut some slices the bream was cooked. Alex put it out on warmed plates, and added the stir-fried vegetables. They sat down at the kitchen table. Alex poured her another glass of Greek wine. She was suddenly very hungry, inhaling the scents of the food.

'Don't add any salt,' he said. 'The fish isn't too salty, but the capers and olives are.'

'And the feta, a little,' she said, putting a white cube into her mouth along with a fragment of fish. 'You're a very good cook.'

'Thank you. I can do any job in the hotel, from portering to cooking, doing accounts and reservations, or waiting at table.'

'Like Milo.'

He smiled. 'Exactly. He trained me. He's a wonderful teacher; patient and long-suffering. He was my father's closest friend.'

'And now he's yours?'

Alex nodded. 'Now tell me about the murder – you were in an office nearby and overheard Sean with a girl?'

She put down her fork. 'They were arguing – the girl said she was pregnant and the child was Sean's, and he must break off his engagement with Nicola to marry her. Sean flew into a rage, then I heard ...' She stopped, swallowing convulsively, staring down at her plate, at the red of tomatoes, the white flesh of the fish.

'Heard her drowning?' Alex gently prompted.

'Yes,' she whispered.

'Then what?'

'Afterwards ... it went so quiet. Sean came to the window and saw me. He looked ... horrified. I fainted. Because I knew I hadn't imagined it, I could see from his face that he realised I'd heard everything. When I came to, I'm afraid I panicked and rushed out. I was so desperate to get away that I never thought of ringing the police. I just had to escape. I drove away, then my head sort of cleared and I started to think. I parked and sat there, realising I had to go back, had to call the police. Which was what I did.'

'But the body had gone, the bathroom was empty, there was no evidence to back up your story?'

She stared at him. 'Who told you all that?' Surely Terry hadn't talked to him about the murder? She knew Alex was close to the Finnigans. Just how close? Was he entirely in their confidence? Was he involved with them in hushing up the murder?

'The police. A Sergeant Neil Maddrell. He inter-viewed me after your accident, and told me the whole story.'

Her face lit up. 'Oh, he's a nice man, he's been very kind to me.'

'Has he?' Alex coolly said. 'You don't surprise me. I gathered that he fancied you.'

A flush kindled in her face. 'That wasn't what I meant.' Changing the subject she quickly asked, 'Did you tell him you planned to bring me here?'

Alex nodded.

'So he knew?' Neil had advised her to go to Greece, he hadn't warned her who was behind the offer of a job here. Why hadn't he said anything? Did he trust Alex? Could she trust him, too? It disturbed her to feel distrust of everyone around her — yet how could she dare risk trusting? She would have sworn that you could trust Terry Finnigan, but he was prepared to have her killed to save his son.

'We talked about it for some time. I promised him I wouldn't say a word to Terry, so that Neil could be sure you would be safe here.' His dark gaze fixed on hers. 'I meant it. You are safe here, Miranda.'

She wanted to believe him, but over the last few terrible weeks she had learnt fear and distrust. When Tom drowned her distress had been compounded by her own underlying sense of guilt, her uncertainty about the wreck of the boat, her dread that Alex was somehow responsible, and was guilty too. She had never shaken off her grief and guilt, and from the day she heard that girl drowning her anxiety had grown worse; her mind was awash with dark emotions and fears. How could she feel safe, anywhere?

Even Charles, who had seemed so nice, and so deeply in love with his wife, had turned out to have secrets.

Terry took his plane up for a brief trip, flying from the airfield to the south coast, to pick up some small components which had been left out of a recent delivery. It only took half an hour to land, load the boxes, drink a cup of coffee and take off again. He had used the collection as an excuse for a flight; a courier could have picked the boxes up easily enough, but Terry wanted to fly for a few hours.

He did not often manage to get up, he was always so busy, and the weather today was so fine and clear. It was a pity to waste a morning like this, he thought, gazing into the cloudless blue sky. There had been so much on his mind lately; he was frequently in a state of depression. Up here he felt more alive, more optimistic.

When he got back home he was surprised to see a dark blue Rolls Royce parked on the drive. He could hear the voices before he walked into the sitting room, one dominating, a husky, flirtatious, laughter-filled voice.

Sandra! Was she alone or had she brought that waste-of-space, Jack, with her?

The question was answered for him a second later when Jack said 'We're on our way to Southampton, going on a Mediterranean cruise. Starting at Toulon, flying back from Istanbul. Twenty wonderful days. Ever been on a cruise, Sean?'

'We went to the States one year, on the QEII.' Sean's voice was apathetic. 'It was OK.'

'How did your engagement party go?' Sandra asked. 'Any piccies, Sean? I can't wait to see your girl.'

'In the top drawer of my desk,' Terry flatly said from the doorway and they all looked round at him.

'Oh, hello, Tel,' Sandra said, looking him up and down.

Jack gave him a placatory grin. 'Hi, there, Terry, how're you?'

'Go and get the photos, Sean, don't just stand there gaping!' Terry ordered. He got angrier every time he set eyes on his son.

'Don't snap at the boy!' Sandra bristled.

Her hair was a brighter gold than ever; courtesy of a recent visit to the hairdresser, noted Terry. It suited her, though; he had to admit he liked it, especially when it had just been done and her dark roots didn't show. She wore twice as much eye make-up as she needed, looking like Elizabeth Taylor as Cleopatra; a very blonde Cleopatra, of course, but with the same sultry stare, the same red mouth, the same long, dangly Egyptian earrings which chimed and shimmered every time she turned her head. The leopard-skin clinging dress she wore was heavily sexy, too.

To his own irritation, Terry wanted her. Bitch. Why did he still feel like this? What was it about her that got him even now? The over-the-top allure, the come-hither smile? Or just plain sexiness? Whatever women needed to have, Sandra had it. In spades. It really bugged him that Jack had her in his bed.

Why had she left him for that loser? He would never know, couldn't fathom it. It couldn't have been money. Terry had more money. What did Jack have? He was a crook; obvious where his money had come from. He and Sandra threw the stuff around as if it would last forever.

But if you spend it, you haven't got it any more. When it was all gone what could Jack do but go back to the old life; to crime and risk. Sandra couldn't have fallen for Jack's looks, either. He wasn't anything special. Just a big, noisy git.

Am I still jealous? Terry asked himself angrily, and knew the answer was yes. He had never got over Sandra leaving him for a man he despised.

Sean came back with the photos, handed them to his mother who began flipping through them, exclaiming.

'She's a lovely girl. You're a very lucky boy. And her father's got all that money, too! Jammy little bastard, aren't you?'

'How's your business?' Jack asked Terry.

'Great. What are you doing?'

Jack's eyes shifted. 'I'm retired, you know that. We've just been up to Manchester to see my family.

My nephew's wife had a baby a month ago, it was being christened. I was godfather.'

'You were?' Terry said, brows lifting. 'I didn't know you had even been into a church.'

Jack glowered. 'It's just a ritual, you don't have to be religious, my bro said. It was a terrific party. All the family there. And while we were in Manchester we visited a few old friends.' He gave Terry a quick, searching look. 'Someone told me you had just been up there. Rumour was you had called in to see Bernie. I saw him, myself, but he was as tight-lipped as a clam about your visit. He's looking old, isn't he? He's paralysed, you know; shot in the spine, a turf fight with the Yardies. He never recovered properly. Don't suppose he's got long.'

'Bernie's tough. He's a survivor.'

Sandra suddenly chimed in, staring across the room at them, 'Why were you up there? You always said you'd never go back, you were out of everything. What's changed?'

Sean moodily swung away, stood with his back to them, staring out of the window, his hands stuck in the back pockets of his old jeans.

'We've got ourselves into some trouble,' Terry carefully said. 'I needed Bernie's help, that's all.'

'Me,' Sean grated without looking round. 'I'm in trouble, that's what he means.'

His mother went over to him, put her hand on his arm, stroked her long, red-nailed fingers up and down. 'What sort of trouble, boysie? Anything we can do to help? We'd be glad to, you know that.'

Terry was silent. If Sean wanted to talk it was up to him. After a minute Sean said, 'Girl trouble. Look, she drowned, somehow; the police haven't found the body, but there was a witness. The police have stuck her away somewhere, we have to find her. Dad thought this guy Bernie might be able to help, might get a cop to tap into the police computer, find her address.'

'She drowned?' Sandra repeated. She had gone pale under her tan. She looked at Terry, who stared back without expression. 'Does he mean what I think he means?' Terry didn't answer. Sandra broke out, 'My God, Sean, how could you be so stupid? If her body turns up they'll put you away for years.'

'It won't turn up, it went into the sea from Dad's plane. If it goes anywhere it will be to Ireland, the Irish coasts were nearest.' Sean looked sulkily at her. 'I know it was a mistake. I lost my head, right? She was blackmailing me, the bitch. She got herself pregnant, then tried to ruin my life. What was I supposed to do? Just give her what she wanted, even if it made my life hell?'

Sandra looked at her ex-husband. 'Couldn't you have paid her off, Terry?'

'I didn't know about her.'

Sean made an angry face. 'And she wasn't after money. Do you think I didn't try to buy her off? No, she wanted me. She wanted marriage, nothing else.'

'Cunning little bitch. So, who was this witness?'

'Dad's PR girl. You've seen her in the office, must have done. She worked for him for three years. Mousy girl. Goody-goody. That's why she was working on a Sunday. I thought the offices were empty, but no, she was there, spying on me. She shopped me and the police have stuck her in a witness protection scheme.'

Sandra frowned. 'I think I remember her. Milly Molly Mandy, I called her; a milk-faced nobody. Butter wouldn't melt in her mouth. And she's the only evidence against you?'

He nodded. 'The police haven't got anything else.'

Sandra looked at Terry, her eyes wide and fierce. 'Then you must find her and make sure she never gets into the witness box. You can't let Sean down. However silly he's been, he's our boy. We have to stand by him.'

'You're a bit late with your mother love,' Terry angrily told her. 'I've taken care of the boy since you walked out on him. I'll take care of this. Bernie's working on it. As soon as he comes up with an address I'll deal with her, don't worry.'

'Jack has friends in the force, he can ask around, too,' Sandra said. 'And sooner or later this girl has to surface, whether they find the body or not. Then you'll have a chance at her. Just make sure that this time there are no witnesses.'

Terry walked out of the room. He had tried so hard to build a good, decent life for himself and Sean, but here he was, being dragged back into the world he had escaped from, and he couldn't see a way out, except by allowing Sean's life to be ruined, and he could not do that.

He couldn't let his boy go to prison for life, Sandra was right. He had to save him. Children were hostages to fortune. Once you had them you went on paying for the rest of your life. Even if he had to sacrifice his business, or his own life, he had to save Sean.

Alex insisted on walking Miranda back to her bungalow after lunch. 'I hope you're comfortable? The staff bungalows were furnished to a high standard. In the hotel there are hundreds of videos, by the way. If you want to borrow one, ask Milo. And before you start work you ought to take a couple of trips to other islands. It only takes three hours to Delos or Mykonos, you can do both in one day, and another day you should take a trip back to the mainland to see Athens.'

'I'd love to do both – are there boats from here? Does the ferry go to Delos?'

'Yes, but you don't want to take the public ferry, it is always very crowded. The hotel boat can take you. Look, I'll take you myself, I haven't been to Delos for quite a while, I love it, there's a very special feeling there.'

Miranda felt a confused mix of emotions – excitement, alarm, resentment. He was like so many men, who feel they can order a woman around as if she were a housemaid, or something – it must be their testosterone. She wished he did not make her senses riot, her blood run faster, excitement burning through her veins.

Chapter Ten

Pandora anxiously apologised next day when Miranda went to see her. 'Alex asked me not to mention him, and I knew you had no need to worry, he only wants to help you, he wouldn't hurt you, but I was afraid you would be upset if you knew he was my brother and owned the hotel.'

'I would have been. Did he tell you anything about me?'

'He said you used to work for Terry Finnigan and you had seen a murder and needed to get away for a while.'

'He didn't tell you about my husband's death?'

'No. Oh, how terrible – was it your husband who was murdered?'

'No. He drowned at sea.' Miranda took a deep breath and went on huskily, 'On one of your brother's ships.'

'Oh.' Pandora stared at her, mouth open. 'Not that one? A few years ago? I remember somebody drowned – was that ... ?'

'Yes. And that's why I wouldn't have wanted your brother anywhere near me, that's why he didn't want you to tell me you were his sister.'

Tears welled up in Pandora's wide eyes, slid slowly down her pale cheeks. 'Oh, I'm so sorry, so very sorry, how dreadful, but it really wasn't Alex's fault, you know. The captain got drunk, he steered on to some rocks, that was what caused the wreck. Alex was very upset about it at the time. I remember how he changed, he wasn't himself for months. Very moody, always flying into tempers. But he's come out of that now, thank heavens. Please ...' She laid a hand on Miranda's arm. 'Please, don't go on blaming Alex. I know you're unhappy about your husband's death, but it isn't fair to hate Alex for it.'

Watching her anxious, colourless face Miranda quickly said, 'I don't any more. Don't worry.' Pandora was so frail, so vulnerable; she did not want to lay any more burdens on those slender shoulders.

Face lighting up, Pandora said, 'Really? Oh, good, I'm so glad. I realise it must remind you, seeing him, but he will be going back to Piraeus next week, so you won't have to see too much of him.'

'He has offered to take me to Delos this weekend, before I start work – is it worth seeing?'

'Oh, absolutely, you must see it, it's the most important place in the Cyclades. The birthplace of . . .'

'Apollo. I know, Alex kept saying so.'

Charles came into the room, smiled at Miranda. 'Settling in?'

She was self-concious in his company, remembering the woman Elena, wondering if Pandora suspected anything. 'Oh . . . yes, thanks.' How could he betray his wife, who was going through so much just to bear his child?

That Sunday, she and Alex sailed to Delos, leaving very early in the morning, before the sun was too hot. Alex took the helm, Miranda sunbathed on deck for a while, in brief shorts and a tiny midi-top which left her midriff bare, but as the sun rose in the cloudless blue sky she felt it was safer to move under the shadow of the awning which ran out from the back of the wheelhouse. She had brought a detective story with her and read it in a desultory fashion, half-asleep in the heat. She still had not acclimatised; but she knew her skin was taking on a flush, a pale apricot colour, even though she had to stay out of the fierce sun in the middle of the day.

The sea was calm, a light spray blown over in her

direction whenever Alex changed course, altering the wash of the wave along the side of the boat.

'There's Delos!' Alex shouted suddenly and she got up and stared forward at a spot of green on the horizon. It grew steadily as they came closer.

A cruise ship flying the blue-and-white Greek flag was anchored in the sea just off the island; as they passed it sailors leaned over the rails to watch them. Alex lifted his hand and greeted them in Greek.

'Ya soo!'

Their cries came back. 'Ya soo, ya soo!'

She knew now that that meant both hello and goodbye, just as *ciao* does in Italian.

The throb of the engine slowed, Alex steered them into place alongside the little harbour wall. A cluster of tourists with sun-red faces and casual clothes were getting into boats there, to return to the cruise ship.

Alex cut the engine and tossed a rope to someone on the jetty, who tied up for them. Miranda collected the thin black linen jacket which matched her outfit, a black straw hat, and a wicker hamper of lunch which Milo had given them. Alex jumped on to the jetty and gave her a hand up to join him while the tourists watched curiously.

Following Alex along the jetty Miranda felt someone staring at her; a woman in a black t-shirt and black shorts whose dyed blonde hair was tied up under a wide-brimmed black hat keeping the hot sun off her face.

It also made it difficult for Miranda to study her features, but there was something familiar about her, although Miranda couldn't remember where she had seen her before.

The other woman obviously recognised her, too, but didn't speak, so perhaps she wasn't sure where she had seen Miranda, either.

One of the men in the queue shouted out, 'Alex! Hi! How're you? Long time, no see.'

Alex paused to stare at the middle-aged man in jeans, cut off and ragged, at the knee, a t-shirt, a crumpled blue linen hat, smiled, held out his hand. 'Jacob, good to see you — how are things with you?'

'Fine. I'm on holiday with my wife and daughters, a cruise around the Greek islands, they're on the ship, they get sea-sick in small boats.' He glanced along the jetty. 'That one of yours? Built it yourself?'

'Uh huh.'

'Nice lines. You on holiday, too?'

'My family live in the Cyclades, I'm having a few weeks with them, then I have to go back to Piraeus to work.'

'Lucky you, sailing in these waters. I'm still sailing, myself; the boat you built me is like a bird. Won a few races this summer. It's easy to handle, very responsive.'

He glanced towards Miranda, who was waiting, as the two of them talked. 'Sorry, I'm holding you up.'

Alex introduced her. 'Miranda, this is Jacob Weingarten, a client and a friend from the States.'

She shook hands, liking the man's weatherbeaten, brown face. Easy to see he was often out in the sun and wind and he had an amiable, laid-back smile. You could tell nothing bothered him much; he was contented.

'Do you sail, Miranda?' he asked.

She shook her head, very conscious of the woman in the queue still watching her, even after she had been helped down into the crowded little boat which finally took off across the sea towards the cruise ship.

Who was she? Miranda searched her memory but came up empty.

Alex shook hands with his friend and turned towards her. 'Ready? Give me the picnic basket, I'll carry that.'

They walked away into long, rustling, sun-blanched grass among which lay marble fragments; pieces of mosaic, statues, fallen pillars, the remnants of walls. Cicadas chirped sleepily on all sides. A lazy hawk floated on thermals above them, wings spread.

'We'll eat our lunch somewhere around the lion terrace,' Alex said, leading the way along a well-worn, dusty path.

'What's that?'

'A row of marble lions, put up at the end of the seventh century BC. There were nine of them, but now there are only five. The others are probably lying around in bits too small to put together again.'

'There are lots of broken statues here, aren't there? What a shame. Isn't there a museum on Delos that could gather up all the pieces, stick them together, and put them on display?'

'The island itself is a museum, an open-air archaeological museum. It was a busy place three thousand years ago, when the cult of Apollo was important in Greece. There was a theatre, which you can still visit; it held an audience of five thousand. There were lots of temples to the god, full of gold and ivory. This was a rich island, so of course it attracted dangerous interest.'

'Who from? It's so far from anywhere else, except Greece itself, and the island must have been Greek, surely?'

'Yes, but people got around a lot more in ancient times than you may realise. In eighty-eight BC the island was sacked by King Mithridates, who spent most of his life fighting Rome but always lost. Anything valuable and portable was stolen. All that was left was what you see in the grass; broken statues and columns. After the Mithridates incident the Romans fortified the island and made it one of their big slave markets. Slaves were shipped in here from all over Greece to be sold.'

She shuddered. 'How horrible.'

They were close now to a row of heraldic beasts on little plinths.

'These are the lions?'

'Yes, they're guarding what was once the Sacred Lake – except that the waters have all dried up, but you can see by the bullrushes where it once was. Apollo is supposed to have been born under a palm tree nearby, which is why the lake was called sacred.'

Alex chose a spot shaded by a cypress, set the picnic basket down, took out a tartan rug and spread it on the grass. They sat down and unpacked the food.

Cooked chicken legs, salad in a plastic box, pieces of feta cheese, little pies stuffed with cheese and spinach, sliced Greek sausages with a strong, rich smell, grapes, a small melon, and finally another plastic box containing *kataifi*, the rolls of shredded wheat pastry stuffed with nuts, soaked in syrup which were one of the specialities of the hotel's restaurant.

Alex poured them both mugs of sparkling mineral water, gave Miranda a little plate, knife, fork and spoon, then they began to eat. The food was delicious in the open air, even though flies and wasps were attracted to the smell of it. Alex fanned them away with a large leaf he picked nearby.

While they ate Miranda stared about curiously. The island was largely flat, with few trees, and there were apparently no modern habitations, just the ruins of stone buildings from ancient times.

'Does anybody live here?'

'Only a few archaeologists and biologists in spring and summer. They go away once the autumn storms start.'

'Is it very cold here in winter?'

'Very.'

When she had finished eating Miranda felt so full up and drowsy that she lay back on the rug, long grass brushing her bare legs, and drifted into sleep. She woke up with a start when a hawk cried overhead, looked around in bewilderment for a second, not remembering where she was, or with whom, until she saw Alex, sitting up beside her, his face in sunburnt profile, staring across the island towards a low hill.

Confused and flushed, she sat up. 'Sorry, I didn't mean to go to sleep. It was the food, I'm afraid, it made me sleepy.'

'Don't worry about it. It was peaceful, I've been reading. Most of the other visitors have gone, to have their lunch at Mykonos I expect, it's only a mile away.

More people will come this afternoon, from other islands, or from cruise ships. They call here every day in the season, spend a couple of hours here, then sail away.'

He got up, extended a hand to her. 'Do you feel like stretching your legs? We can walk to the house of Dionysius to see the famous mosaic floor of the god riding a leopard – or we can visit the house of the Dolphins which has a mosaic floor of the most beautiful dolphins.'

'Can we see both?'

He laughed. 'Why not?'

They spent the next two hours wandering around the ruins of Delos, as the sun rose higher and higher, and the afternoon heat burnt down on them. Although everything was broken and fragmentary, you received a clear idea of how wealthy and important the island culture had been before it was destroyed.

At last they came back to the jetty and got on board the boat. Miranda was relieved to scuttle under the shade of the awning again as they headed off for Mykonos. She was finding the summer heat of Greece difficult to bear and wondered how on earth she was going to be able to work a full day, even with air-conditioning in the offices. But maybe she would get used to it?

'What will you remember of Delos?' Alex asked her

after he set the automatic pilot to take the boat on the right heading.

'Oh. The lion terrace. The long grass full of broken bits of marble everywhere. The sound of the crickets. We do get crickets in England, in the grass, but they don't make as much noise.'

'Here, they're called cicadas,' he reminded.

'Cicadas, yes,' she repeated. 'It was their singing that helped to make me so sleepy. There must be millions of them. And all those white marble pieces of broken statues and columns . . . it is a strange place. Beautiful, but very strange.'

'Haunting, especially in the spring when the grass is full of asphodel.'

'Asphodel, I've heard of that — isn't that something to do with Greek beliefs about heaven?'

'Yes. It's similar to narcissus; a very pale white lily flower, looks like a ghost flower — hence the Greeks thought it grew in the Elysian fields, their idea of heaven. Although they practically invented logic and the use of reason, they were very religious, too. Delos was central to the worship of Apollo. It was forbidden to die or give birth on Delos because it was insulting to Apollo. People who were likely to die, or have a child, were taken off in a boat to Rineia, which is very close.'

She glanced around, and he pointed to another small island very near by, a blue and green smudge in the afternoon heat haze. 'There it is. Can you imagine how it felt to be dying or about to give birth, and have to put out to sea, sometimes in terrible weather, in storms, with wind and rain lashing down. It must have been terrifying.'

'Why was giving birth an insult to Apollo?'

'He was born on Delos, and his priests were determined to make sure nobody else ever was, I suppose. Well, I don't really know.'

Alex stood gracefully, feet apart, body poised, easily riding the soft swell of the sea under him, and she watched him with intense attention, couldn't take her eyes off him.

'We will reach Mykonos soon,' he told her.

'That's inhabited, isn't it?'

He laughed. 'Try overcrowded, in spring and summer. Tourists flock there in season. During the winter the population shrinks away. I prefer it then. It was always a poor island until tourism started, the land is barren, very dry, and sandy. The people lived by fishing. The beaches are excellent, especially around the coast at Platys Gialos, which is why most of the hotels and restaurants are there. You must see the famous white windmills above the town, and walk round the streets, if you feel up to it. You'll be amazed at the shops with top designer names – Versace, Dior, Cartier. American tourists can buy anything there . . .'

He went back to the wheel and Miranda drank some cold water then settled down to drowse, enjoying the rocking of the boat, the cool rush of sea wind over her hot skin.

They spent only an hour at Mykonos, walking round and round the strange, curled white streets which had the convolutions of an ear lobe, making it easy to get lost. Half-blinded by the shimmering whiteness, you followed a lane past walls over which peeped purple wisteria, here a fig tree, there olive branches, and caught glimpses of the blue, blue sea.

Suddenly they were climbing again, up a hillside, past dozens of church towers hung with bells, where Greek Orthodox priests with bushy black beards, in long black cassocks, wearing tall black hats, swung on the bellropes so that the whole town echoed with tintinabulation.

Miranda soon saw what Alex had meant about the international houses which sold goods in this little island. That was almost as bewildering as the sound of bells. What did Paris fashion, American jewellery, high Italian style, have to do with this fascinating place with its own distinct impact – the round windmills on the hill above the town, the white-painted houses, the smell of fish and the whisper of the sea curling up on the sands?

It made money for the inhabitants who had once

lived by fishing, that was all. It gave Mykonos a surreal feel, Alex was right.

'Seen enough?' Alex asked, mouth curving in derisive amusement.

'More than enough!' she said grimacing back.

As they sailed back sunshine danced around them, dazzling Miranda, giving the wide sea a living allure, making her want to sail on forever. It was so tranquil out here, in this wonderful light; sunlight entered her eyes, sank through her cortex into the living brain, stimulating some chemical change which made her suddenly, unbelievably happy.

No wonder the Greeks had worshipped Apollo, god of the sun, of light, of music. Living here in these islands with the blue sky above, the blue sea stretching all around them, the air filled with this marvellous light, they must have been deeply conscious every day of how vital sunshine was to their own wellbeing. She knew she had never been so aware of the necessity of light as she was here, now.

When they got back to the hotel she and Alex went to see Pandora, to give her an olive wood bowl they had bought for her in Mykonos.

'You could fill it with sweets, or fruit, and have it beside your bed,' Alex suggested.

She stroked the smooth, golden, curved sides, smiling. *'Eene oreus, Alex, efkhareesto polee,'* then she looked at Miranda and said in English, 'It's lovely, thank you.'

Someone knocked on the door. 'Come in!' Pandora called in Greek, The door opened. Miranda stared in shocked dismay at the newcomer.

'Elena!'

So Pandora knew the other woman? Did she also know about Elena's involvement with Charles?

Alex had got to his feet. Elena slid a sideways look at him, her eyes slanting and gleaming like polished jet. 'Hello, Alex,' she purred.

His voice was formal, a chill on it. 'Elena. What are you doing here?'

'I'm staying in the hotel.'

'Is your husband with you?'

'Rafe and I were divorced a month ago.'

'Oh. I'm sorry to hear it.'

'Are you, Alex?' she murmured silkily and Miranda picked up an undertone but couldn't decide what it was.

Turning to the door, Alex said flatly, 'Excuse me, I have some work to do.'

'I wanted a word with you, Alex.' Elena followed him out of the room, letting the door slam.

Pandora sighed. 'I wish she hadn't come here! She has no heart, that one.'

Miranda watched her with uneasy sympathy. How

much did Pandora know about Elena and Charles? Tentatively, she asked, 'Is she an old friend of yours?'

'Friend? No. She was engaged to Alex years ago. Her mother had been at school with mine, the two families wanted them to marry – but then Elena met a very rich American, here on holiday and eloped with him. It hit Alex badly.'

Alex? Not Charles? thought Miranda dazedly.

'He was only twenty, and I think he was very much in love. You know how love hurts when you're that age. My mother was really worried about him.'

A stab of jealousy went through Miranda.

'But he's over her,' Pandora ended, not sounding very sure of that.

After their day in the sun and sea wind Miranda was so tired that she had a light supper in her bungalow, just soup and a roll, then went to bed at nine o'clock, and slept deeply, until the early hours of the morning when she woke up from a confused dream, sweating and on edge.

Sandra! The woman on the jetty at Delos, the one in a black hat which half-hid her face, had been Sandra.

If she recognised me, she thought, if she knows Terry and Sean are looking for me, she'll tell them and they'll come to get me.

Sandra had obviously noticed her, but had she recognised her? They had only met a couple of times. Sandra might have sensed she was familiar but not been sure exactly who she was. After all, she hadn't greeted Miranda, hadn't tried to speak to her, just stared.

Even if she had recognised her, would Terry have told his ex-wife what Sean had done and why he wanted to find Miranda? He wouldn't want anyone else to know about the murder, surely? And Sandra was not discreet; she couldn't be trusted to keep her mouth shut. If he told Sandra, she would tell Jack, and out of malice and mischief he would never stop talking about it, the news would spread to all Terry's old friends and even to his customers. A story like that could do untold damage to the business.

But Sandra was Sean's mother – he, or Terry, might have told her.

Miranda couldn't get back to sleep, she was too disturbed, her mind kept chewing over the chances of Sandra ringing Terry to tell him she had seen them.

But knowing that she was here, visiting Delos, wouldn't help Terry find her. She, like Sandra, could be on a cruise around the Greek islands. He wouldn't know where to start looking.

Except that Sandra must know Alex. He had been a customer of Terry's for years. He was a very sexy man, rich, desirable – Sandra wouldn't have forgotten him. She would have recognised him at Delos, and once

Terry knew she had been seen here with Alex he would put two and two together. It wouldn't take him long to check out Alex's home in Piraeus. Not finding her there he would look at the hotel. He would know Alex owned it, and that it was merely a short sail away from Delos.

He'll have me killed, she thought, shutting her eyes in terror. She was starting work this morning. How was she to concentrate when she felt like this?

When she got up next day she saw a pale, haggard face in the mirror. She spent longer than usual on her make-up, trying to create a brighter face, warm foundation, apricot powder, rose lipstick and green shadows on her lids. Surveying her reflection she sighed. Well, she looked a little better.

While she was at her desk printing out letters to possible customers to whom she was sending the hotel brochure Milo came in and smiled. 'How are you coping?'

'Fine, thanks. No problems.'

'I gather you enjoyed your trip to Delos and Mykonos.'

'Yes, very much, it was kind of Alex to take me.'

'He enjoyed it, too. He always tries to get in a trip to other islands. It was a good last day.'

'Last day?'

'Yes, he has left to sail back to Piraeus, we won't be seeing him for a few weeks.'

She stared fixedly at the computer in front of her. So Alex had left. Why so soon? He hadn't mentioned leaving. He hadn't even taken the time and trouble to see her, say goodbye. Had he left because he couldn't be around Elena? Did he still feel the same about her?

Or was there something more sinister behind his departure? If that had been Sandra on the jetty at Delos why had Alex walked past without doing a double-take, without appearing to recognise her? It was such an odd coincidence that Sandra should have been there the same day.

She put a hand up to her mouth, struggling with sickness. Had it been Sandra? What if her imagination was playing tricks on her again?

At times she didn't know what was real and what only existed in her own head. Last night she had dreamt of Tom again, of his drowning cries, and then the dream had changed, she had been in the office listening to the terrifying sounds from the bathroom across the courtyard. Her mind danced with death, day and night, and Alex was part of it all.

What if he had gone away so that someone else might come here, while Alex was safely in Piraeus, with a perfect alibi?

Was someone coming now, to kill her?

Terry got a phone call from Bernie on the following Thursday morning. 'I'm told she is somewhere abroad, definitely not in this country, but her whereabouts isn't on the police computer, so my friend can't find out that way.'

Terry's teeth ground together. Hoarsely he asked, 'Is there a way he *can* find out?'

'Only by going down to London, somehow making contact with the detective in charge of the case. Apparently my friend knows someone in that station, but he's not keen to turn up out of the blue, could be dodgy. Might arouse suspicions in his direction. Obviously he isn't keen to break cover like that. He has a reputation to protect.'

'I'm sure you could persuade him, Bernie.'

'Maybe – but you'll owe me, Terry.'

The casual manner did not disguise the underlying demand. Terry had been expecting to have to pay a price. He was not surprised, but his heart sank. How much more was this going to cost him? He had been paying ever since it happened – in torment of mind as much as money.

'Don't worry, I'll pay up. How much?' he asked resignedly.

Bernie laughed and something in the sound made Terry wince. 'I wouldn't ask you for money, old son. No, no. Not between old friends like you and me.'

'What then?'

'You're into this modern technology ... what do they call it? IT? Doesn't mean a thing to me, but my boys are up to speed on all that stuff and they think you could be very useful to us. They've checked you out and they're impressed. They tell me you're a growing strength in that market.' He paused, softly said, 'Are you ready to help us out if we ask?'

Terry smiled with bitterness. 'Of course, Bernie.' What else could he say? If you ask for a favour you have to repay it. You get nothing for nothing in this world.

'Good boy,' Bernie purred. 'Knew you would, knew you would.' A pause, then he asked, 'Tell me, if you're so hot on technology, why didn't you tap into the police computer yourself? My boys tell me it's possible. What they call a hacker can tap into anything, even the government or army computers, they say. Even break into the revenue boys' computers and we'd all like to do that. Why didn't you try?'

'I did, that's how I knew she was definitely in the witness programme, but I couldn't find an address. I thought there was some other data somewhere under a code key I couldn't find. How soon can your policeman get to London and meet up with Maddrell?'

'I'll talk to him today, try to get him to go down there right away. That will depend how he's placed at the moment, whether or not he can take a day or two off. He won't want to make it obvious, he'll have to have a good reason for going to London. I'll be in touch when he comes up with anything. Oh, and one or two of my boys would like to come down to look around your business, get an idea of what you've got and where you're at. OK?'

'Delighted,' Terry managed to get out. 'Ask them to give me a ring about it first, I'll give them lunch and show them round myself.'

He put down the phone and sat staring out of the window, facing the fact that he was back in that world for good now, would find himself up to his neck in dirty water from this moment on. Easy to imagine the uses Bernie and his boys would put the business to, they would move in here and take over, and there was little he might be able to do to stop it. If he argued he might well end up with a bullet in his head, and then they would run the factory, using Sean to cover what was really going on.

Sean wouldn't have a clue how to fight them. They would blackmail him with the murder, terrorise him; especially if they had already killed Terry himself. The boy had been brought up soft, spoilt. He thought he was clever, thought he was tough – but he didn't know what the words meant.

Terry put his hands over his face, groaning. My boy. My boy. What's going to become of him now?

Chapter Eleven

It was raining heavily as Sergeant Neil Maddrell arrived for work that August morning. Shaking his wet umbrella in the entrance lobby he looked gloomily out at the grey sky. Some August! He hadn't had a holiday so far this summer.' Time he did. Somewhere hot where the weather was reliable. Spain or Italy. He would go into a travel agent and get some brochures, hunt out a cheap trip to the Mediterranean. Spend a couple of weeks lying on the sand, sunbathing. Not thinking. Not worrying. It sounded great.

He found a fax on his desk from Chief Inspector Carol. Merry Christmas to everyone at the station although they were careful never to use the nickname in his presence. George Amos Carol had no sense of humour whatever; he would not have laughed. Heavy in body, heavy in nature, with greyish wrinkled skin and a large nose, like a horn, he prowled the station like a rhinoceros, charging at everyone he met, barking out questions and orders, terrifying young constables who dithered and dropped things under his stare.

'What's he up to now?' Neil asked his boss, who shrugged her plump shoulders.

'A review of the Finnigan case, apparently. He wants to go through the papers with you.'

'What does that mean?'

'He thinks you're wasting police time over it.'

Neil groaned. 'He's going to order me to drop it?'

'He says he hasn't decided yet and wants to hear your side of things, but I think he has.' Her ginger eyebrows bristled. 'The man likes fast results and low costs. This case has dragged on for weeks without any resolution, so he wants to bring down the guillotine.'

'Damn him.'

'I didn't hear that, Neil. Have a quick read of the papers yourself, make sure you're up to speed on it before you see him. One of his favourite tricks is trying to catch you out on some small detail. Don't let him do that.'

'I won't,' Neil said grimly, and spent the next hour going over the case, then wrote a report emphasising every reason why they should continue with it. At a quarter to eleven he took a coffee break, had a mug of black coffee out of the machine in the corridor, then went up in the lift to the next floor.

Inspector Burbage was already with Chief Inspector Carol. They were discussing another case when Neil joined them, but stopped talking to nod to him.

'Come and sit down, Maddrell,' the Chief Inspector grunted, that horn of his pointing at Neil. 'Jessica tells me she has already informed you how I feel, what's on my mind, so let's get straight down to the facts. This witness, Miranda Grey, is the only one who claims to have seen this murder . . .'

'Heard,' Neil interrupted. 'She only heard it.'

'She didn't even see anything, that's right.' Carol licked his right index finger and began turning pages in the folder of evidence in front of him.

'She doesn't give a description of the girl.'

'She didn't see her. But she heard what she was saying about being pregnant with young Finnigan's child, and heard the noise of drowning.'

'Ah, yes, I'll come to that in a minute. So, we have a witness who didn't see anything, only heard noises.' Merry Christmas lifted his hard, dark eyes to stare at Neil, his horn nose pointing belligerently. 'A witness who's well known to be neurotic. Has had a nervous breakdown, was in a psychiatric ward for months, where she kept claiming to hear somebody drowning.'

'Her husband,' Neil reminded. 'He did drown, within earshot of the poor girl. But all that happened three years ago. She has recovered completely.'

'Ah, but has she?' the Chief Inspector pounced triumphantly. 'You can never be sure with nutters. She could be having another breakdown. There was no sign of anyone having drowned, no body was found, nobody else heard or saw anything. The boy has a respectable background, father wealthy, engaged to a very rich young woman, there's nothing against him.'

'But a girl is missing, sir. A girl who knew him, had been dating him for some time.'

'Girls go missing all the time, man! There's no proof she isn't alive. She's probably with some other man somewhere. Sounds to me like that sort of girl. Always hopping into bed with someone, running off with them. The point is, Maddrell, you have no real evidence. Just a neurotic witness who has previously claimed to hear people drowning and has been in a psychiatric hospital for months.'

'I believe her. If you had met her, you would believe her, too, sir. She's a good witness.'

'Look, Maddrell, you have no body, you can't go into court with what this girl says. You can't rely on her evidence. Even if you found a body, the defence would tear her to shreds.' He flicked through the pages of the folder again. 'And without a body we wouldn't have a hope in hell.'

'If the body turns up, sir . . .'

'If it hasn't turned up by now it isn't very likely that you'll find it, is it? The so-called body could be walking around anywhere. No, you're wasting police time and money. Drop it, Maddrell. Get on with your other work. Forget this case.'

'Sir, we shouldn't forget that the witness, Mrs Grey, was knocked down by a hit and run driver immediately after we interviewed her. We have plenty of people who saw what happened and it appears to have been quite deliberate. Doesn't that suggest someone was trying to silence her?'

'It suggests to me that someone knocked her down, panicked, and drove off without stopping. I don't see any connection to the accusations she had made. Plenty of people do get knocked down by hit and run drivers, every day.'

Neil looked helplessly at Inspector Burbage who looked back without expression. She wasn't getting involved, he could see that.

'Forget about this case,' the Chief Inspector said. 'Plenty of other work piling up, deal with that.' He made a gesture of dismissal and Neil rose.

'Sir,' he said with barely hidden resentment. 'By the way, I'm due some leave — could I take it soon?'

'Why not? Now would be a good time. A break, that's what you need, take your mind off this Finnigan case.'

He took the lift down to his own office and stood by the window, staring bleakly out. He couldn't disobey, he had to do as he was told and drop the case.

Miranda Grey was on her own now. He hoped to God the Finnigans didn't find out where she was, that was all. He really ought to get in touch with her, let her know that the case was being dropped, warn her to be careful. And Greece would be the perfect place for a holiday.

Alex Manoussi had had a long, hot, hard morning. He needed to get away from the boat yard, sit in the shade at his favourite harbour-side restaurant, under the awning, drink an ice cold beer, then eat a light lunch – hummus to start with, then salad with fish or maybe lamb.

His table was ready; the waiter quickly brought him a high glass of beer, the sides dewed with condensation from being put into a bowl of chopped ice for a few minutes.

'*Thavmasseeos*,' he breathed, taking a long swallow. 'Wonderful, perfect, I was dying for that.' He took another mouthful, then asked, 'Any specials today?'

'*Streidia*, very good oysters, with shallots and parsley. Or there's a salad of feta cheese and oranges. Or *Kavouras*.'

'Ah, crab, I haven't eaten that for a while — how is it served?'

'Plain, boiled, with green olives, olive oil and lemon juice. Very simple, but good. And the main courses — we have squid, in red wine and oil, a *stifado*, a good casserole with herbs, tomatoes and vegetables. And the meat special of the day is *choirino* — baked pork chops with aubergines, potatoes and green beans.'

'Sounds good. I'll start with the crab and half a dozen oysters, then have the pork chops.'

'And wine?'

'Just your house white.'

'Today that's from Crete, a Gentilini. a good flavour but not expensive.'

'Fine.'

He had just started eating his starter when a shadow fell across him. Looking up he started, eyes widening.

'Sandra? What on earth are you doing here?'

The Greek men in the restaurant all lifted their eyes to stare at the blonde in the clinging leopard-skin tunic which emphasised her large breasts and rounded hips. It clung so close she might as well be naked.

'We're just finishing a cruise around the Greek

islands – flying home from Athens. You remember Jack, don't you?'

He nodded to the other man, noting with distaste the gold earrings, the heavy gold watch, the glisten of oil on Jack's hair.

'Did you enjoy the trip?'

'Yeah, it was OK,' Jack said. 'Is the food good here? Good restaurant, is it?'

'Excellent. I can recommend the fish, particularly.'

'I like the look of those oysters.' Jack's smile revealed even, capped white teeth. 'Good for the sex life. An aphrodisiac, they say, don't they?'

'They say,' agreed Alex.

'The cruise ship stopped off on Delos,' Sandra said.

Alex stiffened, met her mocking stare. 'Oh? Beautiful, isn't it?'

'We saw you there, didn't we, Jack?'

Jack nodded. 'That's right.'

'We were going back to the ship. You were landing.' Sandra paused, watching him. 'You had a girl with you. I recognised her. She used to work for Terry. Did you know he's been looking for her for weeks?'

Alex shook his head coolly.

'I haven't talked to him lately.'

'He didn't tell you he'd sacked the girl?'

'I don't think so.'

'Well, he has. She caused him a lot of trouble, which is why he wants to find her now. Is she here, in Athens? Does she work for you? At your boat yard?'

'No.'

'No?' disbelieved Sandra, her panda eyes wide, red mouth parted and glossy. 'So if we went along there now we wouldn't find her?'

'No, you would not. Everyone who works for me is Greek.'

'Do you know where we can find her?'

He shook his head, took another oyster.

'Well, why was she with you at Delos?'

'I met up with her at Mykonos, recognised her, as you did. When I said I was going to Delos she said she would like to visit it too, so I invited her to sail to Delos with me.' He hoped to God Sandra and Jack had not sailed on to Mykonos on the cruise ship, had not been there when he and Miranda landed that afternoon and strolled round the town, had not seen them together.

'Where did you take her after Delos?'

Sandra had a sharp, insistent way of questioning that grated on him.

'To Mykonos.'

'Was she staying there?'

He nodded without actually answering.

'Did she say when she was going home?'

'No.' He swallowed the oyster, took a sip of the cold wine. Jack watched him, shifting impatiently.

'Time's getting on, Sandra and I'm starving. Why don't we get a table, have lunch here?'

'No, I want to go into Athens, eat at a good American hotel. I don't want any more Greek food, I've had enough to last me for years. Come on.' She gave Alex a hard, almost threatening look. 'I'll be talking to Terry later today. I expect he'll be in touch.'

No doubt he would, Alex thought, watching her and Jack walking away. What bad luck running into the two of them here. The world was smaller than anyone would guess.

Well, at least Sandra clearly didn't know about the hotel, hadn't realised he did not live full time in Piraeus – the question was, did Terry? Terry had visited him here, in Piraeus, years ago, in the early days of their business connection. He had been very curious about Greece, never having been there before.

Alex recalled that his mother had cooked one of her wonderful Greek meals for Terry, who had been very appreciative. They had driven Terry round Athens, shown him the sights, the Parthenon, the Plaka, the beauties of the museum, the gold mask of Agamemnon, dug up in Mycenae, the bronze statues of naked athletes, the mighty bronze of Poseidon hurling his trident, god of the sea and of earthquakes, the bull god, brother of Zeus.

'I'm not too keen on museums, normally, but I must say this is pretty spectacular,' Terry had said. 'How old did you say those bronzes were? Amazing, that people were so clever all that time ago. Makes you think, doesn't it?'

The evening before he left they had taken him to an excellent restaurant where he had eaten the best food Greece could offer; had picked out a live lobster from the large tank along one wall of the room, laughed at the elastic bands on its claws, enjoyed it when it arrived cooked on a great platter, with a fresh lemon mayonnaise sauce.

They had all got on well; talked about business, politics, travel. But had they ever mentioned the other side of their family life – the island, the hotel? Alex could not remember.

He decided to sail home on Saturday morning, see Miranda, warn her that Sandra was going to tell Terry she was in Greece.

Maybe she should move on, find a new place to hide? He grimaced. He didn't want her to leave the island, didn't want her to go away.

*　　*　　*

That Friday evening, Miranda rang her mother and had to wait some time before the phone was answered. Dorothy sounded out of breath.

'Is anything wrong?' Miranda anxiously asked.

'Not at all, I was out in the garden, that's all, shutting the hens up for the night, and had to run when I heard the phone ring. You know, they're laying very well, I've had seven dozen eggs this week, and sold them all to the village shop. Organic eggs get snapped up, especially if they're brown, and my hens lay lots of brown eggs, it's the feed they get. I'm going to get some ducks, Freddy has put a pond into the garden, feeding off the little stream that goes through the village, he's out there now, finishing off. I do love a duck egg for my supper. Scrambled, on toast. Lovely colours, duck eggs; very bright yokes and blueish whites. The flavour is a bit salty, but if you mix some cream with the egg before you start scrambling it helps.' She paused. 'So, how are you, love? Everything OK?'

'Fine, I've finished my first week in the job, and everything has gone well. I like it here very much, and I'm starting to get used to the heat.'

'Sounds blissful. Lucky you. I was thinking maybe I might come to Greece while you're there, spend a few nights in this hotel.'

'That would be wonderful,' Miranda said eagerly.

'I miss you, it would be great to see you. And staff can get better terms for relatives, so let me know if you do plan to come, and I'll see what I can do.'

'I will. Maybe in a month or so. When the heat dies down a little. I wouldn't want to be there while it is so hot. Have you heard from the police in London? That nice Sergeant whats-it?'

'Maddrell.' Miranda's voice took a dive, she sighed. 'No, not yet. They can't do much until they find the body.'

'Well, no, obviously – but why is it taking so long to turn up? What did they do with it?'

'Neil Maddrell seems to think they put it in Terry's plane and dropped it in the sea, but it hasn't come ashore yet.'

'Maybe they weighted it; it may have sunk to the bottom of the ocean, may never come up.'

'Then they will never be able to prove what happened,' Miranda said bleakly, shivering.

'I hope that doesn't mean you will have to stay out of the country for good!'

'Mum, I hope so, too. But at least I should be having my cast removed tomorrow. That will be a relief.'

'I'm sure it will be.'

*　　*　　*

She was driven to the local doctor's surgery next morning. With the cast gone the air felt wonderful on her bare leg. She used a stick for the rest of the morning, but by lunchtime felt able to walk without it.

She was in reception when the hotel bus began depositing new arrivals picked up from the harbour. Miranda waited to see if her services were required. Milo, handing out keys at the desk, smilingly shook his head at her, indicating that the guests did not need a translator, but one of the waiting queue waved at her.

'Hello, Miranda!'

She gasped in surprise. 'Sergeant Maddrell!'

'Neil, please,' he prompted.

The way he was looking at her made her blush. 'N . . . Neil,' she stammered. 'What are you doing here? Has something happened?'

'No, afraid not. I'm here strictly for pleasure, on holiday.'

Milo watched and listened, his dark eyes moving from the man's face back to Miranda.

'Could we have dinner?' asked Neil and she nodded, smiling.

'I'd love to, thanks. What time?'

'Seven thirty, in the bar?'

'OK, see you then.'

That evening as she was on her way to the bar she met Milo who looked her over with raised eyebrows, taking in her tight-fitting blue silk dress, which had a low neckline, the navy blue high-heeled sandals which gave her more height.

'You look delightful, Miranda. Your friend is in the bar — I saw him go in there ten minutes ago. Is he your boyfriend?'

Shaking her head, she casually said, 'Just someone I know.'

Faintly cynical, Milo told her, 'I saw the way he looked at you. He likes you a lot.'

'He's a very nice man but we hardly know each other,' she fenced, rather flushed. 'But if he's been waiting for ages, I'd better join him. See you, Milo.'

She walked into the bar and saw Neil at once as he stood up to greet her.

His roving eyes told her he liked the way she looked before he smiled at her. 'Thank you for coming. I'm very pleased to see you looking so much better. You were so pale and stressed last time I saw you, in London. Now you've got a nice tan and you look far more relaxed and happy.'

'It's a lovely island and the people I'm working with are lovely people.'

She sat down; the barman came over and she ordered a glass of sparkling mineral water.

'Tell me how far your investigation has got,' she asked Neil.

'We're still waiting for the body to turn up. Without that, we can't prosecute.' He hesitated, then brusquely told her, 'My bosses have told me to shelve the investigation until the body does surface.'

Biting her lip, Miranda said, 'They don't believe me, do they? Terry has convinced them I'm nuts.'

'No, no, they just want proof of murder before they act.' Neil's face was sober. 'But you must be very careful, Miranda. Until we find that body you could be in danger, even here.'

She shivered. 'I know. I'm very careful, don't worry.' She hated thinking about it, so she changed the subject. 'How long are you staying here?'

'Not sure – a week, a fortnight. It depends on events. If the body shows, they'll call me back to London.'

After a leisurely, candlelit dinner he walked her back to her bungalow through the gardens, under rustling trees, the sound of cicadas all around them.

'Thank you for tonight,' he murmured huskily, 'It was a wonderful evening.'

Sensing that he meant to kiss her, and reluctant to go too far down that road, she bolted through her front door, muttering, 'Goodnight, Neil.'

In bed in the dark she thought of Tom and was

shaken to realise he no longer haunted her the way he had for the past three years. Was she beginning to get over his death at last? But she had had the old dream only the other night. Yet the cause of that had not been her guilt – she had had the nightmare because of jealousy and misery over Alex, not because of Tom. A realisation that made her guiltier than ever and made her sleep badly again.

Next morning, at seven o'clock, she put on her swimsuit and a towelling robe and carried her towel under her arm to walk through the hotel grounds to the beach.

The sun was rising on the horizon, a burning golden ball, the sky was streaked pink and deep blue, sending shimmering lines across the blue sea.

She had spent half the night restlessly tossing, her mind occupied with memories of the murder, of Tom's death, of Neil, of Alex, and her helpless, stupid jealousy over that woman, whom she saw every day, around the hotel, looking exclusively streamlined in her designer clothes, gold around her neck and on her fingers and wrist. Miranda despised herself for feeling as she did but couldn't stop herself. Her heart was in turmoil – if they never found the body what should she do? Stay here? Watch Alex with that woman? She wished she knew how he really felt about Elena. Maybe she should go home? But that would mean risking Terry or Sean's vengeance.

It sounded so melodramatic, using a word like that, with its overtones of operatic threats, she wished she could laugh the idea off, but Sean had drowned that girl, and someone had tried to run her down in the street.

Reaching the top of the sweep of beach she stripped off her white towelling robe, draped it over a gorse bush growing at the edge of the sand, laid her towel on top, kicked off her flip flop sandals, and began to walk down towards the sea.

As she entered the waves and began to swim a body rose up in the warm blue water right next to her and grabbed her.

Miranda gave a terrified scream.

'I know,' he murmured, holding her closer. 'Poor girl. But I'm watching out for you. Milo and I take it in turns to be on sentry duty, at night, checking that no strangers are in the grounds, that nobody tries to get into your bungalow, or the hotel. I promise you, you aren't in danger while we're here.'

She was astonished, staring at him, lips parted, eyes like saucers.

'You and Milo ... keep watch on me?'

He nodded. 'Day and night, somebody is there, making sure you're safe every minute of the day.

When you're in the office, in your bungalow, in the sea here. One of us is always on guard.'

'I've never noticed either of you around.'

'The last thing we want is to be noticed – by you, or anyone else. If we're easy to spot it would warn off anyone trying to get to you. We want to catch them and have them locked up. There's no other way of stopping these attempts on you.'

She shivered and he frowned.

'You're cold. You need to get indoors, get dressed. Forget your swim this morning.' He stood up, lifting her, and she clutched at him, her arms going round his neck. Her fear had somehow drained away; suddenly she trusted him, felt safe with him.

The swing of her emotions was bewildering: one minute she was terrified, under threat; the next she was soothed into a belief that nothing was going to happen to her with Alex around. She would give anything for a little stability; to have solid ground under her feet for a while, to forget her fears for ever.

Alex carried her to her bungalow, unlocked the door, took her into the bedroom, laid her on the bed and knelt beside her, gazing down at her with an intensity that made her head swim.

'Don't look at me like that!'

'You're so beautiful,' he whispered, then he began kissing her. She drowned in the depth of emotion running between them. His hands touched her, fire scorching her skin, his body moved closer and closer. But never close enough. She yearned to be part of him, to take him into herself, melt into him. This was how she had felt from the first moment she saw him – this need, this desire, had been instant and overpowering. Why else had she felt so guilty when Tom died?

Shuddering, she pushed him away. 'No, Alex, don't.' She rolled off the bed and stood up. 'I must get some breakfast before I start work, but first I have to have a shower and get dressed – would you mind leaving?'

Slowly he got up too. 'Are you still fighting the way you feel, Miranda? Your husband's been dead for three years. It's time you stopped refusing to move on. You're still young, you have a long life in front of you.'

She walked to the door and opened it, silently inviting him to leave but as he came towards her Neil appeared in the doorway, wearing swimming trunks, a large towel over one shoulder.

'I'm going down to the sea for a swim – will you join me, Miranda?'

Alex's face tightened into a cold mask. He walked past Neil, nodding to him curtly.

'Oh, hello, I didn't see you there,' Neil said, startled. Alex walked off without replying. Neil gave Miranda a grimace. 'Did I come at the wrong moment?'

'No, he was leaving anyway. I'm sorry, Neil, I've already had my swim. Maybe I'll see you later?'

'Lunch?'

'That would be nice. My lunch break is at one o'clock today.'

'I'll see you then.'

As Neil swam in the blue sea, under a blue sky, he envied Miranda waking up every morning to weather like this in this lovely place. He would have to go back to dreary, grey, autumnal London, leaving her here.

He wouldn't be able to stop thinking about her, he knew that. Every day she came into his head, he couldn't shut her out. He had never been this obsessed with anyone. Her image was burned into his brain.

Back in his bungalow, he was nearly dressed when the phone rang, making him jump. He reached for it automatically. 'Hello.'

'Hello, Maddrell. Sergeant Cordell here, missing persons. Just had a fax from the Met. They've had information from some fishing port down the coast from Dublin. Port St Patrick.'

'Never heard of it.'

'Me, neither. But, seems a body came ashore there yesterday . . .'

Neil stiffened, heart racing, his knuckles gripping the phone going white. 'A woman's body?'

The other man chuckled. 'Thought that would make you sit up. That's right, a woman's body. Been in the sea a long time, wrapped in an old bit of carpet, weighted down with gym weights, I'd guess from a private gym, they're too small to have come from a public gym, from the sound of it.'

'How the hell did it come up if it had been on the bottom of the sea all these weeks?'

'Came up in a trawl net, Japanese fishermen out in the deep sea, fifteen miles off the UK coast, nearer to Ireland, fishing for mackerel and herring, brought it up in their nets, and put into port with it at dawn. The pathologist hasn't taken a look at it yet, but it could be what you've been looking for. The photo you faxed us isn't any help, I gather. No hair left, no eyes, either, so we can't match them. But the general weight, colouring, could be right, and she has all her own teeth – although some work has been done not too long ago, so if you get hold of your girl's dentist that might help with identification. Shall we send someone else, or d'you want to come back and take a look?'

'Yes,' Neil said fiercely. 'I certainly do.'

'Rather you than me. Remember, she's been in the sea for weeks. Not pretty. And it will screw your holiday up.'

'If this is my missing body it will break the case wide open. It's worth it. I can take a holiday later. Thanks, Cordell. I owe you one.'

'Buy me a drink next time I see you.'

'You're on.'

Neil packed and booked a flight back before going over to the hotel to arrange for transport back to Athens. He then walked through to Miranda's office to say goodbye.

'I've been called back to London urgently.'

Her eyes sharpened. 'Has the body been found?'

He smiled at her. 'You're sharp. Maybe. We're not sure yet, that's why I have to get back at once, to check it out.'

'You will let me know, won't you?'

'I promise.' He bent to kiss her and she lifted her face to meet his.

'Goodbye for now,' he whispered. 'See you soon, I hope.'

He left and she turned to go back to her desk but paused, startled to find Alex in the corridor, watching.

Icily, he said, 'Please keep your private life for your own time.'

When Neil got back to London, he went to Inspector

Burbage's office. She listened, head to one side, watching him with wry amusement from under those ginger eyebrows.

'OK, Neil, go for it. I hope it's the right girl, I know how hard you've worked on this case. Let's hope you're going to be able to charge young Finnigan.'

'I can't wait. I want him so much I can taste it. The cocky little bastard thinks he's above the law. He's been laughing at us all along, certain he had got away with it. Well, he's in for a shock.'

She laughed. 'You really don't like him, do you? Let's hope this is the right body. I'll have a word with Merry Christmas, leave him to me. He'll have to let you open the case again if we've got a body. You'd better take care of that witness of yours, we don't want her ending up in the sea.'

'Don't worry, if this is the missing girl, I shall fly back to Greece to see Miranda, make sure she's safe, and that she will come back to give evidence when we need her.'

She grinned at him. 'Better make it an official trip, then they'll fork out with the cost of the flight, and maybe even a cheap hotel.' She tapped the side of her head with one stubby finger. 'Think canny, Neil. This is business, not pleasure. Even if you do fancy this witness.'

Neil went red. 'I didn't say . . .'

'You didn't need to. I've noticed the way you look every time her name comes up.' Burbage gave him a friendly punch on the arm that nearly knocked him over. She was famous for her fighting skills; was a black belt at judo and had even boxed. 'But don't take any risks, Neil. Don't contaminate the evidence. We don't want the Finnigan brief to dream up a conspiracy between the two of you.'

Soberly, Neil said, 'No, we certainly don't. Look, do you think we should keep this quiet – the body turning up? We don't want word getting back to the Finnigans, do we?'

'No,' she agreed. 'Right, just between the two of us, and the Governor, then. Keep me up to speed, Neil, whatever you're doing.'

He was on his way to Ireland two hours later. He flew to Dublin, where he picked up a hire car before driving along the coast to the little fishing port, a huddle of white cottages with slatey-blue roofs rising up from the walled harbour. He went first to the police station, built of flint and local stone, with a mock-Gothic tower at one end, looking more like an illustration from the Brothers Grimm than a modern police station. Inside, however, procedure was what he would expect of his own station.

He waited for five minutes until he was joined by a balding, middle-aged detective from the local Garda.

Inspector Declan Murphy wore a crumpled grey suit and a tweed tie which had slipped sideways like the noose of a hanged man.

They weighed each other up, shaking hands.

'So, you're here to see our body? Someone you'd been looking for, I was told?'

'Cross fingers,' Neil said, performing the action.

'You're not going to recognise her. Even her own mother wouldn't know her, poor soul. She'd been in the sea for a long time.'

'I know. Can we go to see her right away?'

'Surely.'

They drove up the winding little hill to the town's cottage hospital; built around the same time by the same architect, as the police station, decided Neil as they parked and he got the chance to stare at the place.

'What's your population?'

'Oh, around twenty thousand.' Declan Murphy gave him a dry look sideways. 'This is a far cry from London.'

Neil laughed humourlessly. 'I'm sure.'

'We get bodies drifting up on the beach now and again, but mostly we just have the odd burglary, petty shoplifting, vandalism, taking and driving on a Saturday night, when the pubs kick out, and a murder around once every couple of years –

often domestic, the last one a man hit his wife on the head with a meat hammer, and before that a wife poisoned her husband because he was sleeping around.'

'Sounds a nice quiet life.'

'It's very much a community life. We know most people, they know us. When a house gets done, we go round and lift the usual suspects. They're not too bright upstairs, our criminals. We often find the goods stored in a garage, or under the stairs. We have a good clear-up rate.'

'I might move here.'

Declan laughed. 'Have you found somewhere to stay for the night?'

'Not yet. I came straight to the station.'

'Ah, well, now, I'll find you somewhere.'

They were walking round to the back of the hospital. The morgue was housed in a stone building not much bigger than a garage. Neil shivered at the coldness inside and Declan gave him one of his shrewd, piercing looks.

'Sure you want to do this?'

'Yes,' Neil said, hesitated, then confessed, 'I need to see she's really dead.'

'Did you know her?'

'No, but for a while I thought my witness might be lying, or crazy.'

'Ah, sure, you want to set your own mind at rest. I understand. OK, Michael, bring her out.'

The attendant pulled out a drawer from the row of metal cabinets along one wall, then whisked back the white cotton sheet.

The body was horrific; swollen, silvery, glistening like some great fat fish, no features left on the inflated head for him to recognise. His eyes flashed briefly to the naked body then away again as sickness rose in his throat.

'Enough?' Declan asked, watching him.

Neil managed a nod. He reeled out of there and leaned on a low stone wall.

As they drove back to the police station, he kept his eyes shut, the window open beside him and a rough, clean wind from the sea filling his lungs, helping to expel the after-taste of the morgue. That scent of decay and antiseptic was deadly. He hated it.

Back in his small, shabby office Declan opened a drawer and got out a bottle and two glasses.

'Join me?'

'Please,' Neil said through white lips, afraid he might throw up any minute, which would be humiliating in front of this stranger. He had seen dead bodies often enough before, but that one had been the worst in his experience.

Declan put a file box on the desk. 'X-rays —

she'd been to a dentist recently, she broke an arm in childhood and it was set badly, and there's a scar on the abdomen. Appendix. Forensic says it's quite old; she was maybe late teens when she had that done.'

'Yes, that fits what we know.'

'Did you know she was pregnant when she died. Around three months gone.'

Neil nodded. 'I was told she said she was.'

'Ah, but it's sad. I always hate it when the corpse is pregnant. Two deaths for the price of one, God help us, and the babe with no life at all. You should be able to get a fix on her with all that, though.'

'Oh, yes. I'm sure she's the girl I've been looking for – what about the lungs?'

'The lungs?' Declan stared at him blankly.

'What does forensic say about how she died? Did she drown in the sea?'

Declan flipped pages, leaning forward to read, stabbed a finger at a page. 'Ah, you're right, there – sorry, I did notice it, but I'd forgotten. I'm working on a few other cases at the same time. You know how it is. There's no salt water in her lungs at all, she was dead when she went into the sea. But there's water in the lungs – only it's tap water. Probably died in a bath.'

Neil began to smile. 'Got him.'

'Ah, it's a joy, entirely, isn't it?' Declan sympathised. 'Come on, now, and I'll find you a bed for the night.

I know a nice quiet place where you can get bed and breakfast for twenty pounds. My wife and I would be very happy to have you eat your dinner with us. She's making braised steak in Guinness tonight. With dumplings, light as air. I tell you, man, you'll think you've died and gone to heaven. Maureen is a wonderful cook. I'm a very lucky man. Are you married, Neil?'

'No, not yet, but I'm working on it.'

Declan grinned. 'Good man.'

Terry Finnigan got the phone call early next morning while he was eating toast and marmalade and drinking coffee in a misty morning light.

'Not good news, I'm afraid,' Bernie told him, wheezing. 'They've found the body. It came up in a trawler's net, off Ireland. They identified it by the teeth, and some old operating scar — and she was pregnant, of course.'

Terry shut his eyes, breathing carefully. What bloody bad luck. All these weeks and then some fisherman nets it. In another couple of months there would only have been bones; no evidence left. Why couldn't it have stayed down there?

He swallowed, asked flatly, 'Has your man tracked down the other girl yet? Miranda.'

'Not exactly, but he did pick up some gossip

about the detective on the case flying to Greece last week. He wasn't booked for a holiday, maybe that's where she is?'

'Greece?' Terry was astounded, his mind racing.

'Yeah. Anyway, warn Sean to expect a visit, get your brief on side, ready for when they come. Keep me in touch with what's going on, won't you, Terry?'

'Sure, of course.'

'My two boys are coming to see you tomorrow. Andy and my computer expert, Liam. Ten o'clock, at your office, OK?'

'OK,' Terry said indifferently, no longer caring. What did his business matter compared with what might happen now to his son?

Sean was still in bed, his blinds down, the room in soft shadow. Terry crashed open the door, yanked the sheet off him as he walked past to pull the blinds up and drench the room with morning light.

'What the hell d'you think you're doing?' Sean spluttered, sitting up.

His father looked down at the boy's naked body in that tumbled, heated nest, his temper rising. Look at him! All he thought about was enjoying himself; partying all night, sleeping all morning. It was Sean's self-indulgence, his obsession with his own pleasure, that had brought all this about. If he hadn't slept with that girl none of this would be happening.

Rage filled him. He slapped his son round that sulky, flushed face, still stupid with sleep, and saw incredulous amazement come into Sean's eyes.

He had never struck the boy before. He should have done. Maybe some of this was his fault? He had brought the boy up as if he were a prince, given him everything he ever wanted, often before he had even realised he wanted it. No wonder Sean thought he had a right to take what he liked, do what he liked. He had never before met real life, been forced to pay for what he had done.

'Get up, get dressed, come downstairs. We've got to talk.'

'You hit me, you bastard!' Sean's hand curled into a fist. 'I'm not a kid. You've no right to lay a finger on me! I should knock your face through the back of your head.'

'They've found the body.'

Sean was very still, staring. 'They can't have.'

'They have.'

'I weighted it down . . . it couldn't float up.'

'It didn't. It was dredged up in fishing nets.'

Sean went white. 'Where?' he whispered.

'Ireland.'

Desperately the boy gasped, 'But by now it must be . . . unrecognisable. It's been down there for weeks. They won't be able to tell who it is!'

'They will. These days they've got all sorts of ways of proving identity. They can take a hair from her hair brush and get her DNA. And they're like death and taxes, they never let go. They'll prove it, somehow, and God help you when they do.'

'Even if they can tell it's her, they can't prove I did anything.'

'With Miranda's evidence they can.'

Sean swore hoarsely. 'That bitch! We've got to shut her mouth. With her out of the picture the police won't be able to make a case.'

Terry sighed. Sean was right. 'Bernie says that detective, what's his name ... the one who's dealing with the case, has gone to Greece. I wonder if that's where Miranda's been hiding?'

A car rolled up the drive, wheels grating on gravel, and Terry frowned. 'Now who the hell is that? Not them, already?' He looked at his son almost despairingly. 'Get up, get dressed, come downstairs.' Then he ran down the stairs two at a time and pulled open the front door, staring at the couple confronting him.

'Sandra? I thought you were on some cruise.'

'We just got back.' She swayed past him on very high, glossy black heels. Jack followed her like a dog, keeping close to her, as if afraid Terry might hit him.

The idea did occur, but Terry decided not to indulge himself. He had enough problems without getting into a punch-up with Jack, or quarrelling with his ex-wife. 'Coffee?' he offered, walking into the dining room. 'This is still hot.' He lifted the steel vacuum jug and waved it.

Sandra sat down, crossed her legs, her black dress sliding upwards to reveal supple, tanned thighs.

'Lovely. I fancy some toast, as well, please.'

Terry slid two slices of bread into the toaster on the sideboard.

'Where's Seany?' Sandra cooed, pouring black coffee for herself and Jack, who was jingling his gold bracelets in a sleepy way.

'Getting up. You going back to Spain right away, or staying on over here for a while?'

'We're flying to Spain day after tomorrow.'

Sean appeared in the doorway, his hair still damp from a shower, wearing a sleek casual outfit: pale biscuit slacks, a chocolate brown shirt, a cashmere beige cardigan over it.

'Sean baby, you look great – you've got real style, I love the gear,' his mother said, extending her arms, and he reluctantly allowed himself to be engulfed in them and kissed.

'You look pale,' Sandra said, leaning her head back to look closely at him, then turned accusing eyes on

Terry. 'The boy looks pale — what have you been doing to him?'

'What have I been doing to *him*? Sandra, he's been lying about on sofas watching videos, or sleeping late, while I've been running around like a blue-arsed fly, trying to save his bacon.'

'No need for language like that! He's not well, poor boy. But never mind. Sean, I've found that girl for you. What's her name — this PR girl you've been looking for.'

'Mum!' Sean burst out, 'You aren't kidding me, are you? Where is she?'

'Greece,' she said, stroking his hair. 'Seany, you ought to blow-dry this hair right away. You don't want to catch a cold, it's dangerous to go around with wet hair.'

'I'm OK, Mum,' he wriggled, pulling out of her arms.

'What d'you mean, Greece?' Terry grated, looking at her with dislike, taking the brown toast from the toaster and dropping it on a plate which he pushed in front of her.

She pulled the marmalade dish over and began spreading. 'You know — that country on the other side of Italy. Greece. We went there on our Mediterranean cruise and we saw Miranda.'

A rush of angry colour flowed up Terry's face.

'Don't be such a drama queen, Sandra. Stop pussy-footing around and tell us the facts. Where exactly did you see her, and when?'

'The cruise ship stopped at this little island called Delos. We all went ashore in little boats. While we were queuing up to go back to the ship, after . . . and, God, it was boring. Just a lot of grass and broken bits of statues. Anyway, I saw that girl landing in another boat – and guess who she was with? That Greek chap you do business with. Alex something. It was his boat.'

'Alex?' Terry sat down, breathing thickly. 'Are you sure it was him?'

'Certain.'

'And we saw him, in that place near Athens, when we arrived back from the cruise,' Jack chimed in. 'He was eating lunch. Sandra stopped to talk to him. You asked him about the girl, didn't you, Sandra?'

'Yeah. He admitted she'd been with him, claimed he'd picked her up in Mykonos, that's another little island, not far from Delos, but at least they have great shops and no broken statues. I bought a wild silk blouse there, Yves St Laurent – a lovely damson colour.'

'Delos?'

'No, I told you, Mykonos. They have great bars, too.'

'Tavernas,' Jack said. 'Greek drinks are weird, though. I hated retsina, and ouzo tastes like that French stuff, aniseed, what's it called? Pernod?'

'Do shut up about Greek drinks,' Sandra snapped at him. 'Alex said the girl was having a holiday on Mykonos, he'd met her by accident.' She shrugged and bit into her toast, crunching noisily. 'Who knows? Maybe it was the truth.'

'When was this?'

'End of last week,' Jack said.

'God Almighty,' Terry erupted. 'Why didn't you ring and let me know at once? Don't tell me you didn't have your mobile with you? Or that there were no phones on this ship?'

Sandra swallowed her toast, gave him an indignant stare. 'I tried to ring here a couple of times but you weren't in, then I tried the office, and left a message – but I couldn't tell your new assistant I'd found that girl, could I? It might have been a dodgy thing to do. If the police were listening to your calls and heard that they'd have known you were looking for her, and it could have gone against you.' She wiped her crumbed fingers on a paper handkerchief. 'I was using my brains, don't know why I bothered. As soon as we landed we came straight here to give you the news. And all I get is insults and bad temper. We might as well still be married.'

'Sorry,' Terry said, grimacing. 'I'm anxious, that's all. Look, did you get the impression Alex was telling you the truth? Do you think he did just meet up with Miranda like that?'

She stood up, her blonde hair catching the light. 'I don't know. Well, I'm not sure – but no, my instincts told me he was lying. Now, don't ask why, I can't say. I just felt it, instinctively.' She looked at her watch. 'We'd better get going. I want to do some shopping in the West End.'

When she and Jack had departed Terry stood on the steps staring at the sky.

'So Bernie was right,' Sean said. 'She was in Greece, that's why Maddrell went there.'

Terry nodded grimly. 'And that's why I'm going, too. We have to find that girl and silence her before the police can move her on somewhere new.'

'If you go to Greece it will look suspicious!'

'Ah, but I've got a great excuse. I do a lot of business with Alex Manoussi. I'm going there to liaise with him on the spot.'

Chapter Twelve

Miranda had settled into her job now and was enjoying it. There was sufficient variety to keep her interested all day, especially when she had to deal with hotel guests. A number of Americans stayed there, few of them spoke Greek, she was often called upon to translate for them.

The hours were quite long, but she had one afternoon off a week. Alex went back to Athens on Sunday evening and on Tuesday she broke off work at mid-day to eat lunch with Pandora in her room, the meal served by Milo from a trolley. They had egg and lemon soup to start with, then salad with feta and olives. Pandora ate very little and seemed listless, silent.

'Aren't you well?' Miranda asked anxiously, still wondering about Charles and Elena. That kiss she had seen — what had that meant? Did Charles love his wife? Milo clearly did not like him — why not? What did Milo know, or suspect?

'I'm so bored lying in bed all day. I wish I could go out just once in a while.'

'But why can't you? If you were wheeled out to a car you could be driven anywhere.' Miranda could easily understand how she must feel. Outside the window the sun glittered on the grounds; on the silver birch shimmering in shadow, on roses and lavender carefully watered every evening to keep them alive. People walked past in swimsuits, carrying towels, making for the beach, or one of the swimming pools. Children scampered, laughing. 'It must be a drag to have to stay indoors in weather like this.'

'Oh, it is, especially when I'm alone for hours. Charles is always so busy. I know running a hotel is a full-time job, I just wish I could go out now and then.'

'I don't see why not. Ask your doctor if you can.'

'I seem to have been in this room forever. Ever since we got here, anyway. Do you really think they would agree?'

'There's no harm in asking, is there?'

Pandora picked up the phone beside her bed and dialled. 'Charles? Can you come here? Miranda's had an idea I want to put to you. OK, in five minutes.'

Putting the phone down she gave Miranda a half-pleading, half-rueful look. 'You don't mind if I blame you? You never know with men, how they're going to react. Charles wants me to stay put until the baby comes, he doesn't realise how depressed I get, and I don't like to make too much fuss.'

'He loves you, anyone can see that.' Miranda pushed away the memory of Charles kissing Elena. The other woman was probably more interested in Alex, who was free and available. 'He'll want you to be happy. I can't see why there should be any real objection, so long as you don't overstrain yourself, try to walk, get out of the car. A short drive could make all the difference to your mood, and that's important, especially at the moment. You need to be cheered up. Tell him.'

'He may not be able to spare the time.'

'Then get Milo to take you. Or me! I can drive.'

Charles came in, overheard what she was saying and raised his eyebrows. 'What are you two plotting?'

Pandora told him in a rush, her voice shaky.

He scratched his chin uncertainly. 'I think we should ask the doctor if it's OK, first, don't you?'

'Ring him now, then,' urged Miranda, getting up, but Pandora caught her hand.

'Wait – if I can go, come with us. We'll drive to

my favourite church, you can go in and say a prayer, light a candle to the virgin.'

Charles made the phone call, put the question to the doctor, listened intently. 'Yes, she's very depressed. I think it would do her good to get out even if only for half an hour.' He listened again, smiling. 'Yes, thank you, I promise.' Putting the phone down he turned to his wife. 'He says you can have one hour's drive today, he'll be along to see you tomorrow morning to make sure it wasn't too much, but you are not to put a foot to the ground.'

She let out a long sigh of pleasure. 'Wonderful. Can we go at once? You will come, won't you, Miranda? Or had you other plans for your afternoon off?'

'No, I've nothing special planned, and I'd love to come.' She walked to the door. 'I'll wait in reception while you get ready.'

'I haven't worn outside clothes since we got back here. I just lie about in my nightdress, all day. It's so boring. Just getting dressed is going to be fun.'

In the reception area Miranda found Milo and told him what was afoot. His face lit up.

'That's good news. I was getting worried about her.'

'Me, too.'

'She's been more and more depressed this week. I wonder the doctor and Charles couldn't see it. They're so concerned about this baby that they aren't thinking about Pandora herself.'

Miranda gave him an affectionate look. 'You're very fond of her, aren't you?'

'I've known her since she was born, she's almost my own child. Can I get you anything while you're waiting, Miranda? Tea? Some sparkling mineral water spiked with fresh lime and lemon? Very refreshing on a hot day.'

'Some tea would be nice.'

'Milk or lemon?'

'Lemon, please.'

'Sugar?'

'No, thank you. I find it more refreshing without sweetness.'

He brought it in a tall glass in a fretted silver holder; a slice of lemon floated on the top. There was a faintly herbal scent to the tea, Miranda sipped it happily.

'Delicious, thank you, Milo.'

'My pleasure.' He gave her that characteristic little bow of the head, his smooth, discreet, olive-skinned face warm. He was one of the nicest men she had ever met. He made her feel safe, cherished. But he also had a quiet authority – he could be anything, she thought – head waiter, hotel manager, prime minister, archbishop, absolutely anything.

She finished the tea just as Charles pushed Miranda

in her wheelchair through the swing doors. Milo came forward to take Pandora's thin, frail hand, lift it to his lips and kiss it.

'*Agapeete moo!*' he said gently and Miranda knew enough Greek now to realise he had called Pandora 'my dear'. She was pleased with herself. She had been having Greek lessons for weeks now and was gaining a little of the language every day, but learning a language was not easy for her.

'I'm going for a drive! The doctor said yes,' she eagerly told him and he smiled down at her.

'Enjoy yourself. You're looking better already.'

It was true, she was, her eyes brighter, her face mobile and excited. She had put on a loose, dark red linen kaftan embroidered around the neck in gold, and falling to her feet; the reflection of the colour on her skin gave her a healthy flush. That worrying listlessness had gone; she was alive and alert once more.

As they were getting into the car Elena walked over to them. 'Going somewhere nice?'

'Just for a drive,' Charles said.

'Well, have a good time. Tell me, when is Alex coming back?' Was she waiting here until he did? thought Miranda bleakly.

'He never tells us.'

They drove out of the hotel grounds five minutes

later and headed into the hills to the little village Pandora had talked about, a few dozen pastel-washed houses – pale apricot, blue and yellow – surrounded with ancient olive trees, their silvery green leaves fluttering like butterflies in a gentle breeze, their great, gnarled trunks growing out of terraces marked off by low stone walls. In the centre stood the church, pale terracotta, with white-painted windows. The colours blurred and shone in the afternoon sunlight.

Charles parked outside the church and took Miranda inside, out of the hot, bright sun into the deep, cool shadows where the icons of saints glowed round the walls, silver and gold backgrounds to the faces.

'The church was started in the eleventh century, but took many years to finish because whenever the village ran out of money they stopped work.'

'It's beautiful,' Miranda said, staring at the offer-ings attached to icons, thank-yous for the saint who had cured a disease, helped a woman have a baby. She walked around the circle of walls, under the dome, to look at the Byzantine faces; strong and stern, St John, St Basil, the Apostles staring down, grouped around Jesus.

Her favourite was the Adoration of the Magi painted in gold, black and flame-like red, with a very plump baby Jesus waving a palm leaf at his mother who had a faintly bewildered expression, as if not quite sure who he was. Around them stood saints and kings whose faces were quite blank of expression except that they had great dignity and pride, enrobed in their magnificence, with golden halos round their heads.

Before they left, Miranda knelt in front of a dark, tender icon of the virgin and lit a candle for Pandora, as she had promised, praying silently that the baby would be born safely in due time. Charles also lit a candle, knelt beside her; she sensed that his prayer was the same as hers. It must be very hard for him too, this difficult pregnancy, especially, as Pandora said, when he was kept so busy running the hotel.

When they rejoined her, Pandora was leaning back in her seat, watching a small gecko on a stone wall near the car, his throat gulping, eyes closed as he absorbed the hot sun into his greeny-grey body.

'I love lizards, don't you?' she whispered, then as they got back into the car a chestnut-headed little bird dived down out of the bright blue sky and flew off with the unfortunate lizard wriggling helplessly in his beak.

It all happened so quickly it made them jump.

'A woodchat shrike!' Pandora said, shivering. 'Horrible birds, they impale lizards on thorns and keep them to eat later – you can see their larders in the woods. A row of pathetic little bodies waiting for dinner time. Ugh. Enough to make you turn vegetarian.'

'Let's go home now,' Charles said, watching her anxiously. Her emotional reactions were too fierce; she was white again, trembling. 'Don't upset yourself, darling.'

'I'm fine,' she insisted obstinately. 'Charles, I want to buy some rolls from the shop across there. I've been smelling the bread while I waited, it's made me hungry.'

'I'll go,' Miranda said. 'It will give me a chance to practise my Greek.' She had been working for an hour a day at the language, but reading it was one thing — speaking it another.

There were several women in the shop; tanned so deeply they were almost black, with headscarfs over their hair, all of them in well-washed cotton dresses. They stared and she shyly said good afternoon.

'*Ya soo, thespeenees.*' they chorused. Hello, miss.

She pointed at a wicker basket of rolls. '*Psomakee, parakalo.*' Holding up her hands, counting off fingers, she indicated that she wanted six.

The shopkeeper shook her head and said, '*Ne!*' Why did they always shake their heads and make a negative sound when they meant yes? Were they trying to be awkward, or trying to deceive any enemy watching? She did not know of any other people who did that.

As the rolls were put into a bag she noticed a bowl of fresh figs and asked for a kilo of them. The other customers watched her without comment or expression. Were they hostile, or simply being polite? The trouble with a foreign country was that you did not instinctively pick up the secret, subterranean language.

She paid and walked back to the car. Pandora immediately began to eat one of the golden rolls, taking bites out of a purple-black fig, too, from time to time as they drove along.

'It's odd, I'm suddenly hungry,' she said.

'That's good, you haven't eaten much for days,' her husband said, smiling.

The figs had glistening, sensuous pink flesh; Miranda watched Pandora's teeth tearing at them. Her mouth watered. They looked so good. There were always figs on the buffet table at lunch in the hotel; she must have some tomorrow.

'I really feel so much better,' Pandora confessed, yawning. 'Just having a change of scene, and some sunshine, and fresh air, has given my spirits a boost.'

'Well, whenever you want to go out, just tell me, in future,' Charles said, pulling in through the gates of the hotel grounds.

'There's Alex!' Pandora gasped, leaning forward to stare.

Miranda's heart crashed.

'What on earth is he doing back here so soon?' Pandora said. 'I hope nothing's wrong!'

Alex was casually dressed in pale grey trousers and a dark pink shirt, but he looked pale, almost grim. He kissed his sister's cheek. 'Glad to see you looking so well, Pan.' Then he shook hands with his brother-in-law. 'How are you, Charles? I've just had half an hour with Milo, so I know business is good.'

'We're fully booked for the next fortnight. There isn't a single room free.' Charles was looking self-satisfied. His brother-in-law smiled at him.

'I know. Well done.'

'I'll just pop Pan back into bed, then I'll join you in the office,' Charles said, but Alex shook his head.

'Not yet. I'll see you later. I need to talk to Miranda.' He took her arm, his fingers incisive, and hurried her away, through the grounds to her bungalow.

She felt Pandora and Charles staring after them. 'What is it?' she asked Alex anxiously. 'Has something happened?'

'Yes,' he said in that terse, harsh voice. 'Where's your key?'

He opened the front door of her bungalow and let

them in, followed her inside and walked over to open the shutters which the maid always left shut after cleaning the room. Daylight flooded into the cool, shady room.

'You're going to need a cup of tea and I could certainly do with some strong coffee. Let's put the kettle on.'

'I'll do it,' she said, but he was already busy. She watched him move about finding cups, a teapot, the coffee and tea bags.

'Alex, tell me what's happened, before I scream!'

He looked round at her broodingly, that dark, Byzantine face shimmering gold in the afternoon sunlight. 'They've found the body.'

The shock made her sit down, a hand to her mouth as if to keep down a scream. As soon as she could speak she whispered, 'When?'

'Yesterday.'

'Where?' She only seemed able to speak in mono-syllables.

'It came up in some fishermen's nets and was taken to the nearest port in Ireland.'

'Has it been identified?'

'Yes, there's no doubt it is the missing girl. And she was three months pregnant.'

'Oh, poor girl!' she breathed, biting her lower lip so that she didn't cry.

He poured her tea, put it in front of her and sat down next to her with his own strong black cup of coffee.

'That detective rang me – the sergeant who talked to me in London.'

'Neil,' she nodded.

Alex gave her a narrowed stare. 'The one who was here. Yes. He says he's coming again, quite soon, to see you, and he wanted me to tell you the body had been found and events were moving at last.' He took a sip of coffee then flatly added, 'And then I had a phone call from Terry Finnigan.'

She looked at him, her nerves jumping. 'What did he want?'

'Well, he said he was flying to Greece to see me about a new improvement in one of the navigational computers. He didn't say a word about the police finding the body. I suppose he didn't think I'd know.' Alex's mouth twisted cynically. 'He's arriving tomorrow. I had to come here to warn you. I'll make sure you're protected, don't worry. Milo will move you back into the hotel. It will make it easier to keep an eye on you day and night.'

She was touched by his concern, but shook her head, frowning. 'I love my bungalow, why can't I just stay here? The grounds are patrolled by security men, aren't they? Nobody could get at me. And I prefer the independence of living here rather than in the hotel.'

Alex looked impatiently at her. 'There's far less risk if you're in the hotel. What if somebody does get through the security cordon? What if your bungalow is broken into? At least in the hotel there are plenty of other people around.'

'You don't honestly believe Terry would come here and try to kill me! Sean's the killer, not his father. Have the police arrested Sean?'

He shook his head. 'Not yet, but I imagine they will, now they've got the body. That detective told me they had now found plenty of forensic evidence.'

She sighed. 'Poor Terry. He must be desperate. And he loves his son, you know. Sean is the centre of his whole life. I feel so sorry for him.'

They arrived first thing in the morning before even Terry was up, let alone Sean. Tousled, flushed, in a gaudy Stuart tartan red dressing gown, under which he was wearing nothing, Terry stumbled downstairs to open the front door.

Neil Maddrell flashed his warrant card, walking past him as he did so. 'Your son here?'

'He's still asleep. Hey, wait a minute, you can't just barge into my house without permission!'

Neil was already in the hall. 'Get him up, Mr Finnigan. We're taking him to the station for questioning.'

'You wait a minute. I'm getting my lawyer.'

'Your son's going to need him. Tell him to meet us at the station. Because I am taking Sean there, so please get him up, or would you rather we did it?'

Putting on a calm air, Terry argued. 'Why all this urgency? You've already talked to him for hours and you know you can't charge him. There's no evidence against him except for what you were told by that neurotic bitch who worked for me.' They must not know that he had been informed about the body brought up out of the sea. That would make them suspicious of him, of his contacts.

Life had become so complicated since Sean killed that girl. He often felt he was walking through a minefield, always watching where he put his feet, intensely afraid of an explosion that could blow his whole world to smithereens.

'We've found the body, Mr Finnigan. We've identified it beyond a shadow of doubt, through DNA, dental records, medical records — and she was three months pregnant and the baby's DNA will give us your son's paternity, I've no doubt.'

Terry swallowed, realising for the first time that the unborn child had been his grandchild, his flesh and blood. That had been his dream for years, to have grandchildren, but this child, this first one, had died with its mother.

'I'll get him up,' he hoarsely agreed.

When he looked down at his son he had a terrible impulse to punch him in the face hard. How could Sean sleep so soundly after what he had done?

Terry saw the ruins of his life around him and hated the boy for a second, but was it partly his own fault? A child was always the product of his upbringing.

When you were young you had no idea what effect your every casual, impulse-born action would have. He and Sandra had made Sean what he was; loving the child they had always indulged him, given him anything he asked for, made Sean feel he only had to put out his hand and he would get what he wanted. Taught him to feel no guilt for whatever he did. They had rarely smacked him, they hadn't believed in it. If Sean was naughty they forgave him at once.

How could he be forgiven for killing the mother of his unborn child, and the child with her?

'Wake up. Sean, wake up.' He was afraid to lean over and shake him; afraid if he touched him at all he would end up battering the stupid boy senseless.

Sean blinked, lids fluttering, yawned, looked up.

'The police are here. And they're taking you away with them. Get up, wash, get dressed.'

'Get my brief!' Sean sat up, glaring, issuing his commands as if his father was a servant. 'And do it now! I'm not talking to them without him, get it?'

Terry looked at him bleakly. 'You stupid, arrogant little bastard!' His love for his son was turning to something like hatred.

But he went down to his office and put through a call to his solicitor. There was nobody in the office yet. The secretary came in at nine, it was only eight thirty. He left a message on the answer phone, stressing the urgency.

Then he stood by his desk staring out at the garden, watching birds looping through the trees calling. It was a beautiful autumn morning; golden and glowing. He had always loved days like this, but his spirits were too low for him to enjoy it now. He felt despair clogging up his throat. You think you've built a wonderful future for yourself and your family, then one day it is all destroyed. All because a stupid, selfish boy couldn't keep his trousers zipped and then couldn't face up to the consequences of his own folly.

He had booked to fly to Greece this morning. Should he still go? Or should he stay here, in case Sean needed him?

'Aren't you coming with me?' Sean demanded behind him and he slowly turned, looked at his son as if from a far, far distance.

'You're a big boy, I'm sure you don't need me there.'

'Well, if you don't want to come ... well, don't!' Sean's lower lip stuck out petulantly. 'Did you ring the brief?'

'Yes, he'll come along when he can.'

'That's not good enough! Ring him again, tell him he either shows up at once or we'll get someone else.'

The police loomed up. 'Time to go.'

They seized Sean by the arm, one on each side.

'You hear me, Dad?' Sean resisted them, glaring at his father.

'I hear you,' Terry wearily said.

He had just remembered that Bernie's son was coming today to look over his books, check out the firm's situation and prospects. The day that had started so badly was probably going to get worse.

He would have to ring up and postpone his flight to Greece after all. There was no way he was going away with those bastards coming. He had to be there to protect his interests.

Miranda had dinner with Alex that evening, in the hotel restaurant. While they were eating a dessert of figs and crème caramel which was both very rich and very subtle, Milo brought him a folded slip of paper.

'This just arrived from the office in Piraeus. They faxed it to us at once.'

'Thanks, Milo.'

When Milo had gone Alex looked at the printed words, his black brows rising. He glanced across the table at Miranda.

'Finnigan isn't coming after all. He says an urgent matter has arisen. He'll make a new appointment when he's free.'

She breathed a long sigh of relief. 'Thank heavens for that! I wonder why he changed his mind?'

'No doubt the police have charged his son and Finnigan has to stay there to deal with the fall-out. Perhaps he and his lawyers are trying to get bail for the boy.'

'Do you think they'll succeed?'

'I can't see the police agreeing. This is a murder charge. They won't want a killer roaming the streets. Not now they've got the evidence they needed to charge him.'

She sipped her white Greek wine, staring at the candles on the table. Their flames flickered and dipped as someone walked past, pausing beside them.

'Hello, Alex,' slurred a sexy, sensuous voice and Miranda looked up to see Elena in a sensational white crepe dress which clung to every slender inch of her body.

'Elena,' he said, rising. 'You look like a Greek goddess. Still enjoying your holiday?'

She leaned towards him, her red mouth brushing his lingeringly. 'Mmm . . . yes.' Her dark eyes shot to Miranda's face. 'I don't think we've met, have we?'

They had, of course, and she was sure Elena remembered.

'Miranda is the hotel translator,' Alex said.

'Oh, just one of the staff,' Elena dismissed.

Miranda flushed under the icy sting of her scorn. But it was true, wasn't it? She was just one of the hotel staff, whereas Elena was an old family friend who had once been engaged to Alex. She had hurt him badly once – was he still in love with her?

'We must have dinner, Alex, talk about old times,' Elena said.

'Yes, we must do that,' he agreed, standing. 'Miranda, I'll walk you back to your bungalow.'

They were silent as they walked through the gardens. What was he thinking about? she wondered, glancing sideways at his hard, tanned profile. Elena?

He insisted on going into the bungalow first, to make sure nobody had got inside, went into every room to check the place was empty. Miranda waited at the door. The emergency was over, Terry wasn't coming, she was safe for the moment, perhaps for ever.

Poor Terry. She couldn't help being sorry for him. It wasn't his fault his son was rotten. Some people might blame the parents, people often did blame parents for what their children did, but Sean's weakness and viciousness was in his face, must have been visible all his life. His genes were to blame, not his upbringing. Heredity had determined how he would react that day. Who knew from which set of genes his weakness came — from his mother's family, or his father's?

Terry was a worker, tough, determined, with guts and character. She couldn't believe his family had provided Sean's genes.

Sandra was silly, self-indulgent, pretty worthless. She pursued her own pleasure whatever it cost others; her son included. She had left him behind and gone off because she wanted the life Jack offered her. Sean even looked like his mother; fair, with a smooth, epicene softness to his face, and the same greedy eyes and mouth.

Poor Terry.

Alex came back. 'Everything's OK.' He walked over to her, gazing down into her face. 'You look tired, poor girl. Better get to bed at once. You've had a busy day.'

She leaned her cheek on his chest, listening to the beat of his heart underneath her. 'How long are you staying? Now that Terry isn't coming do you have to go back at once?'

He put his face down against her hair. 'Do you want me to stay?'

She nodded, too shy to say it aloud, to beg, as she wanted to. Please stay, please don't go away again, I need you here, I feel safer with you around.

Alex slid his index finger under her chin, lifted her face so that he could look into her eyes. Her lids flickered up and down, she was afraid to meet his stare.

'Miranda,' he whispered huskily, then his mouth was on hers, heat between them, a fire that consumed her entire body, made her shake and shocked all the air out of her lungs.

Her arms went round his neck, she clung to him, kissing him hungrily, wanting him in a way that was totally new to her, totally unexpected. If she hadn't been so inhibited she would have told him, cried out her desire, babbling like an idiot, I want you, I want you.

She didn't need to say it, he gave a groan, said, 'Oh, God, Miranda . . .' then picked her up and carried her to the bed.

He undressed her, hurriedly, roughly, while she trembled and burned, waiting for him, staring up at his white face, barely able to breathe.

Their bodies merged with a shock like the collision of trains running out of control, unable to stop. She cried out in pleasure and need, twining with him, arms and legs around him, their mouths hotly devouring each other.

It was too intense, too agonising; tears ran down her face, the piercing desire almost broke her body in two as she rode under him, with him deep inside her, driving her up the bed. She had never been so aware of being animal. Her mind wasn't operating. Only her body worked, reacting to his, more and more wildly, until the clamour and tension broke and she let out a high shriek of exquisite, unbearable pleasure.

She had known, the minute she first saw him, on that ship, that this was how it would be if they ever made love. The gentle affection between her and Tom had been a million miles away from this fierce mating. That was why she had rejected Alex, denied her true feelings, hidden them deep inside herself. She could not admit to them because they betrayed her love for Tom. Her guilt had made it impossible for her to face up to what she wanted. Now she had. The sharp, tortured desire emerged from where she had hidden it all these years, she moaned it out into the night air, sobbed and wept with it.

Afterwards they lay still together, their breathing

slowing, the heat in them dying down, the room no longer spinning round for them.

Had she told him she loved him? She had no idea, could not remember anything she had said, or if she had spoken at all. All she knew was that she had never realised pleasure could be so painful, or pain so pleasurable.

She felt she had died in this bed, with him; died and gone to heaven.

But life was never that easy or simple.

'I'd love to stay all night,' he huskily murmured. 'But I have too much to do. I'll have to go.'

He unwound himself and got up, naked and golden in the glow of the bedside lamp. Why was he leaving her? she thought, anguished. To find Elena?

Pain pierced her breast. She had lost all control, had eagerly offered herself, lost to everything but her need for him. He had taken what she gave, but did he feel anything more than desire for her? Was it still Elena he loved?

Chapter Thirteen

Bernie's son and another man arrived promptly at ten o'clock. Terry greeted them himself in reception, forced a smile and made polite remarks as he escorted them up to his office. 'How's your father? I hope he's well? And your mother? We go back a long way, you know. You won't remember me but I remember you as a little kid.' He laughed. 'You've grown a lot since then, of course.'

Andy Sutcliffe resembled his father as Terry remembered him years ago; wiry and potentially powerful, with rough brown hair and the same quick, easy, cheerful smile. He gave the impression of being laid-back, easy-going, but then so had Bernie. The charm was deceptive, hid a ruthless focus on getting his own way. Power, that was what Bernie had always wanted, and had got, by one means or another.

'I've heard my parents talk about you. Afraid I don't remember you, myself; I guess I was too young to notice much when you were around. Oh, this is our computer anorak, Liam Grady,' he introduced him and Terry looked hard at the other man, shaking hands.

'I suppose you could say I was a computer anorak, too,' he smiled. His obsession with computers in the beginning had led him to another world, a new career. What had begun as a passion had become a business. Sometimes he regretted that, wished he still felt the same eager excitement.

'Yeah, well, we all need to understand computers and use them, or lose out in the modern world.'

Liam Grady was dogmatic, a small, sharp Irishman with spiky yellowish hair, bright blue eyes and a touch of belligerence in his manner. No room for discussion or argument in his view of life. Liam Grady knew what he was talking about and anyone who didn't agree with him had to be taught he was right. He was the type to have a fight in every bar he walked into. Terry had known a lot of men like Liam Grady when he lived in Manchester and moved in the Irish Catholic enclave centred on the local church and the social life held there in the club.

He had been that way himself, when he was young, before he caught on that fighting wasted energy you could better use in making a success of your life.

'You're right,' he said amiably, smiling at Grady.

Andy looked at his watch. 'I want to get back up to Manchester this afternoon, I have things to do in the office there, so do you mind if we cut corners? We need to see how your firm works — your order books, your accounts, everything. My father told you that, didn't he?'

'He told me. Come along.' Terry led them into another room. The computers were all switched on and waiting, ticking like wound-up clocks, their screens blank but alive, shining in autumnal morning sunlight. Terry sat down, punched in the code to give access. The machine began to hum, to whir.

Terry stood up again, impatient to get away. He found it hard to be polite to these intruders who were going to fumble through his business like policemen searching somebody's knicker drawer.

'You'll find your way around without needing me here. I'll leave you to it. If you do want me my internal number is on this pad. And the access codes to the computers are on it, too.'

Liam nodded abstractedly. 'Fine. OK.'

He sat down in the chair Terry had used, immediately attentive to the screen in front of him, and began operating keys. The screen changed, numbers and figures swam up from somewhere. Liam read them, his fingers hovering over keys.

'Can we have a tour of the premises later?' Andy asked.

Terry nodded. 'Certainly. Just give me a ring when you're ready. We can have some lunch across the road in the pub you can see from the window here. It's an old house, but the food is pretty good and they have a huge range of beers and spirits.'

'Sounds great then. See you later.' Andy went over to another computer and sat down.

Terry left, glad to escape their presence. He was too afraid of losing his temper.

Since Sean's engagement party and what happened next day, his mood was always volatile. After years of being amiable and even-tempered he had become aggressive again, just as he had been when he was young, but he could not risk losing his temper with Bernie's son. Bernie would turn nasty if he did. When they met in Manchester, the old man had seemed a burnt-out case, a lion whose teeth had been drawn, but Terry was not deceived. Bernie would be a bad enemy to make.

He was a bad friend to have, come to that. Ruthless, acquisitive, greedy, he was going to eat into Terry's company, if he could, but if they were still, on the surface, friends, he would not go too far. If Terry let his temper rip, though, Bernie might turn nasty and step up his demands, no longer feeling he needed to pretend or mask his intentions.

The strain of keeping calm was unbearable. He shut himself in his office and tried to concentrate on some work. His new secretary was not efficient; he had to check every letter she sent to make sure there were no spelling mistakes, bad grammar, stupid little errors of fact. She didn't always get the name of the client right, and her filing was erratic, she was always losing documents. As he couldn't shout at Andy Sutcliffe, he shouted at her all morning, reducing her close to tears several times.

'Oh, don't turn on the water works! Just get it right next time, and save me the trouble of telling you where you've made mistakes.'

She went off, sniffing, a delicate little handkerchief dabbing at her eyes and nose, but he sensed the angry resentment underneath. She would probably start looking for another job but Terry did not care. There were plenty more fish in the sea.

He got a call from his solicitor just before lunchtime. Edward Dearing sounded as weary and bored as usual.

'How's it going?' Terry asked and Edward sighed.

'They've broken for an hour, to eat lunch. They've

sent sandwiches down for Sean, and a bottle of beer. I've gone across the road to eat a Chinese.'

'How's Sean bearing up?'

'Not too well. To be frank, Terry, your son is far too aggressive with them, he keeps shouting. That never works. He's making enemies.'

That didn't surprise Terry, Sean was an arrogant, hot-headed young fool. But it worried him. How did you guard against the boy's own folly?

'What about the evidence? Do you think they've got anything we need worry about?'

Edward was dry. 'Terry, they've got the body, and these days that can tell them a lot. Forensic evidence can make a case, and they have a lot of circumstantial evidence, too – that he was involved with the girl, that he had a strong motive for wanting to get rid of her. It all mounts up.'

'Surely they can't have much evidence from the body after all that time in the sea?'

'I'm afraid so. They've got DNA evidence, proof of identity, and that carpet … they know where it came from. They've got photographs taken in your office flat that show an identical carpet, in the hallway. Do you know if any was left over, when it was laid? Was there a spare roll some-where?'

'In a cupboard, yes.' No point in lying – they would

only check with the cleaners and find out. It had been there ever since the flat was furnished.

'And is it still there?'

'I haven't looked.'

'Then do so, at once! We need to know exactly what we're up against. Well, we'll put up what defence we can, but, frankly, it isn't looking too good. I think they're going to charge him, perhaps today, maybe tomorrow — but the probability is they will charge him sooner or later.'

'But even if they can prove he knew this girl, that he slept with her, and it was his baby she was carrying, that isn't enough to prove he killed her. I can say I threw the carpet away.'

'You will say you threw it away,' Edward pointedly told him.

'Yes, yes, that is what I'll tell them.'

'Hmm. They'll want to know where you tipped it, and when. They'll also be relying on the evidence of this witness, this girl who worked for you. She is the bedrock of their case, I think. She heard the murder, she links everything up. Have you found out where she is yet?'

'She may be somewhere in Greece.'

'Try and find her, Terry.' A pause, then Edward said, 'Of course you won't threaten her, or anything. But we need to know exactly what she might say. Ah, my lunch has arrived. Beef in black bean sauce – smells great. I'll talk to you tonight.'

Terry put down the phone and stared out of the window. He would have to go to Greece. Miranda was now even more of a danger. If Sean was charged her evidence would be vital to the police case.

He might be able to get away tomorrow; just for a few days. He had had a wonderful time in Greece last time he was there. The Manoussi family were charming and hospitable, he had loved being there.

It had been a culture shock for him, seeing how they lived, visiting the Athens museum, glimpsing the Greek past, the incredible statues, the gold, the beauty of ancient jewellery. It had all been so strange to him; the food, the buildings, the markets in that place ... what was it called ... the *agora*? Or had that been the old market, no longer in operation? He had loved the narrow alleys and lanes filled with stalls selling junk for tourists, reproductions of Greek vases, little statuettes, or selling army surplus boots, or fruit, or modern curtains. The noise, the bustle, the cheerful friendliness ...

Oh, yes, he had loved Athens.

This time would be very different.

*   *   *

Miranda woke up next morning in a state of depression, hating, despising herself, for allowing Alex to use her the way he had. He must despise her, too. She had collapsed in front of him, like a crumbling wall – she had made it easy for him to take her then walk away.

How was she going to face him? She wasn't hungry and skipped breakfast, walked into the office feeling very shy, wondering if people would be able to see what had happened between her and Alex. One of the other two girls was at reception as she passed, dealing with a telephone query. She waved a hand and winked at Miranda, who waved back, forcing a stiff smile.

As she passed the manager's door she saw it was slightly ajar; she could hear Alex's voice inside. Was he talking to Charles?

She paused, listening, to see if she could pick up Charles' voice, and meaning to go in to talk to Alex, then realised Alex was talking on the phone. Through the open door she could glimpse the whole office. Alex was alone; standing by the window gazing out while he talked, one hand raking back his thick black hair.

'Stop worrying,' he said. 'I've kept her here for you, haven't I? She won't get away – this is an island, remember? She'll be here whenever you want her. Come over and get her any time.'

Miranda went cold, a frown etching itself between her brows. Who was he talking to?

No prizes for guessing who he was talking about. Her. He meant her.

What did he mean, he had kept her here and whomever he was talking to could come and get her any time?

'Terry. Look,' Alex said abruptly, then stopped, listening. 'Right, OK, I'll expect you. What flight will you be on? I'll make sure you're met. I'll go back to Piraeus today.'

Miranda's legs were trembling under her, she could barely walk, but she made it, somehow, to her own office, staggered to her desk and collapsed on to her chair.

Alex had betrayed her. Had lied to her all along, was in league with Terry. It had all been lies, his concern about her, his desire to keep her safe ... oh, yes, safe until Terry could come and ... and ...

And Terry would kill her, to make sure she never gave evidence against his son.

Alex's love-making, his passion, had all been phoney, a lie. She felt sick, remembering her own abandoned desire, the intensity of her own feelings. She had been cheated, deceived. Alex had made a fool of her. How could he be so heartless, luring her here and making love to her only to hand her over to Terry, knowing she would be killed?

The Angel of Death she had called him once.

Her intuition had been spot on; she had known from the beginning that he brought death, first to Tom, then to that poor girl who had been murdered by Sean – and now to her.

She heard footsteps, the outer door was flung open. Elena swayed through it, sinuous in a black suit with a low, plunging neckline and tight waist, a very short skirt that showed off her beautiful legs.

'Oh,' she said, looking around. 'I'm looking for Mr Manoussi, where will I find him?'

'The next door along the corridor.'

Elena left, not bothering to close the door behind her.

Miranda glared, hating her. She went to the door to shut it, and saw Elena open the door of the manager's office, glimpsed her entwining herself with Alex, cooing up at him.

'Darling Alex . . .'

He didn't exactly push her away, either. 'Good morning, Elena, how are you? I hope you slept well. I'm sorry but I'm busy. Maybe we could have lunch?'

Miranda shut her own door and sat down at her desk again. Her temples were throbbing with pain. A migraine, she felt it gathering, darkening her sight.

She had been such a fool. She put both hands over her eyes, pressing her palms down.

She wished she were dead.

For a few minutes she sat, breathing slowly, feeling the aching in her head lessen. Then the door opened, and she let her hands drop, fought to appear calm.

Alex came over to her desk. 'Good morning. How are you today?' His voice was warm, held a hint of passion.

'Fine,' she said, her stomach churning with sickness and pain. How could he cheat, lie and pretend like that?

'You look beautiful.' He ran a hand over her hair, cupped her chin, forcing her to look up at him. 'Every time I see you, I can't believe how lovely you are. It's going to be hell to leave you again. But I've got to, I'm afraid. I have some important business to deal with. I'm sailing back this morning.'

When he had gone, would Terry arrive to kill her? Fear choked her, fear and misery over Alex's betrayal. She pulled her head away, refusing to look at him. How could he live with himself afterwards, knowing he had abandoned her to her fate? Or was he leaving so that he needn't be here when she died? Maybe that was his version of a conscience? What he didn't have to see he need not feel guilty about?

'I'll miss you, I hate to leave you,' he said huskily.

He was a consummate actor. Men could be such liars.

She couldn't bring herself to answer him; she couldn't pretend, the way he did.

'I wish you would move back into the hotel so that it would be easier to keep an eye on you,' he said. 'Why don't you do that while I'm away?'

She forced herself to answer that, her voice rusty. 'No, I told you, I prefer to be independent.' Why was he so insistent that she move back into the hotel? Was it because he knew Terry would come here and stay in the hotel, and having her under the same roof would make it so much easier for Terry to get at her?

'You obstinate vixen!' he said, sighing. 'Well, I must go. I'll ring you tomorrow to check up on you.'

He kissed her averted cheek, then was gone and she sat bleakly listening to his departing footsteps.

When would Terry arrive? Today? Tomorrow?

What was she to do? Just sit here like a trapped rabbit and wait for the final blow? Yet what else could she do? Well, she could take the ferry to the mainland and fly back to London, of course. But her passport was locked in the office. Milo had taken it weeks ago for some official reason to do with the Greek police she thought.

He probably had it locked away for safe-keeping. If she asked for it she would have to explain why she wanted it, she would have to say she was leaving – but she couldn't say why because Milo would think she was crazy.

Later that morning she saw on her computer screen that Elena had checked out. Had she gone back to Athens with Alex? Was that why he had left so unexpectedly?

She went back to her bungalow when she stopped work, ate a light salad for supper and went to bed early, exhausted by the tension and misery she had suffered with all day.

That night she had the old dream which she had had for years, where Tom was drowning and she could not reach him, however hard she struggled. He called her name and she cried out, 'I'm coming, Tom, I'm trying to get to you,' yet knew she wouldn't. The marbled sea tumbled her over and over. Her head rang with echoes. Miranda, Miranda, he called, and in her sleep tears ran down her face.

'Oh, God, Tom . . . I'm sorry.'

This time, though, she heard another voice, luring her towards him. 'Miranda, Miranda, come to me,' She quivered with weakness and the green sea took her, drifted her, into his arms.

'Help Tom,' she begged. 'Save Tom, never mind me.'

He kissed her passionately, his mouth demanding,

and her body grew limp, weak and helpless, kissing him back, despite the guilt she felt.

Alex put his hands around her neck. They tightened and tightened, the fingertips biting into her flesh. He was going to kill her, she realised. He meant to strangle her.

She woke up screaming, her face wet with tears. The room was shuttered, warm, dark, a womb of sleep. She listened to the sounds outside: the soft shushing of the palms, the rustle of fronds, the distant whisper of the sea on the beach. There was no sound from the other bungalows, no light pierced her darkness. She could have been alone on a desert island.

The last time she had been this unhappy had been during the months after Tom's death. She had been haunted by grief and guilt. This time her misery came from knowing Alex had lied to her, betrayed her, plotted her death. Yet she still loved him, her Angel of Death, she always had, from the minute she first saw him, and that was why she had felt so guilty over Tom. In wanting Alex she had always felt she betrayed her husband, and now she had betrayed herself, too, by letting Alex make love to her. He did not love her. Oh, God, why was she such a fool?

Sean was charged that evening. Edward Dearing saw

him alone afterwards. By then Sean was pale and drained, his face puffy, as if he had been crying, his body limp.

'I want to see my dad.'

'I'm afraid he can't come today, Sean. He's had to go away for a couple of days.'

'Gone away?' the boy repeated blankly. 'While I'm going through all this, he's gone away?'

'Yes, but he'll be back soon.'

'Where the hell has he gone that's so important just now?'

Dearing hesitated, frowning. Walls had ears, especially in police stations.

'I can't tell you that, but, believe me, he only has your welfare at heart.'

The boy's face contorted viciously. 'Oh, yeah, sure. He hasn't scarpered because he doesn't want to be mixed up with me now I'm up on a murder charge?' He lay down on his front, on the cell bed and hid his face in the crook of his arm.

'Buzz off if you can't do nothing for me, you useless bastard,' he muttered.

Edward looked at the back of the boy's head with dislike. That was all the thanks you got for slaving away all day on his behalf. It had been a long and difficult day, and Edward was very tired. He bit back the angry retort that had risen to his tongue, knocked on the inside of the cell door, and left without a word.

Left alone, Sean wept angrily.

Why was this happening to him? He had always thought of himself as lucky. His life had seemed a charmed one. Not any more. Everything was going wrong.

Miranda could not get back to sleep, so at first light she got up and put on her swimsuit, slipped into a towelling robe and sandals, to walk down to the beach, carrying a towel. A swim would help her face the day ahead. After that largely sleepless night she was overheated, weary, stupid with misery and fear.

As she walked along the winding paths through the gardens, she watched the sun coming up out of the sea, a bright orange, hot and glowing, as if made of fiery iron, streaking the sky with colour, pink and red, like blood seeping into the pale, pale blue, beginning to fill the world with light, showing her the way down to the beach. She heard the waves louder and louder, the cry of gulls, the tumbling waves crawling up the beach.

Only a short time ago she had come down here at this hour and found Alex in the sea. He had come up out of the water and grabbed her.

Her heart hurt as she remembered being in his arms that morning, felt his kiss on her mouth.

She ran a sweating hand over her face. She wouldn't think about him. It was over now, she must begin to forget or she really would go mad.

She slowly took off her robe and laid it down with her towel on top of it, kicked off her sandals and placed them beside the robe, then began to walk down the beach. The water was chilly at this hour of the morning, before the sun warmed it up. She slid down into the sea, gasping, and struck out. A moment later she saw a boat round the high rocks guarding one side of the bay.

White sails billowed. There were two men on board, moving about, pulling on ropes, navigating.

Miranda began to swim, staying cautiously in the shallows. It was safe enough, on this beach, if you stayed close to shore, but she feared the sea. It was as unpredictable as a wild cat, striking at you when you least expected it. It had taken Tom. She had never got over that.

The boat came nearer. One of the men on board hailed her in Greek. She trod water, lifting her head to hear him.

'*Meea keereea* ...' The other words were drowned by the sound of the waves sloshing about around the boat.

'*Leepa me*,' she said, after saying she was sorry, she didn't know enough Greek to understand what he had said.

He leant over the side of the boat and she swam closer to hear him better.

He reached down his hands and caught hold of her shoulders.

'What are you doing?' Miranda breathlessly said in Greek, feeling herself being lifted, pulled up into the boat. 'Let go of me!'

A second later she was over the side and slithering wetly down on to the boards in the bottom of the boat.

The man who had dragged her up into the boat bent and picked her up. Terrified, she struggled, screaming.

He carried her into a small cabin and dropped her on the bed. She tried to get off but was caught again and hauled back. As she yelled up at him to let her go he forced her down on the bed and tied a gag around her mouth, then tied her hands behind her back.

She kicked and wriggled, making stifled, angry noises. He ignored her and tied her ankles together.

A minute later he had left the cabin, locking the door behind him, and Miranda was alone, on the bed, unable to move.

Fear drove the blood from her heart. What were they going to do with her?

Chapter Fourteen

Terry was sitting in Alex's office promptly at two o'clock. Alex arrived ten minutes later, flushed from hurrying.

'Sorry, I sailed here and the weather was a bit rough. Did you have a good flight?'

'Calm and trouble-free. I came last night, actually, and stayed in Athens overnight. Nice hotel in Syntagma Square. Excellent food and the rooms are very comfortable.'

He laid a large file bulging with papers on the table. Terry looked down at it.

'Is that the details of the new navigational aid?'

Terry nodded. 'I think you're going to like this one. All you have to do is type in your destination and it plots your course for you. It even changes course if it receives information about storms in your path ahead.

Any weather warnings are received automatically from your ship's radio and it acts on them at once. You could almost leave it to captain the boat for you while you put your feet up.'

'Sounds interesting. I could have done with it on my trip here.'

Terry gave him a casual, friendly glance. 'Where were you coming from?'

'Delephores.'

'Oh, yes, of course. That's an island, in the Cyclades, isn't it? And you have a hotel there.'

'Uh huh.' Alex leaned back in his swivel chair, his long legs stretched out to the side, and tapped his fingertips on the leather top of his desk, frowning. 'Did I tell you about it?'

'Somebody did, maybe it was you. While I'm here I'd like to see it, could that be fixed? Does a ferry go there?'

'Yes, once a day. But there really isn't anything to see, just hills and beaches, little bays, with a few old churches. The sort of scenery you get on the mainland, and here there is so much to see. If you want to take a trip I'd advise you visit Mycenae – see the beehive tombs of Agamemnon and Clytemnestra, the ancient tombs up in the acropolis of the city, the lion gate that leads into it. There are tours by coach every day, leaving Athens in the morning, stopping en route for lunch at a little taverna where you eat real Greek cooking and end up with eating fresh grapes picked from the vines you sit under. Very romantic. You'd love it.'

'Sounds marvellous,' agreed Terry. 'Well, I'll think about it. I was looking forward to seeing your little island, though. But, anyway, first of all, can we look at the specifications on the new navigational aid? It won't come cheap, but then look at what it does . . .'

Neil Maddrell landed in Athens on the first flight of the day and took a taxi down to Piraeus. He walked along the rows of ships and boats studying the names. It took some time before he found the one he was looking for; his legs were aching and he was very hot. It had been raining in London when he left, the temperature had been low. He had worn a raincoat and carried an umbrella. Now he carried his coat over his arm and his face was red and perspiring as he walked up the gangplank.

A large Greek barred his way. *'Keeree e?'*

'Sorry, I don't speak Greek,' Neil said. 'I'm Neil Maddrell. I'm going to Delephores, to stay at the hotel.'

The weathered face broke into a smile. *'Ne!'* he shook his head.

Did that mean no? Neil hesitated uncertainly – was this the right boat or not? The Greek in the white t-shirt carrying a logo waved his hand along the boat to an open door.

'*Ne parakalo, keeree.*'

Neil made his way along the boat and sat down on one of the padded sofas in the cabin indicated. A few moments later he heard the engines start, then the man who had welcomed him aboard appeared and bowed his head with great courtesy.

'Please – you want drink?'

'Beer?' Neil hopefully enquired and the Greek nodded vehemently.

'Greek beer. Very good.'

Neil hoped so. He had had no idea Greece made beer, but he was so hot he didn't much care at the moment. He would have drunk anything. His throat was parched, his face burnt, he was so tired he could fall asleep sitting here.

The beer was icy and refreshing; he drank it almost without tasting it, needing the coolness it spread down his throat, throughout his body.

By then they had left Piraeus behind and were sailing steadily into the blue distance.

He did in fact doze briefly while they sailed; his head falling back against the chair, his body slumped sideways. He was too tired to dream and when he woke up was flushed and still drowsy. Yawning, he sat upright and looked about. The windows were blurred with sea spray and the boat was bucking back and forth like a difficult horse.

He felt the boat slowing noticeably and went out on to the deck which was wet and slippery now. Ahead of them he saw the island, green and grey, with a few scattered houses to be seen.

The Greek seaman appeared. 'Delephores,' he told Neil, pointing a long, brown finger. 'Delephores, sir.'

Neil nodded his understanding. The boat was heading for the harbour – they would probably land in twenty minutes or so, he calculated. He would see Miranda very soon.

The thought excited him. He had missed her badly, was worried about her; she was a very special person.

Now that the body had been discovered and Sean Finnigan charged with murder it wouldn't be long before she came back to London. Not yet, though. It wouldn't be safe until the actual trial when she would have to come back to give evidence, and even then, she would need a police guard until the trial was over.

He would be glad to do that, to take care of her, in his flat, make sure the Finnigans didn't get a chance to hurt her or stop her giving evidence.

*　　*　　*

The boat had stopped moving. Miranda heard the cabin door open abruptly. She turned her head, lying very still, her heart banging inside her.

The two men came over to the bed and pulled her up off it, carried her between them out on to the deck. They wound a chain around her waist; from it hung something heavy — she couldn't see what it was, but it clanked against the chain. They were weighting her body, she realised with a sinking of the heart. Walking to the rail of the boat they lifted her, swung her between them, faster and faster, then hurled her into the sea.

Her body sank instantly under the blue waves. *Déjà vu*. This had happened to her before, except that the last time she was flung into the sea she had had her hands and feet free.

The two men watched the upward splash of water. The girl did not resurface.

They walked away and the boat began to move again.

Terry was talking to Alex in his office when the phone rang. Alex answered impatiently.

'I told you not to interrupt me. What is it?' He listened, then looked at Terry, one black brow lifting.

'It's for you.' He handed the phone to Terry, who leaned forward to take it.

'Hello? Yes, it is. Who . . . ?' He fell silent, his face suddenly blank. 'You're certain? Oh, right. So that's that. Thank you. Well done.'

He hung up and leaned back in his chair as if exhausted. Alex stared.

'Are you OK? You've turned very pale. That wasn't bad news, I hope?'

Terry gave a long, unsteady sigh, lifted his hand, glanced at his watch. Got to his feet. 'I'm afraid it means I must go back to London, at once.' He held out his hand. 'Sorry to break this up, but I hope you'll be confirming this sale very soon.'

'I'll let you know before next week.' Alex followed him to the door.

'No need for you to see me out, I know the way,' Terry said roughly, and walked off very fast, like a man who couldn't wait to get away.

What had that phone call been about? Alex wondered. One minute Terry had been eager to go to Delephores, completely set on it. The next he was leaving to get back to London.

What had happened to change his mind?

A shaft of terror struck him. Miranda. Terry had come all this way to find her, Alex was sure of it.

Had he just heard something that no longer made it necessary?

Alex picked up the phone, his hand trembling, and rang the hotel. 'Give me Milo, will you?'

The switchboard operator recognised his voice. 'Yes, sir.'

'Hello?' Milo said in Greek. *'Ya soo?'*

'Is Miranda OK?' demanded Alex hoarsely.

'We can't find her,' Milo admitted, his voice tense. 'I was just about to ring you. She isn't in her bungalow, she isn't in the hotel, or in the grounds, we've just searched them thoroughly.'

Cold sweat stood out on Alex's temples. 'When was she last seen?'

'A security man saw her going down to the beach to swim, as usual, at around six thirty. We found her robe, sandals and towel on the sand. But there's no sign of her.' His voice soothed. 'She's an excellent swimmer. The tide is running fast, but if she got swept off course she might have made land further along the coast and be trying to get back here on foot.'

Alex's mind worked fast and anxiously. 'Get some boats out, look for her, out to sea and along the coast. Get the coastguards involved and the police. Tell them why we're very concerned. Tell them she's a witness in a British murder trial, and someone could have harmed her. I'm coming back at once. I'll fly, it takes too long by boat. I should be with you in a couple of hours.'

If she had been murdered he would never forgive himself.

Neil Maddrell arrived at the hotel to be met by Alex, looking pale and haggard. As their eyes met Neil felt fear strike him.

'What's happened?'

'Miranda,' Alex said, confirming Neil's worst fear.

'What? What?'

'She's vanished. We think she went swimming. She may have drowned, or . . .'

'Or?'

'A small boat was seen coming into our bay by a fisherman. They could have picked her up, abducted her.'

'Or killed her,' Neil whispered, white to his hairline.

Alex didn't answer but his sigh said all that needed to be said.

'Have you contacted the local police?'

'Of course. They've searched the island too, but found nothing. And the coastguard have been up and down in their boat, looking out for any sign of her. It was them who got word of a strange boat coming inland. On a small island like this somebody always sees something. A fisherman, mending his nets outside his cottage, keeps looking at the sea — it's their instinct, their habit. And old women, widows who've lost men at sea, they look too and talk to neighbours.'

'Thank God they do. Nosy neighbours are a great help to the police.'

Alex smiled at Neil. 'Thank God, yes. We need them. The police have been in touch with other islands, with the mainland, asking everyone to keep an eye open for this boat, but we don't know where it came from or where it was going. If it slips back into some tiny port it left at dawn this morning, nobody will think twice about it.'

Neil hesitated, biting his lower lip, then blurted out, 'I don't like the Finnigan family's way of drowning people who become inconvenient to them.'

Alex shut his eyes, groaned. 'I know. Do you think that hasn't occurred to me? Terry was in my office talking of coming over here to Delephores when he got a phone call and suddenly changed his mind, went rushing off to the airport. I wish to God I knew what he was told on the phone. Was the caller a man he had hired to deal with Miranda?'

Neil breathed hoarsely, 'And is she alive now?

That's what I can't stop thinking about, that's what's scaring the life out of me. Finnigan doesn't want her testifying against his boy.'

'Will the case collapse if she isn't there to give evidence?'

'It will be a nuisance to us, but not a disaster. There's too much forensic evidence to show motive and probability. After all, who else had the opportunity to wrap the girl's body in carpet left over when the Finnigans had it laid in their flat? Oh, the boy won't get off, but Terry Finnigan may think he will. He may believe if he gets rid of Miranda he will save his son.'

'If that boy gets off and Miranda was killed, I'll kill him myself,' Alex grimly said.

Neil said nothing but his expression was just as bleak.

Terry Finnigan flew home and went straight to the office to do some work. He rang Edward Dearing first and heard that Sean was now in prison but he could visit him at certain times.

'You have to ask permission, first. I'll take care of that, get you an appointment.' Edward paused. 'How did your trip to Greece go? Everything settled satisfactorily?'

'Yes,' Terry said curtly and rang off a moment later.

The atmosphere in the office was charged. Nobody was looking at him, people's eyes slid away when he spoke to them. His son's name was not mentioned, yet he knew what they were all thinking about, no doubt whispering about, when he wasn't around.

An hour after he arrived his secretary walked in rather self-consciously and handed him an envelope.

'What's this?' Terry opened it, read it, dropped it on the desk. It was her notice, handwritten. 'Have you got another job?'

She nodded, eyes down, her face cold.

'More money?'

'No, about the same.'

He did not ask her why she was going; he could guess, she had a tight-lipped face, her eyes disapproved of him and his son. She did not want to be mixed up in murder. Clear off, then, he thought – and anyway he hadn't been satisfied with her work, he wasn't sorry to see her go.

Crisply he said, 'Clear your desk, take all your possessions, and leave immediately. You can settle what you're owed with Accounts later.'

He turned away contemptuously, reached for the phone to ring an agency and ask for a temp.

She banged the door deliberately as she went and the next time he went past her office the room was empty. She had gone. And he could not even remember her name, try as he might.

The only name he remembered was Miranda's.

It rang in his head like a bell across the sea. Miranda, Miranda, Miranda.

When he left the office late that afternoon the press were waiting. Terry didn't understand at first, blinking in the first battery of flash-bulbs, deafened by the shouting of his name, the crude insolence of the questions.

'Terry, Terry . . .'

'Did you know all about it? Did you help Sean murder the girl? It was your plane he used to dump her in the sea, wasn't it?'

Where did they get that? Who gave them information that should not be public property, at least until it came out during the trial? Did they bribe policemen on the desk in stations? Did they have a source inside the force? It had never occurred to him before – he had read the gutter press without thinking about the way they gathered their stories, whether what they wrote was true or not.

'Terry, look this way . . . hey, Terry . . .' they cooed

like bilious pigeons, ducking and diving in a flock, cameras levelled his way. He ignored them, fighting his way through to get to his car.

It took him some time, but at last he was in the car and driving off. But if he thought he would get away from them all he soon saw he was over-optimistic. They got into cars, too, and followed him.

He decided to go to his country home – if he had realised the press were outside he would have stayed in his flat in the office building.

Or would he?

He hadn't used it since the murder. The idea of sleeping there made the hair rise on the back of his neck. He had been over there; the atmosphere was ... he hesitated to use the word, but how else could he describe it? Haunted. The flat was haunted. You almost felt you could hear the screams of that girl, the violent splashing, the gasps and smothered groans of someone drowning.

Was that how Miranda had felt after her husband drowned? Had she kept thinking she heard him ...

Terry put his foot down, accelerating away from the pack of reporters on his heels.

He was being stupid. The flat wasn't haunted. He didn't hear that girl drowning. He was just letting his imagination run away with him, and it had to stop. He would go mad if he didn't forget all about her, that girl he had never even met.

What had she really been like, the girl who would have been the mother of his grandchild? Would he have liked her? Would she have made Sean a good wife?

And the baby – had it been a boy or a girl? He would never know, unless it was mentioned during the trial. No doubt they had found out the sex of the child when the autopsy was done, but it might not come up in court. Why should it? That had no bearing on the case.

The only person interested was himself. He groaned, his eyes fixed on the road ahead and burning with unshed tears.

He wanted to know, he needed to know. He had always dreamt of grandchildren; of having them climbing on to his lap, warm and comforting, with their talcum smell and their open, innocent faces, calling him Grandpa, giving him hope for the future.

But the child had died with its mother. Murdered by its father.

He drove even faster, half hoping he would crash and end all this misery. How could you live with these thoughts churning round in your head?

But he didn't crash. He reached his house at dusk

and let himself in with his front door key a minute or so before the hounds behind him arrived.

They prowled around the locked gates, some tried to climb over the walls, cameramen with long distance lenses took photos of the house, reporters peered up the drive, shouting his name.

But Terry was upstairs in his bedroom, taking off his clothes. He had a long, hot bath for half an hour, feeling the warmth seeping into his chilled flesh, staring at nothing, listening to the distant uproar which the press were making outside.

When he climbed out he put on a towelling robe, brushed back his wet hair, and made a phone call to the local police.

His son might have been charged with murder, but Terry had always had a good relationship with them, contributed to their benefit society, bought tickets for the police ball, gone along to watch them play rugby at the police sports ground.

They arrived quite promptly. He watched from upstairs as they talked to the reporters, wondering exactly what they were saying.

The other cars moved off after a few minutes. Soon there was only the police car left. The uniformed officers rang the bell. Terry opened the gates electronically, went down to the front door to talk to them. He knew them both. Decent guys, polite and sympathetic.

'They will probably camp outside your gates, Mr Finnigan, we can't stop them parking on the highway, but they won't invade your grounds, we made it clear that we wouldn't stand for them trespassing. You'll be all right, so long as you don't leave the house.'

'I won't,' he said. 'Thank you very much, I'm very grateful to you.'

They drove away and he went into the kitchen to make himself supper. First, he pulled down all the blinds so that nobody could watch him. He heated up some vegetable soup and ate it at the kitchen table, listening to the radio. The programme played old pop classics, songs he knew and remembered from his youth. It seemed so long ago, a place he had visited once, briefly. He had thought he was happy. Now, with hindsight, he saw he had merely been content enough.

He had never been happy. Never, in his whole life, except the day Sean was born and he thought he had glimpsed a future for them.

The future was never within sight, though. You never saw what was coming, and just as well, or you wouldn't want to live to meet it.

He made himself a toasted sandwich — filling it with grated cheese and brown pickle. Comfort food, reminding him of his childhood. His mother had made these sandwiches at the fire, on a long-handled toasting fork, first toast, then cheese inside, then she pressed them together and cut them into triangles. He had loved them. He had loved his mother. But he had to get away from the sordid muddle of that life. He had escaped to safety and reassurance, had thought he would always be safe.

You never were.

The phone rang; he answered it warily, afraid it would be the press, but it wasn't. It was Francis Belcannon, sounding harsh and angry.

'My daughter is breaking off this engagement, she'll send her ring back to your son. Just make sure you keep our names out of this. I don't want to see my daughter splashed all over the gutter press, is that understood?'

'Yes,' Terry wearily said. 'Look, I'm sorry, Francis . . .'

Belcannon hung up so violently that Terry's ears were almost shattered.

Well, he couldn't blame the man. That poor girl, how she must be suffering; she had loved Sean. Why, why, why, couldn't Sean have loved her, been faithful to her?

A sob choked in his throat. The engagement was over; there would be no marvellous marriage. Sean had killed that girl for nothing. Had murdered his own child for nothing.

The phone shrilled again. He sat staring at it, not

wanting to talk to anyone, but eventually picked it up again.

This time it was Bernie. 'I've been trying to get hold of you for days. Where have you been?'

'Greece.'

'Ah.' A significant pause. 'And?'

'And what?'

'Did you deal with your local problem?'

'Yes.' Another pointless, stupid death. He regretted Miranda almost as much as he did his dead grandchild. He had liked Miranda; had liked and admired her. She was beautiful and good at her job. She hadn't deserved what happened to her.

None of this need ever have happened.

'Well, good,' Bernie said briskly. 'Now, my boys tell me we would do well to move into your line of business, they were very impressed by what they saw. We need to have a meeting, soon, to discuss terms.'

Whose terms? Terry thought with dreary resignation. The last thing he wanted was to have a partner forced on him, to lose control of the business he had taken years to build up.

But to fight Bernie would use up energy he needed to fight for Sean.

Well, why should he fight for Sean? His son had cost him his business as well as his grandchild and his peace of mind. He wasn't worth fighting for.

'Next Wednesday, two o'clock, here?' Bernie suggested. 'Easier for you to come up to Manchester than for all of us to come down to London.'

'Very well,' Terry accepted. 'If I can't make it for some reason I'll let you know the day before.'

'I hope you will make it,' Bernie said with cool insistence. 'Be there, Terry.'

Terry replaced the phone, his teeth gritted and his whole face aching with tension.

Miranda knew she must not struggle, if she were to have any chance of survival. As her body sank she tried to stay calm, to think rationally. Her fingers fumbled with the heavy weight on the chain. How was it fastened? If she could only shed it. Fish swam around her in the blue water. Up above light glowed; the distant sun penetrating the waves.

She did not want to die.

The weight had been hooked on to the chain; she dragged at it, fighting to lift it up, and off.

It resisted, then suddenly she felt it coming upwards, managed to force it away and felt it fall. Released, her body bobbed up like a cork, surfaced in the warm Aegean, and she felt the sun shining down into her face. She blinked, trying to look around, searching for a sign of the boat from which she had been flung.

Ah, there it was — heading off into the distance, leaving a shining track behind it, like some great water snail. The sea was calm here, there was little wind, the weather was different to the weather when they left Delephores.

Where was she? How far from land?

Nobody would ever know what had happened to her — except Alex, perhaps. Had he known she would be drowned? Had Terry told him?

Her body was chill, despite the heat of the sun. She wished she could hate Alex, but her Angel of Death had got under her skin, she loved him more than life itself, which was ironic. How else could you love the Angel of Death?

She would have to float. She had learnt to do that when she was taking a rescue badge at school. You had to wear pyjamas, with the jacket sleeves tied to stop you using your hands, and float until your partner rescued you.

She would do that now. Relaxing, she let her body bob up and down on the gentle waves, turning her head from side to side slowly, to look round the horizon. If another boat came along she would be picked up, saved from death. All hope was not over.

But there were no other boats in view. How long could she keep up, stop herself sinking?

Panic rose in her throat; she felt herself grow heavy, dragged down under the glittering, blue, sunlit water. Oh God, Oh God, she thought, prayed, terror streaking through her. Please don't let me drown.

Chapter Fifteen

Nicola walked out of the house while her aunt was having one of her marathon phone calls in the drawing room. Nicola could hear her high, Home Counties voice talking on and on and on, interspersed with shrill laughter.

'You aren't serious! She didn't? Heavens, Daphne, did she really? And what did he . . . ? He didn't?'

She had left Nicola in the conservatory, doing a watercolour of some flowers Aunt Eloise had arranged for her.

'When you've finished that you can go upstairs and start packing. I know we aren't going to New York until the day after tomorrow, but you'll need time to pack, you're going to have to be selective. There's this tiresome weight problem, you can only take one suitcase, so choose carefully, and remember, we'll be able to buy anything you need in New York and we'll be coming back by sea so there won't be a weight problem coming back.' She had given one of those unreal, insincere smiles Nicola hated so much. 'Now, just concentrate on your painting, sweetie. I'll look in on you later.'

Aunt Eloise was her mother's sister and looked like her. Nicola had never liked her much, which didn't matter as Eloise lived in Manhattan and rarely came to London, but her father had invited her over to, in his words, 'be company' for Nicola at this time. What he really meant was be a jailer, watch Nicola like a hawk, keep her away from Sean.

She had not seen Sean since he was arrested. Her father had almost had a fit when she said she wanted to visit him.

'In a prison? My daughter, walking into a prison to see a murderer? Certainly not. The idea is ludicrous. Now, never suggest it again. Eloise, can't you think of something? Keep her occupied?'

'New York,' Eloise had said. 'Why don't I take her back to the States with me? Show her a good time, find her other young men to stop her thinking about . . . about that one?'

'Excellent,' Francis Belcannon had said in relief. 'Absolutely. Take her at once.'

But Aunt Eloise had wanted to do some shopping

in London, meet with old friends she rarely saw, take in the latest exhibitions and visit the best boutiques. She had not been in a hurry to go back to New York just yet. Francis Belcannon had paid her fare and was putting her up; she was having a free holiday and hadn't got bored with London yet, although she would. Eloise de Haviland always got bored with everything. She was a great traveller; drifting from Peking to Moscow, from Cairo to Istanbul, buying and chattering, floating like a gilded dragonfly over the surfaces of life everywhere. Even her native New York was largely foreign to her. She never visited some parts of it. Manhattan and Long Island, they were her chosen spots. Everywhere else was uncertain; dirty or dangerous, or full of disturbing people, people without money or influence, who might want something from her, might attack her or steal from her.

She had a beautiful, exquisite, apartment looking over the park, with the sort of security she could trust. Shops delivered. She had carefully checked staff. She never had to do anything for herself.

She had friends, the right sort of friends. She no longer had a husband; he had thoughfully died, leaving her enormous sums of money. She had squads of hopeful men friends, none of whom would ever get to first base because she had no intention whatever of marrying again. A husband merely cramped your style, although a girl like Nicola must marry young, get it over with, get a good divorce and then really start to live with lots of money and lots of freedom to do as you please, get what you want, never have to compromise or do anything for anyone else.

That much Nicola had learnt over the last few days, listening to Aunt Eloise talking in her brittle, lively way.

The life she was being urged into was not what Nicola had dreamt of; she did not want to turn into Aunt Eloise, to be enamelled and self-obsessed, drifting over life endlessly without ever experiencing any depths or experiencing anything fully.

'Certainly not, you cannot go and this ... this what-ever.'

'Sean.'

'Don't even say his name. Don't think it. Forget you ever heard of him.'

'I love him.'

Aunt Eloise had opened her mascara-ringed eyes, her dark red mouth a circle of distaste. 'After what he's done? Sweetie, where's your self-respect? He was cheating on you with some shop girl and got her pregnant, then killed her. He's a bastard. You can't still love him.'

Nicola did, though. Oh, she had been shocked and horrified by what she had been reading in the papers.

Their home had been surrounded by press, cameras flashing, men jostling on the London pavement, ringing the door bell, banging on the door. Every time it opened to let Papa in and out, to admit visitors, or permit them to leave, the men outside had surged forward, tried to force their way inside. They had shouted Nicola's name but had caught no glimpse of her because she was upstairs in her bedroom, weeping on her bed, or spending hours in the bath, where at least she could avoid Papa's preaching and later Aunt Eloise's talk, talk, talking.

Nicola had read all the newspapers, curled up on her bed, staring at the grey photographs of the girl whose body had been fished up from the sea by Japanese fishermen.

Why? Why had Sean ever done it with her? What had she got, this flashy looking blonde?

He hadn't taken Nicola to bed, had said they would wait until they were married. If he wanted to sleep with someone, why not her? Why go elsewhere for what she would have given him eagerly?

Hadn't he ever loved her? Hadn't he fancied her, hadn't he wanted to sleep with her?

Bewildered, hurt, aching with frustration and wounded passion, she had needed to see him, ask him, get him to tell her . . . why? Why, why, why?

But her father and Aunt Eloise would not allow

her to visit him in prison, so she had to escape and get her own way. Aunt Eloise kept proclaiming the importance of getting your own way, after all.

The press had given up hanging around. Nicola was able to slip quietly out of the front door and got a taxi right outside; pure luck. She would have walked to Hyde Park Corner, nearby, and got on a bus, if she had to, but a taxi was better. She went to Oxford Street and bought herself some inexpensive jeans and a cheap little thin white sweater, changed into them in the restroom at the Savoy, put the green Dior dress she had been wearing into a bag and left it to be collected. She could pick it up sometime before she left. After all, how could she visit a prison wearing a dress that had cost over a thousand pounds? The quality stood out a mile, just as the cost of the clothes she was wearing now were getting some sideways looks from the staff in the foyer of the Savoy.

But this was one occasion you had to dress down for. She didn't want to stand out, or attract attention, at the prison. She had also bought a cheap anorak with a hood which she could pull forward over her head, disguising her blonde hair and hiding her face.

All the same, she got stared at by the other prisoners as she waited for Sean to come and sit opposite her.

He looked astonished as he saw her, his face going red.

'Hello, Sean,' she whispered shyly, not quite meeting his eyes.

'Hello, Nicola,' he muttered. 'I didn't ever think you'd visit me, in here – your father's solicitor came, told me the engagement was over and I wasn't to try to see you again, or write, or anything.'

'He doesn't know I'm here. He didn't want me to come, but I had to see you.'

He shifted uneasily. 'Look, I'm sorry, OK? I won't give you excuses, there aren't any. But I am sorry.'

'Did you ever love me?' The question was quiet, but even someone as selfish and dim as Sean could have heard the pain burning behind it.

He swallowed, audibly, looking at her. 'Yes, yes, more than I realised, myself, and before you ask I never loved her. I just needed to ... do it, right? I couldn't with you. I knew that. I respected you too much. But I'm only human and I'm a man. And she was there, and offering. But that was all. It was just sex.'

Her small, pale, delicate fingers twisted together. She looked at him through her wet lashes. 'I wish I could believe you.'

'I wish you did, not that it makes much difference now, it's too late, I know.'

She kept looking at him, tears dropping from her big blue eyes. 'You look different. Thinner. I don't know . . . different in other ways, too. Older. Sad. Oh, Sean, it's all such a mess.'

He groaned softly. 'I know. But I do love you, Nicola. I wish to God none of it had ever happened. Honestly. If I could go back . . . I got scared when she said she was going to have a baby. I must have been mad for that one minute. And now your dad will never let me marry you, even if I get out of here, if I'm not found guilty, say. Even then he wouldn't let me marry you. It's all over for me.'

She didn't deny it. She knew her father. 'They're sending me to New York, I don't know when I'll get back here. But I'll write to you, I swear. I'll write whenever I can.'

He looked at her with desperate attention. 'Will you, Nicola? I'd love that. It would give me something to hold on for. But . . . will you forgive me?'

She whispered. 'I love you, silly. I really do. I always did. I can't help forgiving you.'

Sean's face crumpled like a child's; a tear slipped down his cheek.

Neil went out with the coastguard, on his orange boat, trawling the sea for any glimpse of Miranda. Alex was looking, too, in his own boat, but Neil preferred not to go with him. Alex was the master in his boat, he made the decisions, making Neil prickle with resentment, and his jealousy of Alex ground inside him like swallowed glass every time the other man spoke of Miranda. He felt far easier with the coastguard, who was a guy he could talk to, and who had never even met her.

It was like looking for a needle in a haystack, said the coastguard whose name Neil could not pronounce He was a small, wiry Greek with blue and red tattoos on both arms. He had been a sailor working a Greek cruise ship and spoke rough but comprehensible English.

'You see, she could be anywhere. Where do we look? The Aegean could swallow a whole ship, let alone one little girl.'

Alex was thinking the same. His black eyes searched the horizon. There wasn't even another vessel to be seen now. He had sailed out of sight of the island. He must head back in again and search another quarter.

They hadn't told Pandora yet. Charles was afraid of upsetting her. She might lose the baby.

'She's asking why Miranda hasn't been to see her, of course, but we lied, said she was out with you, sailing.'

'Soon enough to tell her the truth when ... if ... we don't find Miranda,' Alex had said.

Charles looked sideways at him, hesitated. 'She

... she could be ... could have ... drowned, you know.'

'I know.' Did Charles think he hadn't considered that possibility?

'Lots of people do drown here, they take risks, swim out too far, get cramp ... it happens all the time.'

'I know. But Miranda was a good swimmer and she knew the Aegean, she's been here long enough to know to be careful. I'm going to go on looking for her while there's still hope.'

'Of course. Let me come out with you.'

'No, we need you here, back at the hotel, while Milo and I are out at sea. But thanks.' He had clapped a hand to Charles' shoulder, smiled at him. 'I appreciate the offer.'

'Are you serious about her?' Charles had asked, but got no answer, so he had asked, 'What about Elena?' But to that he had been given no reply, either. Alex did not talk about his feelings, he kept them to himself.

So, Alex had left, urgently needing to be at sea, looking, doing something, anything. Time was going by and hope was fading, he knew that. Oh, he knew. So many things could have happened to her. She could have been abducted, could have been killed, could have drowned.

But he would not contemplate those possibilities.

He had to believe she could be alive, somewhere, and that they would find her.

Miranda was alive but she was very cold, her skin below the water goosepimpled from being in the sea for so long, yet burning from the heat of the sun. She was experimenting with gentle movements to keep herself afloat. She began by moving her feet, flexing them rather than kicking, flicking them sideways. At first it put her off balance, her heart leapt into her mouth as her body sank in the water, so that it lapped at her mouth. She had to fight to keep calm, not to panic.

Gradually the tiny movements became easier; she floated round and round in a circle, beginning to move her body as she kicked, flexing her stomach and hips too, and the chill wore off a little, her muscles warmed up and the cramp died away.

But it was tiring; she increasingly wanted to give up, float, stop fighting, but that would end only one way, in death. She knew that. So she kept up her movements.

Now and again she turned her head sideways to dip her face under water. Her skin was getting badly sunburnt; on shoulders and face. The Greek sun was so hot.

How long had she been in the sea? She had no idea. It seemed like forever. How much longer could she keep going? She couldn't guess that, either.

At the back of her mind was the memory of hearing Alex talking to Terry Finnigan on the phone, saying he had kept her on the island so that Terry could come and get her when he liked.

The pain of the memory was intense, far worse than her sunburn or the weariness of her tired muscles.

Alex . . . how could he? She wished she could hate him, but she couldn't; she still loved him. She must be insane. She must stop feeling like that. He had made love to her knowing what he meant to do; it had all been lies, everything he said to her. How could she go on loving a man like that?

Something brushed against her. What was that? She stiffened, shooting a sideways look in shock.

Right beside her gleamed an eye; large and round and shiny.

Her throat pulsed with fear — what was it? She hadn't heard anything moving. It touch her again, nudging her with its nose like a dog.

Only then did she recognise it, realise what it was that had silently stolen up on her. A dolphin. It was a dolphin.

The silky, bluish silvery skin was cool to the touch. She leant her head towards it and pushed her cheek into it, delighted to have company. It swam closer, curving against her, supporting her, almost as if it understood her predicament.

Suddenly it lowered its head beneath the sea; she felt a strange vibration from it – what was it doing?

Ten minutes later another dolphin swam towards them; the two of them touched noses, blowing into each other, made funny little chuckling noises – were they talking to each other? she wondered.

The second dolphin swam to the other side of her, pushing into her, supporting her, so that she was sandwiched between them, and the strain of trying to stay afloat eased.

The dolphins began to move, taking her with them. Miranda flicked her ankles lightly to keep abreast of them. She could see nothing but sea and sky. Where were they taking her?

She tried to remember everything she had ever heard of dolphins, but could only remember that they were not fish, they were mammals, marine mammals.

It was easy to believe; under the sleek blue and silver skin she felt the pulse of warmth, of blood moving in veins. Her body responded to theirs as if they were human, too.

Some people believed they had a language, could communicate with each other, she remembered.

Had that been what the first dolphin had been

doing when he made the water vibrate? Had he been calling for help?

They were believed to like human beings, to enjoy human company – and hadn't Charles told her on that first day, when dolphins swam round the boat as they were sailing from Piraeus, that they had rescued people from the sea before?

Moving with them, between them, she thought how elegant they were, their bodies sleekly adapted for moving in their watery environment.

Their round, rather mischievous eyes were almost human in their expressions and when they opened their long mouths in a grin she couldn't help laughing back.

Having their company made the whole world look different, gave her hope. She pushed away the painful thoughts of Alex. He had betrayed her, but the dolphins healed the wound of that memory.

She almost fell asleep, so tired it was hard to keep awake. To help herself stay alert she lifted her head and gazed about her.

Was she imagining it, or was that a coastline she could see? Above the waves it ran like a rippling yellow line, coming closer all the time. A beach? Was that where the dolphins were taking her?

A sound cut through wind and waves – an engine? Was it an engine? Was there a boat coming?

She raised herself again, staring in the direction from which the noise came, and saw a yellow boat's prow cutting through the water, churning up white, marbled spray.

They might sail past without even noticing her. Desperately she lifted her head even higher, hoping they would see her.

The engine cut and the boat slowed; the dolphins stopped moving forward and waited, tails lightly flicking. Somebody in a yellow life-jacket leaned down, hands seized her shoulders, began to pull her firmly but gently upwards.

She bit back a cry of pain. Her skin was so sunburnt it hurt just to be touched on the shoulders.

Slithering over the side of the boat she fell into a man's arms and looked up into Neil Maddrell's face.

'Neil!' she hoarsely said, almost surprised to find her voice still worked. 'Oh, thank you, thank you.'

'Who the hell did this to you? Did you see? Did you recognise them?' He was undoing her ankles.

'Greeks, I'd never seen them before.' She tried to stand up but her legs crumpled underneath her. 'Must thank the dolphins ... they saved my life.'

Neil picked her up gently, her head against his shoulder, her legs dangling.

'Yes, we saw – that was what made us look, the dolphins – and then we saw you, between them.

Amazing; I'd never have believed it if I hadn't seen it for myself. You do hear these stories about their superintelligence, people say they do these things, but it seems so incredible, doesn't it?'

'They were marvellous,' she said as he carried her to the side of the boat to look down into the water from which she had only just escaped.

It looked so pretty, blue and glittering, sun dancing on the surface. Who would believe it was so dangerous, so deadly?

The coastguard was throwing raw fish to the dolphins; they leapt out of the water to take it, silvery and lithe, swallowing the fish whole, their white teeth visible briefly in that friendly grin of theirs.

'Thank you, thank you,' Miranda called and they looked at her as if understanding, grinned up at her, made more of their strange chuckling noises, swam once around the boat in a pair, nose to nose, then leapt out again, flicking their tails, before sinking back into the water and disappearing.

Miranda was sad to see them go — she wished she spoke their language, could tell them how she felt, but her head was going round now, she was sick and dizzy.

Neil carried her limp, shuddering body into the little cabin and laid her down on a padded bench, pushing a cushion under her head.

He looked down at her, frowning. 'You have terrible sunburn.'

'I know.'

Her face was blotched red, her eyes half-closed, swollen like boiled eggs, the irises mere slits between those puffy, dark red lids. Neil grimaced. 'Is it painful?'

She was shivering violently. 'I feel weird. I'm very hot, but I'm so cold, too. How can you be hot and cold at the same time?'

He gently laid a blanket over her and the warmth was marvellous; it seeped into her very bones. Even this rather hard bench felt wonderful under her.

'Would you like a hot drink? Chocolate? Are you hungry? I could get you a sandwich. We have ham, cheese — what would you like?'

Her lids were closing now that she no longer needed to stay awake and aware. She was weary, dying to sleep, to give up, give in, let go of everything.

'Chocolate, yes,' she whispered. 'Lovely.'

'Sandwich?'

'No.' She made a disgusted face. 'I feel too sick.'

'OK, I'll be back in a minute. There's instant chocolate in the galley, we had some earlier. Will you be OK if I leave you alone?'

'Mmmm . . .' she said, almost asleep.

He went away. So did Miranda, sinking into warm,

soft sleep and dreaming of dolphins and blue seas and fear like a poison in her blood.

Neil talked on deck to the coastguard. 'We must get her to a hospital. She's in shock, that could cause serious worries. She also has bad sunburn and hypothermia. Is there a hospital on the island?'

The coastguard shook his head. 'We have a small clinic, attached to the doctor's surgery, that deals with minor medical problems. Cuts and bruises, that sort of thing. But for anything serious people have to be taken to the mainland. We have a helicopter. I'll get on to them right away, tell them we'll need them as soon as we land.'

Neil went back with the hot chocolate a moment later, but found Miranda asleep, breathing heavily. He put a hand to her forehead and winced at her temperature.

The sooner they got her to a hospital the better.

After contacting the helicopter, the coastguard talked to Alex on the radio, too. 'She isn't injured, but she's been in the water for hours, she's in shock – in fact, she's sleeping now, and she's suffering from sunstroke, and hypothermia. She needs immediate treatment for both, which means going to the mainland, to hospital. I've been in touch with the helicopter, Georgio will take her at once, as soon as we make land.'

'Wait for me to get back, Stathatoo,' Alex urgently said. 'I should be there in half an hour.'

Alex ended the call and put on more speed, bouncing over the water, his body tense with the drive to get to her. He had been so sure she was dead, that he would never see her again alive.

But she was alive, thank God. And not seriously injured. But she had obviously had a bad time; she must have been scared stiff. The bastards. How could they do that to a woman? It was barbaric, inhuman. If he found out who had done it, he'd kill them — and not quickly, either. No, he would cut their throats and let them bleed to death.

It took longer to make land than he had anticipated. At last he got there and tied up at the harbour only to see the helicopter taking off.

The coastguard met him as he climbed the ladder on to the harbour wall.

'I'm sorry, the English policeman insisted on leaving at once, he wouldn't wait for you. He said he was worried about shock — she was getting worse and he wanted her to have medical help as soon as possible.' A pause, the coastguard was embarrassed, couldn't meet his eyes. 'And he said ... said he would rather you did not see her just yet, anyway. She needed complete rest.'

Alex held on to his temper, refusing to let other people see how he felt. His teeth gritted, he gave a curt nod and said quietly, 'Well, thank you, for all your help. We're very grateful. You probably saved her life.'

'Oh, the dolphins did that. They were keeping her afloat, keeping her company. What marvellous creatures they are. I fed them my dinner – a potful of fresh-caught fish I got before I went out to sea. I was going to stew them with some tomatoes and garlic, but I had to thank the dolphins somehow, so I chucked the lot to them.'

'Come back to the hotel and we'll give you the best dinner of your life,' Alex said.

He drove the coastguard up there and left him in Milo's care, in the bar, then went to his own room to shower and change into clean clothes that did not smell of the sea.

After that he lay on his bed and stared at the square of the window, angry with Neil for his high-handed arrogance in taking her away. He wants her himself, Alex thought, he always has. I've seen the way he looks at her. His teeth ground together. But if he thinks he'll steal a march on me by taking her away so fast he's wrong. I'll cross back to the mainland tomorrow.

*　　*　　*

In a small room in a hospital Miranda lay listening to the sound of cicadas in a garden outside. The room was quiet and shadowy, beige linen blinds closed against the light.

She had had treatment, was sedated now, sleepy but comfortable, dazedly remembering what had happened to her, the hours of discomfort and fear, the dolphins, the rescue.

Neil came into the room and she started, looking at him blearily. He had changed out of his damp, salt-stained jeans and was wearing a suit again, looking very English.

'Neil . . . where am I? On the island?'

'No, we're in Greece now. You needed hospital treatment and there's no hospital on the island, so we flew you here.'

'Is Alex here?'

'No, I thought it was wisest not to wait for him to get back to the harbour, but I expect he'll come to see you tomorrow.'

'No!' she burst out, her hand clutching at his sleeve. 'Don't let him. I don't want to see him.'

Neil tensed, studied her, eyes narrowed. 'Why not?'

'I think . . . I think he may be in league with Terry Finnigan. I heard him talking on the phone. I think it was him . . . he arranged for me to be snatched and thrown into the sea.'

Chapter Sixteen

Alex Manoussi was volcanic with rage. He had flown back to Greece the morning after Miranda was rescued and gone immediately to the Athens hospital where he knew she had been taken by Neil, who had sent him a fax confirming this, only to be denied admittance to her private room. Two Greek policemen stood guard outside, shoulder to shoulder, big men in uniform, with darkly tanned faces and watchful black eyes. They wore guns at their belts and looked as if they would use them without hesitation.

They were very polite to Alex, polite but firm. 'I am sorry, sir, but our orders are that no one may be allowed to see her.'

'Who is your superior? Where do I find him?'

Expressionlessly, they gave him a name and telephone number, but when Alex tried to talk their superior officer into allowing him to see Miranda he came up against a brick wall.

'She has narrowly escaped death, she has to be protected. She cannot see anyone except police officers.'

Alex took a deep breath, forced himself to seem calm. 'There is a British police officer from London, a Sergeant Neil Maddrell – do you know where I could find him?'

'He is staying at the Syntagma Hotel.'

But when Alex went there he was told Sergeant Maddrell was not in the hotel. No, the receptionist had no idea where he could be found. Alex left a note asking Neil to get in touch with him, but got no reply.

He sent a fax to the hotel the following day. Neil faxed back that it was considered essential that no one at all should see Miranda, and he hoped Alex would leave her alone. She was very shaken, and needed rest.

Alex's language turned the air blue.

A week later, Miranda flew back to London, looking almost normal. Her swollen eyes had shrunk back to their usual size, her reddened skin no longer had a rough rash, instead it had begun to peel off in strips. Her head didn't ache any more. But the attack on her had left a long-term legacy – she was still sleeping badly, had nightmares every night and was jumpy and nervous.

Neil took her to his flat which was a short walk
from one of London's many parks. From the window
of the tiny box room she would be using she could see
trees, many of which were stripping now for winter,
their yellow, russet and orange leaves blowing off like
ancient coins, drifting down the streets, filling the
gutters and choking the drains. A brisk autumn wind
rattled the windows, rain spattered lightly.

She shivered. Autumnal London was dreary compared to the blue skies, blue seas and hot sun of
Greece.

'Will you be OK in here?' Neil asked uncertainly
and she turned to smile gratefully at him.

'It's fine, thank you, you're very kind.'

'I just want you to be safe. They won't get at you
in here. It won't occur to them that you'll be staying
with me. Or to Alex, I hope. He's been trying to see
you ever since you left the island.' He looked at his
watch. 'I've got to go in to work, I'm afraid. You won't
be nervous, alone, will you?'

'No, I'll be fine.'

'Good. Before I go, can I get you a meal? My freezer
is well stocked, or there's a Chinese restaurant in this
block. It wouldn't take me five minutes to get you
something from them.'

She shook her head. 'Thanks, but I'm not really
hungry.'

'Well, if you change your mind, take what you like from the kitchen. I've got plenty of stuff in the freezer, frozen foods, chops, a couple of steaks, I think, and I've also got eggs, bacon, salad, vegetables – everything you could need. Just help yourself.'

He left, warning her not to leave the flat or open the door. She watched television for an hour, then rang her mother.

'Where have you been? I was getting worried,' Dorothy Knox said. 'I had a call from that Greek, Pandora's brother, saying you had left Greece and asking if you were with me. He wants you to get in touch with him, he needs to talk to you.'

'I don't need to talk to him,' Miranda said flatly.

Surprised, her mother asked, 'What's this all about? I thought you were nicely settled over there – why have you left so soon? Have you quarrelled with Pandora's brother? What about Pandora, how is she?'

'She's OK, as far as I know; I haven't spoken to her for a week. She's still staying in bed all day, and getting pretty bored, but at least the baby is stabilised.'

'What about the brother? What's he done to make you so cross?'

'I don't want to talk about Alex.' Miranda sounded stiff and sulky.

'Oh. I thought you liked him.'

'I did. Now I don't, but I really don't want

to talk about it, Mum. Honestly. Please, drop the subject.'

Reluctantly Dorothy did, asking instead, 'Where are you?'

'London, I can't tell you where, it isn't safe. Did you know Sean Finnigan has been charged? But the trial may not happen for another year, maybe even two – it takes forever to come to court, apparently. It's going to make life difficult, because I can't risk them finding out where I am. They had another go at killing me on the island.'

Dorothy was horrified, her voice shaking, 'Oh, my God! What happened?'

'They tried to drown me.'

'How terrible – where? I mean, in your bath, like that poor girl, or . . .'

'In the sea.'

'Who did it? It wasn't Terry Finnigan, was it?'

'No, it was two Greeks. He must have hired them, though. Who else would want me dead?'

'It couldn't have been an accident? I mean, are you sure they meant to kill you? What exactly happened?'

'They caught me swimming, dragged me into their boat, tied me up, hand and foot, and threw me in the sea miles out from land. It wasn't an accident, Mum. No way. They meant to kill me.'

'Were you hurt?'

'I had sunstroke and I was in shock, but otherwise I wasn't hurt. But it was scary.'

'It must have been. You poor girl.'

'The most amazing thing happened, though. I was floating out there, in the middle of the sea, when I was rescued by . . . you'll never guess what! Dolphins!'

'Dolphins? What do you mean, rescued?'

'Two of them swam beside me, keeping me between them, supporting me and moving me along . . . it was extraordinary, I'll never forget it. I might have died if it hadn't been for them.'

Dorothy exclaimed excitedly. 'How wonderful. I've heard of dolphins helping people, but that's amazing.'

She talked about dolphins for some time, then asked, 'So, was Alex Manoussi involved?'

'I think he may have been. That's why I left to come back here. Neil thought I shouldn't stay there any longer. I'm glad to be home, but, I must say, I miss the Greek weather – London is so grey, but it was still sunny and warm back in Greece.'

'Why don't you come here? Freddy will look after us both. You'd have a full-time bodyguard.'

'I wish I could, but . . .'

'Why can't you? With me and Freddy to watch over you? You'd be quite safe.'

Miranda was tempted. It was going to be boring staying in this flat and never going out.

'I'll talk to Neil.'

'Neil?'

'The policeman in charge of the case.'

'Oh, I remember. Nice man. All right, talk to him. Ask him to ring me and I'll talk to him, too.'

She spoke to him that evening when he returned, but he shook his head.

'I know it will be dull for you here, but it is the last place they'll think of looking, whereas your mother's home is the first place they'll go.'

'Alex has already rung her.'

'There you are then!'

'But he will have realised she still thought I was in Greece. He won't go there. And even if he did, I'll have her, and Freddy, to take care of me. I won't be alone.'

'Freddy?'

'Her current boyfriend – he's an ex-policeman and he's living there at the cottage to keep an eye on her because the attack on her in London scared her. He can keep an eye on me at the same time. Neil, you know I'm very grateful to you, but I'll go mad if I have to stay shut up in a tiny London flat forever.'

He looked at her soberly. 'Miranda, if anything happened to you I'd never forgive myself.'

'It won't. I'll be twice as careful this time. I had such

a shock when those Greeks tied me up and threw me in the sea. I was more frightened than I've ever been in my life.'

'You and me both. When I arrived and found you were missing I really thought you'd had it that time. It was such a relief to find you alive. I'm not taking any more chances with your safety.'

'But Freddy and my mother will stand guard day and night. I'd have company. It's very sweet of you to go to so much trouble to take care of me, but I can't live locked up in your flat for the next year. I'd go crazy.'

He rang her mother and spent half an hour talking to her, and was finally persuaded to let Miranda go and stay at the cottage later.

A week later he drove her down to Dorset at night, under cover of darkness. As they parked outside the cottage, a dark shape reared up in the garden and shone a torch into their faces.

'What the hell . . .' Neil burst out.

'It's Freddy,' Miranda said, laughing.

Neil groaned. 'Well, I can't say he isn't alert, I suppose!'

He came to meet them, wearing camouflage trousers and jacket with a hood. 'I'm camping out here, in a tent, to make sure nobody tries to break in. Sorry if I startled you.' He offered Neil his hand. 'Hello. I'm

Freddy – a friend of Dorothy. I was in the job myself until they retired me.'

'So I gather. I must say, I'm very relieved that Miranda will have you here to look after her.'

'You can rely on me, don't worry. I've spent years sitting around in patrol cars at night watching someone. I've got good ears and I can do without sleep, I nap during daylight hours. I've rigged up poacher traps at the back of the cottage – black wires tied between bushes that set off alarm bells. I was taught how to do it by a gamekeeper. Nobody can move about out there without tripping over one of my wires. And they're quite invisible at night.'

'Sounds perfect,' Neil said, furtively studying Freddy's ginger moustache.

Freddy let them into the cottage, switching off a burglar alarm before stepping over the threshold. Once they were all inside the hall he turned on the electric lights and Dorothy came out of her bedroom and stood at the top of the narrow stairs, peering down at them. She was in blue, brushed-cotton pyjamas over which she wore a shortie blue velvet robe and her bare feet were pushed into blue velvet slippers.

'Everything all right?'

'Yes, hello, Mum. You remember Neil, don't you?'

'Of course I do.' Dorothy came downstairs, smiling

at him, and he blinked at her with the same stunned expression men had always worn when they first met her mother. Even now Dorothy had ... whatever it was ... sex appeal, beauty, magnetism, a combination which turned men's heads, in spite of her age.

Freddy was looking at her with the same entranced attention.

'You'd better get back outside,' she said to him softly, and he nodded obediently.

'Yell if you need me!'

'I will. Thank you, Freddy.' She brushed a hand up his arm, smiling gratefully at him.

He blushed. 'No problem.'

Dorothy had him wrapped around her little finger, thought Miranda, and then thought, was her mother going to marry Freddy? She wasn't sure how she would feel about that.

She liked him, but her mother had always enjoyed her independence – how would she submit to being married, tied down again?

'You must stay the night, Sergeant,' Dorothy said to Neil. 'I'm afraid the spare room is just a little box, but the bed is comfortable.'

'That's very kind of you.'

'Now, about food – have you eaten? I can quickly whip up supper for you both – how about ome-lettes?'

'That would be lovely,' Miranda said. 'Can I have a tomato omelette?'

'Of course — and you, Sergeant?'

'The same for me, thanks.'

'Chips with them? Or would you rather have salad?'

'Chips, please,' Neil said.

'Salad for me, Mum. Can I come and help you?'

'I don't need help to make a couple of omelettes! You go and lie on the sofa, you must be very tired, driving all this way. Put the electric fire on in the sitting room, and there are rugs in the cupboard by the window.'

Miranda knew that if she lay down with a rug draped over her, she was so tired she would fall asleep within minutes, so she sat upright, switched on the television and watched a documentary about African national parks to keep herself awake.

'Aren't big cats beautiful?' she thought aloud, staring at the screen. 'Look at the way that leopard is moving. Poetry in motion.'

'Pity they eat people,' Neil drily replied and she laughed.

'Well, we eat cows and sheep — where's the difference?'

'You aren't a vegetarian, are you?'

'No, just a member of the Be Fair to Leopards

Party. I do love them, don't you? What strikes me about big cats is that household cats, ordinary tabbies, act in exactly the same way. Clean themselves, move, eat, just the way wild cats do. They're just as beautiful and bloodthirsty. We had a cat once who used to kill mice, shrews, birds – bring them into the house and arrange them on the mat in front of my mother, like trophies. He used to eat their heads, poor little things, and leave the rest. Too lazy to pluck or skin them.'

Neil shuddered. 'Sounds horrible.'

Dorothy pushed a trolley into the room and handed each of them a tray on which was set their cutlery, a glass of home-made apple juice, their omelette on a plate, thinly sliced bread and butter, and the vegetables they had asked for. A delicate little salad for Miranda, crisp golden chips for Neil.

'This is delicious,' Neil said, eating ravenously.

When she had finished, Miranda felt even more tired and could not stop yawning.

'Bed for you,' Dorothy said. 'What you need is a good night's sleep.'

'And me,' Neil grimaced. 'It has been a very long day.'

No sooner was Miranda in her bed than she fell deeply asleep, and woke up to find the room filling with pale grey and lemon light. The sun was just floating up behind the trees, a pale yellow slice in the champagne sky.

It was the first night she had spent for a fortnight without bad dreams. She stretched, yawning, feeling clear-headed, healthy, full of energy.

After a shower she dressed and went downstairs. Her mother was in the kitchen making apple and blackberry jelly. The rich scent of the fruit filled the room. Dorothy stirred attentively, humming to herself. Along the kitchen counter stood clean empty pots, waiting for the jelly to fill them.

Hearing Miranda's footsteps she turned her head and smiled. 'Sleep well? Yes, I can see you did. You've got some colour this morning and your eyes are clear. You looked terrible last night. Sit down, I'll get you some breakfast — how about some porridge? I must just get this jelly to the right consistency, give me two minutes.'

'I'll be happy with toast, I can make it myself, don't mind me, just look after your jelly.'

Miranda cut a slice of bread, found the old toasting fork and opened the grate door of the Aga and began toasting her bread at the bars. The heat glowed, the bread turned golden brown. She spread it with marmalade and bit into it as she boiled the kettle and made herself some instant coffee.

'Can I make you some coffee, Mum?'

'Mmm, thanks.'

Neil didn't appear for another hour. When he finally came downstairs, he found the two women sitting with mugs of coffee in the kitchen, talking quietly, rows of filled jars glistening red along the counter.

'Sorry, I overslept, I meant to be up and away an hour ago, but I must have slept through my alarm,' he said with a sheepish grin.

'You obviously needed more sleep,' Dorothy soothed, getting up. 'I expect you've been under a strain lately, and working far too hard. 'Now, what would you like for breakfast?'

'Oh, just a coffee will suit me, then I must run.'

'Nonsense – how about piperade?'

He looked confused. 'What's that?'

'Fried peppers and tomatoes cooked with scrambled egg – it's delicious and very good for you.'

Neil hesitated. 'Well, it sounds gorgeous – if that isn't too much trouble. Thank you.'

It was cooked within minutes and Neil ate it slowly. 'It's a surprising mixture, but I love it. I might try to cook it for myself.'

He left half an hour later. 'Don't forget, keep indoors for a few days, don't tell anyone where you are, and let me know if you notice anyone hanging around.'

'I know, Neil. I'll be careful,' Miranda said, and waved as he drove off back to London.

'He's in love with you,' her mother said.

'I hope not, because I could never feel the same way, and he's a very nice man, he deserves to be happy.'

'Hmm,' Dorothy said thoughtfully, staring at her.

'What does that mean?'

'Oh, nothing,' her mother said, going back into the house.

'Where's Freddy?' asked Miranda, following her.

'Asleep in his tent. He sleeps all morning, but he won't come into the house. He wants to be ready if we get unwelcome visitors.'

As the slow, quiet days passed, and the nights of deep, untroubled sleep, Miranda felt her tension and misery lift. She still dreamt of Alex now and again, but her dreams about him now were different. And with better health she began to be restless.

'I need to work. I think I'll get a job somewhere down here.'

'Would that be safe? Will Neil agree?'

'I shan't tell him. I can't do nothing all day, and I need to earn my own living. I don't suppose I'll get a job in publicity, but anything will do.'

A few days later they had lunch at a hotel in Dorchester and Miranda saw a job advertised; for a secretary for the hotel office. She immediately applied, was interviewed and given a short test on the office computer system.

Flushed and excited she rejoined her mother in the car park. 'I got it! I start work next Monday. The salary isn't as good as I was earning in London, but it's OK. I get a free lunch, too. They seem a friendly lot in the office, too; it's a small place and I didn't get the impression it was over busy.'

'It will take you half an hour to drive here every morning, and half an hour back, you realise.'

'There's a bus that comes to Dorchester from your village, the manager said. Several of the staff take it.'

'You don't want to go by bus!'

'I can't use your car, it would leave you without transport.'

Dorothy groaned. 'You are the most awkward, obstinate girl! Well, try it to begin with, then you can borrow my car if it doesn't work out.'

But it did. Miranda enjoyed the morning drive on the bus, in misty half-light at first until the sun was fully up and the countryside swam into full view, rolling fields with neat hedges, filled with browsing sheep and cows, oaks and a few moth-eaten elms, woods and valleys and soft green hills. Dorset was a gentle, domestic landscape, very different to the dramatic Greek island she had been visiting.

The office was orderly and quiet, her fellow

workers amiable and easy-going, with their burring Dorset accents. They were never in a hurry but worked methodically, got the job done. She enjoyed walking around Dorchester during her lunch hour, after eating a light lunch in the kitchen. She got to know the hilly streets, the shops, the museum where Thomas Hardy's study was reproduced and where ancient farming tools and machines were on display.

One day when she got home her mother told her Alex had been there, demanding her address.

'I had a lot of trouble getting rid of him. I had to threaten to call the police in the end. He's a very intimidating man, isn't he?' Dorothy gave her a shrewd, searching stare. 'What exactly happened with him, Miranda? He didn't look like a killer to me.'

'What do killers look like? Sean looks like a slightly plump cherub, I would never have suspected he could be capable of killing anyone.'

Her mother shuddered. 'Don't!'

'I believed Alex was on my side, you know. He completely convinced me I could trust him. Looks can be very deceptive.' She tried to keep the hurt and bitterness out of her voice but her mother knew her too well.

'Are you in love with him?' she asked softly.

Miranda did not answer and carefully avoided

meeting her mother's eyes, but she knew she had already betrayed herself.

'Oh dear, oh dear,' Dorothy sighed. 'I can't blame you. If I was your age I think I'd have fallen for him, too. He's very sexy, isn't he?'

'Yes,' Miranda said shortly, remembering her dreams. Alex was very sexy, but she didn't trust him, and trust was essential in a relationship.

Terry Finnigan sat in his office staring at the documents in front of him. Bernie had been greedy. He wanted more of Terry's firm than Terry wanted to let him take, his lawyers had drawn up contracts which would give him control of the firm in future.

If Sean was found guilty, he might spend twenty years in prison, although their counsel seemed to think the sentence would be much lighter than that.

'We'll plead a moment of madness brought on because Sean was afraid of losing the woman he loved if she found out about the baby,' he declaimed, fingering his jacket lapels in a courtroom gesture. 'He hadn't planned to kill the girl. He blacked out for a minute, then panicked and tried to hide his crime, but he regrets it deeply, wishes he had not done it. If we can get the charge switched to manslaughter, he would go down for a few years — two, three, at most four.'

If Bernie's family took over their business, though, Sean would come out to find the company was no longer in their control.

Terry ground his teeth. Damn Bernie. Why should he put up with being blackmailed like this? It was too big a price to pay for getting very little information from a bent copper. Of course, Bernie had helped him to get the names of Greek contractors who would get rid of that girl, but even there, apparently, they had fallen down on the job. Miranda had lived, for which, now, Terry was glad. But he didn't feel he owed Bernie half his company.

And he wasn't going to hand it over, either. Let Bernie do his worst.

He picked up the contracts and tore them up, pushed them into a big brown envelope and addressed it to Bernie. No need for a letter to accompany them. Bernie would get the message.

A week later as Terry was getting into his car after a long day's work he was shot dead from across the street.

The police were baffled. They had eyewitnesses, but the descriptions of the killer were too vague;

tall, dark-haired, youngish, wearing a black leather coat. Nobody noticed his face; they had all been too frightened.

'It was a contract killing,' the officer in charge told Neil. 'No question, a real pro job — he was shot through the head once, killed outright. No amateur could be responsible.'

'I wonder who ordered it?' Neil thought aloud. 'We'll have to dig deeper into Terry's past. Before he came to London, what was he doing? Who wanted him dead?'

When they told Sean in prison he collapsed and had to be sedated. For the following week he was on suicide watch. After a shock like that, in his situation, he was a prime suspect for taking his own life.

Miranda heard the news from Neil and was appalled. 'Oh, poor Terry! I always liked him, you know, he was a friendly, cheerful man. Before ... before the murder.'

'You can't remember anything he was involved in that could explain why someone should murder him?'

She shook her head. 'No, but he must have been involved with some pretty nasty people if he knew how to hire people to murder me, especially so far away in Greece — mustn't he?'

'Yes, we're looking into his past history, his life

before he came down to London. He never mentioned what he was doing before that, did he?'

'No, never. In fact, I used to wonder what he was keeping so secret.'

'You should have joined the police. You're a smart little cookie,' Neil said, smiling at her.

She went pink. 'Thanks.' Then sighed. 'How has Sean taken it?'

'Badly, I'm told. They were surprised by how badly. Everyone thought he was a selfish little prat who didn't care about anyone but himself, but he was badly shaken by hearing his father had been killed.'

'He probably blames himself. Everything was going so well before Sean had his little fling, killed that girl. And Sean must know it, and feel guilty.'

'My colleague tells me that the ex-wife has appeared and taken over running the firm with her new husband. I don't think she's overwhelmed by grief.'

'Maybe she did it?' Miranda grinned at him. 'I never liked her.'

A year later the trial began in London, at the Old Bailey, the Central Criminal Court. Miranda was called to give evidence on the second day, first thing in the morning. She was so nervous she was white and at first she could not bring herself to look at Sean in the dock. She answered the opening questions of the prosecuting counsel, staring at him rather than glancing round the high-ceilinged, panelled room.

When she finally risked a look at Sean she was struck by the changes the last year had made in him. He had lost weight, was pallid, looked much older. Their eyes collided, she quickly looked away, suddenly sorry for him.

The judge asked her a question and she turned to answer, feeling strange. There was a surreal feel to being here, with this judge in a white wig and red gown trimmed with ermine, behind his high chair the blaze of colour from a coat of arms on a shield.

Was that the royal coat of arms? Yes, she thought it was – there were the lion and the unicorn. The old nursery rhyme floated into her head. The lion and the unicorn were fighting for the crown. The lion beat the unicorn all round the town . . . what did it mean?

There was probably some real historical incident behind the rhyme. There always was. Nursery rhymes were the last remnants of the old street ballads that served the same office as today's newspapers.

Her mind had wandered; she was brought back to awareness by another question from the prosecutor.

'Exactly how long would you say it was between the

moment when you ran out of that office and when you returned and rang the police?'

She was honest. 'I have no idea. Half an hour, perhaps, or as much as an hour. I didn't look at the time. I was too upset.'

The morning wore on interminably. Question and answer, question and answer ... it was strangely boring as well as very tense. She had to fight a desire to yawn. Yet her nerves were jumping.

The prosecutor finally stopped asking questions and sat down, but then she had to face the defence counsel.

He decided to start with questions about Tom's death, about her mental breakdown, her hallucinations. He had her medical reports from that time.

'You kept hearing people drowning, apparently?'

She swallowed. 'For a while. Yes.' She wasn't going to lie about that. Where was the point? There would be other witnesses to the fact.

There was a suppressed ripple of reaction from those watching, a gasp, then a whisper of comment, and Miranda nervously looked round the court, then, for the first time.

And saw Alex.

Her heart leapt and she began to tremble.

He was sitting just a few feet away from her, wearing a dark suit and white shirt, a blue silk tie, looking magnificent. His skin had a deep, smooth tan that made his hair seem blacker than ever and his black eyes watched her in a way that was unnerving.

She moistened her dry lips with her tongue, looking away. Was he still involved with Elena? Would he be marrying her? Or had he already done so?

'You were obsessed with drowning, in fact,' the defence counsel said.

'I wouldn't say that,' she whispered.

'You wouldn't say it, no, perhaps not,' he repeated. 'But is it true? I shall be calling a psychiatrist who worked with you three years ago who says that in his opinion . . .'

The prosecutor was on his feet. 'Objection, your honour. Hearsay. Not substantiated in evidence as yet.'

'I agree, Mr Ruddock,' the judge coldly nodded. 'The jury will disregard the defence counsel's last sentence.'

Miranda wished she could sit down; she felt cold and weak. Through the high windows she watched the grey cloudy sky move by relentlessly. Was it raining in the streets? It seemed to her to be raining in here. Her eyes were misty with unshed tears.

When she had finished giving evidence she left the court, to avoid Alex, but found he had anticipated her action and was waiting outside.

His dark eyes were intense, glittering. 'Miranda...'

'Leave me alone!' she cried in panic, and began to run but he caught up with her, his legs were longer than hers, he could move faster.

'Why have you turned against me? I don't understand!' he said, taking her arm in his long, hard fingers, and making her stand still.

'Why do you think?' she hissed at him, aware of people staring. 'Don't bother to go on pretending. I know you were in league with Terry.'

He stared in apparent amazement, his expression so convincing she almost believed him. 'What are you talking about?'

'I heard you, on the phone. You said he had asked you to keep me on the island until he could come for me.'

'That wasn't Terry, that was Neil I was talking to! I'd promised him I'd keep you safe.'

She drew a sharp, painful breath. 'I don't believe you!'

'Ask Neil,' he shot back.

'I have, I've talked to him about it and he never said ...' She stopped, thinking back. What exactly had she said to Neil?

Had she told him what she had overheard? Now that she thought about it, she had a feeling she had been vague, not wanting to go into details, trying to hide her hurt and anger, hating to admit Alex had made such a fool of her.

'Here he comes now,' Alex said, looking back up the stone steps. 'Ask him.'

Neil arrived, breathless and a little flushed from running. 'What's going on?' He looked from her to Alex, back again, frowning. 'What are you doing, Alex? I told you she doesn't want to see you again.'

Huskily, Miranda said, 'Neil, listen, I have to ask you something. I overheard Alex talking to someone on the phone last year. He said something about having promised to keep me on the island until this other person came to get me. I thought he was talking to Terry Finnigan, but he says he was talking to you. Do you remember that? Did you ask him to keep me on the island?'

He frowned. 'Well, I did ask him to keep an eye on you while you were over there, to make sure you didn't leave the island until I could come and get you. I was afraid of you being abducted.' He paused, then added, 'As you were, in the end. Just as I was afraid you might be. So I was quite right, wasn't I?'

Miranda couldn't speak, she was too overwhelmed. She walked on out of the Old Bailey into the close-set streets surrounding it. Alex caught up with her. She stopped and looked up at him. He was so strikingly foreign in this grey place, with his deep tan and jet hair.

'I'm sorry,' she whispered.

'So you should be! If only you'd said something, told me what you were thinking . . .' He stopped, seeing her wince. 'Never mind that. Let's go somewhere and have lunch.'

He put his arm around her and guided her to the kerb, flagging down a black taxi which was heading towards them.

'I asked her first!' protested Neil, furious.

Alex turned a dark gaze on him, his face belligerent. 'You've probably seen a lot of her over the past year. I haven't.'

The taxi stopped. He urged Miranda into the back and told the driver, 'Charlotte Street, please.'

Miranda couldn't look at Neil. She leaned back as the taxi moved away. Alex watched her, very close.

'How could you do that to me?' he said huskily, voice low. 'Don't you know how badly you hurt me? I went mad, trying to get to see you. I didn't know what I'd done, I thought maybe it was guilt, that you felt badly about sleeping with me, felt you had betrayed your husband. I kept trying to work it out, but how could I guess that you suspected me of conspiring with Finnigan? All this time, Miranda — all these months without setting eyes on you.'

'Isn't Elena enough for you?' she jealously muttered.

'What?' He stared at her rigid, averted profile. 'Elena? What are you talking about?'

'I know you were in love with her ...'

'Years ago, when I was twenty!'

'And now ... when she turned up on the island ... I could see you still cared ...!'

'How could I care a pin for her when I'd been in love with you for three years?'

She drew a sharp, incredulous breath, staring into his dark, insistent eyes.

'Elena was simply a nuisance. She thought she could walk back into my life the way she had walked out of it and find everything the same. But all I wanted to do was make you see how I felt about you. I couldn't wait to get rid of her so that I could concentrate on you. And then you ran away from me, too, without giving me a clue why.'

'I'm sorry,' she whispered. 'I was hurt, too, can't you see that, Alex? I thought you had been stringing me along, didn't really care two pence for me – I've been so unhappy.'

He turned her face up towards him. 'Then let me make you happy. God, Miranda, I've missed you.'

'Me, too.'

Their mouths met, she wound her arms round his

neck, clung, close to tears as she realised it was over, she was safe now, and with Alex again.

While they ate a marvellous Greek meal later, Alex told her about his sister's baby boy, who had been born a month early and had had to stay in an incubator for the first day, but was now a healthy, bouncing nine-month old.

'They've called him Nicos. Wait till you see him! I don't think Pan wants another one; she hated being kept in bed all those months, and now she's got this boy she and Charles are satisfied.'

'I'm so glad for them! I felt guilty, leaving like that.'

'When you come back, Pan will have a lot to say to you about walking out! Tell me what you've been doing – have you had a job? I hope you can give notice at once and come back to Greece with me.'

She laughed. 'You're rushing me!'

'I'm not going to let you escape again.'

Two days later Sean was found guilty of manslaughter and sentenced to three years in prison, of which he would probably only serve half, Neil said.

Alex and Miranda were in court. She felt very sorry for Sean. What he had done was very wrong, but he had paid a terrible price. The consequences of his crime had devastated his life. The law's punishment was nothing compared to the loss of his father, and Nicola.

She and Alex flew back to Greece the following week, and three months later were married, in Dorset, in a medieval church in the village, surrounded by family and friends.

She threw her bouquet deliberately to her mother, who caught it, then looked at it in amazement.

Freddy beamed.

CHARLOTTE LAMB

DEEP AND SILENT WATERS

Laura would never have gone to Venice if she had known she would meet Sebastian Ferrese there: for the past three years, she has fought her attraction to the enigmatic film director and has no wish to lay herself open to temptation yet again.

But her nomination for an award at the Film Festival proves too much of an enticement — and when Laura sees Sebastian, she finds herself swept up in his overwhelming magnetism once more. It is a dangerous infatuation. For death seems to follow Sebastian around — and Laura begins to suspect that he is no innocent bystander ...

PRAISE FOR CHARLOTTE LAMB:

[Her novels] 'are rip-roaringly, mind-bogglingly ... heart-poundingly successful'   *Radio Times*

'One of the secrets of [her] phenomenal success is her magnificent moody heroes'   *News of the World*

'The secret of her success is that both reader and writer get their fix, identifying totally with the heroine' *Daily Express*

Charlotte Lamb (Mrs Sheila Holland) has written more than 150 novels — from romances to thrillers, from historical sagas to tales of the occult — in a writing career spanning more than a quarter of a century. Her worldwide sales are well in excess of 100 million copies. Born in Dagenham, she comes from a long line of Cockneys, but now lives with her husband and eldest daughter (herself a novelist) in a house overlooking the sea in the Isle of Man.

HODDER AND STOUGHTON PAPERBACKS

CHARLOTTE LAMB

WALKING IN DARKNESS

Two worlds separated them. But the dark eyes that watched over each were the same ...

Beautiful heiress Catherine Gowrie had spent her life protected by one of America's wealthiest families and married to one of Britain's most successful men. Now her all-powerful father was close to his greatest ambition – nomination as Presidential candidate. Nothing must be allowed to stand in Don Gowrie's way.

Sophie Narodni shared only Catherine's beauty. Her father killed before she was born, the young journalist from Prague had worked her way out of poverty to travel the world. But with her she carried a secret: a secret that could destroy everything Don Gowrie had dreamed of. If he didn't silence her first ...

PRAISE FOR CHARLOTTE LAMB:

[Her novels] 'are rip-roaringly, mind-bogglingly ... heart-poundingly successful'   *Radio Times*

'One of the secrets of [her] phenomenal success is her magnificent moody heroes'   *News of the World*

'The secret of her success is that both reader and writer get their fix, identifying totally with the heroine'   *Daily Express*

HODDER AND STOUGHTON PAPERBACKS

CHARLOTTE LAMB

TREASONS OF THE HEART

When Claudia and Ben meet in Paris, the sexual frisson between them is powerful, instantaneous — and mutual, until Claudia's home is burgled and she is violently attacked. She begins to suspect Ben is less interested in her than in Hugh, the enigmatic Englishman who owns her apartment. Hugh had been her father's best friend and took care of her when her parents died. When she tells him Ben is in Paris, Hugh is obviously troubled.

Fleeing in terror to Hugh's villa on the beautiful Cap d'Antibes, Claudia is pursued by Ben and other sinister figures — including the ghosts of the past. What secret does Hugh know about the long-dead Duke of Windsor and why does it threaten their lives?

As she struggles in a web of treason and old lies, Claudia has to decide whether Ben is lover or deadly enemy.

Walking in Darkness, *In the Still of the Night* and *Deep and Silent Waters* are also available from Coronet.

'The romantic city of Venice and the glamorous and illusory world of film-making are the subjects of bestselling author Charlotte Lamb's latest novel. Deep and Silent Waters ... lose yourself in this irresistible mystery'
Woman's Realm

HODDER AND STOUGHTON PAPERBACKS